All the
Wrong Men
and
One Perfect
Boy *A Memoir*

Spike Gillespie

Simon & Schuster

SIMON & SCHUSTER
Rockefeller Center
1230 Avenue of the Americas
New York, NY 10020

Designed by Leslie Phillips
Manufactured in the United States of America

10 9 8 7 6 5 4 3 2 1

LIBRARY OF CONGRESS CATALOGING-IN-PUBLICATION DATA
Gillespie, Spike.
    All the wrong men and one perfect boy : a memoir / Spike Gillespie.
        p.   cm.
      1. Gillespie, Spike—Relations with men.   2. Women—United
States Biography.   3. Single mothers—United States Biography.
I. Title.
HQ1413.G53A3   1999
305.4'092—dc21
[B]   99-25766   CIP
ISBN 0-684-83983-0

The author gratefully acknowledges permission to reprint extracts from
the following:
    "Everything's Alright." Words by Sir Tim Rice and music by Sir Andrew
Lloyd Webber. Copyright © 1970 by MCA/PolyGram Music Ltd. All rights
controlled and administered by MCA—On Backstreet Music, Inc.
International copyright secured. Used by permission. All rights reserved.
    "Hand in Hand" by Elvis Costello. Copyright © 1978 by Sideways Songs
administered by Plangent Visions Music Limited.

Acknowledgments

There are no words or sentiments deep enough, no gratitude near great enough, to heap sufficient thanks upon all those who have helped me, to date, through this wacky life of mine, who have not judged me for my own misjudgments, who have stood beside me through the many trials. I would like to say a big merci beaucoup to the following:

Bob Mecoy, for tracking me down at the virtual soda fountain and casting me in the dream role of author. Elizabeth Kaplan for sealing the deal. Constance Herndon and Andrea Au, for hopping on the merry-go-round so late, but so very enthusiastically. Louis Black, Nick Barbaro, Kate Messer, Margaret Moser, and everyone at the *Austin Chronicle*, for allowing me to test my writing wings and supporting me over so many years. Coury Turczyn and Hillari Dowdle. That Whittle Trinity: Keith Bellows, Bill Gubbins, and Tom Lombardo. Andy, Marty, and Lenny—my three wise men and financial "consultants." Paula Judy, for a lifetime of love crammed into fifteen years. Jonathan Van Meter, for teaching me love. Angela Atwood and Ross Harper, for everything. Magan Stephens, for all the assistance, tolerance, receipt of kvetching, and overall dedication. Jason Levitt and Patrick Burkhart, for pushing me to get online. Jimmie and Stephanie Walker, for so many things. Kristie and Blair, for the girlfriends' club. Elena and James and Bern and Kenny, for all those first draft babysitting stints. Jason and Shannon, for art and love. Hope Edelman, Katie Granju, and Michael Sledge, for their writerly advice and so much more. Elizabeth Royte, for all of the letters and support through all of the men and gigs and years. Elisabeth Vedrine, for whipping me into shape emotionally and physically. Hettie Vedrine, for transcending our language difference. Hilary Liftin and Ana Pouso and all those at Prodigy Services and on the WOL BB who believed in me. Evan Smith, for moving past that failed blind date and keeping me going. Julia Null-Smith, for all the early advice. Sabrina, for understanding. Peter Moore, Ariel Gore, Deb Stoller, Michael Fay, the Rev. W. Blake Gray, Claire Connors, Barrie Gillies, and all the editors who took a chance publishing my work. Richard and Suzy, for the wheels. Michael McCarthy, for the greatest gift of all. Kerry and Stephen, Jen Goodman, Bonnie Bain, Dr. Martha Schmitz and her staff. Uncle Jack, and Murphy Mom-mom. The whole Foster/Lasser/Gilbert family, for embracing me as one of their own. Dawn Carpenter-Jones, Amy Wright, and Ronnie Earle, for all the legal help and moral support. Montessori House of Children. Diane Fleming. Lauren at the Spot. Chandler Stolp. Michael Bertin. Kathi and Stephen and Ollie and Charlie. Macduff and Mary, for the endless inspiration. Paul Klemperer. Michael Stravato and Claudia Kolker. Tom and Mary Kirk, for insisting I try "one more step." Genevieve Van Cleve and Deanna Capaldi. And Greg Welch, for an impossible amount of patience. Finally, to the very many others not named here, who helped us so much through our unplanned moves, our legal and physical nightmares, and some very dark days and darker nights. Thank you so very, very much.

This book is for three perfect men—
Jonathan Van Meter, Martin Berger,
and Ross Harper

And the ultimate little boy—
my darling Henry Mowgli Gillespie

Thank you for
giving me the love
I've craved
forever

No, don't ask me to apologise.

I won't ask you to forgive me.

If I'm gonna go down,

you're gonna come with me.

Elvis Costello, "Hand in Hand"
(*This Year's Model*, 1978)

Dear Henry,
This is a book about the truth.

The biggest truth about us—you and me—is that I haven't yet told you the Whole Truth. To me, this isn't lying, I just didn't think you were ready for some of it yet. You didn't need that burden. Sometimes, I think that if I didn't remind you of what happened, you'd never have to remember it. Your future would never have to be affected by your past.

But I know better than that. We have to remember things. I remember my first day of kindergarten. My first crush. So many things that only now I am able to see how they fit into the puzzle of who I have become. And so, unlike my parents, who tried to keep me from remembering too much, I want to keep you from forgetting too much.

Like the baby.

I wonder, if I never mentioned it again, would you remember the other baby? The baby that wasn't. Would you just put it out of your mind? Would you forget? I want you to remember.

I want you to know the truth. About the baby. About a lot of things.

I need to tell you about the many places we lived when you were just a baby. And all the people we lived with. It took me such a long, long time to get us to this house we now have and to leave behind the drinkers and the junkies and the hard times. You might only remember ice cream and smooth sailing. But me, I remember so much more.

I have lied a number of times in my life. But I have never been able to lie well enough to deceive anyone. Except for this one woman. And, I'd say, if you don't count her, I've only lied a dozen times in my life. Most of those times, I got caught.

Never by her, though. She kept believing me so I kept on lying. It was an exhilarating game. Until, finally, I realized I was destroying her with my fiction.

That woman is me. I tried to convince myself I didn't care about things I actually cared far too much about. Mostly, men. I met so many, loved so many, wanted so much more than I ever could have gotten from any one of them. Because for so many years I looked for the right thing from the wrong men.

Still, I convinced myself. Told myself if only I tried hard enough, dressed nicely enough, kept my mouth shut long enough I would find the perfect man. The man who could sweep away my self-loathing, take away the hurts I inflicted on myself.

I'm learning how to tell myself the truth now, son. And so much of that is because of you. I don't ever want you to lie to others and I certainly don't want you to lie to yourself. There is a saying about the truth setting you free. But I assure you that before you feel the joy of freedom, you must suffer the pain of acknowledgment. I hated so many truths about my life. Tried desperately to turn a blind eye to them. No more.

Now I know. I will wade through the pain to get to the relief of these truths.

I remember the day we lost the baby. You had drawn me a picture while I was asleep. Grace showed it to me. She knows about this art therapy stuff—she's worked with the *homeless and elderly and battered forever. She helped me figure out what you were trying to say.*

In the picture are four images: a magician, a pair of hands floating above a keyboard, a circle with two faces—one happy, one sad—and, finally, a blue circle around a red circle around a yellow circle, all three rings encompassing a big question mark. Except for the colors in these circles—and you had many colors to choose from—everything is black.

We had a hard time trying to figure out the floating hands, but the rest seemed obvious. The question mark was you wondering where the baby had gone. The happy/sad faces showed me you had hope. As for the magician, Grace said that was you, your desire to wave a wand over us and make it all better, make the pain disappear so we could find some magical calm and order in all of the chaos.

Order from chaos—it's what we're all seeking. It's why we take what happens to us and try to put it all together in neat pictures, pictures that we can bear to look at.

But the biggest truth is that life doesn't really fit into simple sentences or pretty pictures.

I'm asking that you keep something crucial in mind: Understand that there are many characters that shaped this truth of mine. Some are here, in these words, but a whole lot of others aren't. Still, they really existed. They still exist. Some I've played up. Some I've played down. Some I don't mention at all. I can't help it. That's just how I remember it.

New Jersey

1

TWICE in my life, my father reached out to me.

The third time, I ducked.

No, wait, that can't be right. Because I have seen for myself an 8 mm film where he is, right there, making contact at least one other time. The sort of contact he did not dole out regularly or willingly, the way I imagine other fathers did, when I imagine other fathers, of what it would have been like if . . . Casual touches. Spontaneous hugs. I did not receive these things. Some children suffer the pain of wrong touch, incestuous touch, violent touch. In my family, though, it was a given that we did not touch—as if this were weakness, or unnecessary, inappropriate.

He is holding me as we ride the merry-go-round on the boardwalk in Wildwood, New Jersey. We are both grimacing but maybe it's just the sun hitting our eyes. After all, I'm only a baby.

Or maybe we *are* already angry with each other. Maybe this film is some sort of prophecy of how things will be forevermore. Us, going round and round, eyes squinting, discomfort obvious to anyone who views us. Right up until this very day.

We never liked each other much. And I am convinced now he does not love me, never did. This is not a complaint, not anymore. I'm too old for that now. This is merely my observation, looking back, searching for one bit of happy comfort felt in his presence. Search as I will, I can find none.

I have a remarkable memory. It startles people. Be careful what you tell me, I joke, when friends start talking. I can recall phone numbers of people I haven't spoken to in ten years. Birthdays of ex-boyfriends and relatives I haven't seen in forever. I can quote others on things they have forgotten saying ages ago. It's a gift. And a curse.

Family members have told me again and again that I exaggerate. That it can't be the way I remember it. They tell me I am too harsh in my recollection of my father. That of course he loved me. My mother always says, "He does love you. He always did. In his own way."

I know better. It is three decades plus past that baby me, frowning on the carousel. Near two decades since the first time he touched me. A decade and a half since the second and final time we connected. The last time he tried, even that, is fully ten years gone now. But that moment is still fresh in my mind, in this memory of mine. Like a photograph.

They think I cling to this story of our mutual disgust for one another so I can walk the world full of self-pity. They think I hang on to this thing they call myth so I can have someone else to blame for what I've done. They cannot understand how much I want to see it the way they do. To believe them when they say I'm giving it all too much weight.

Photographs. There must be photographs. I look for proof sometimes. Search for hard copies of the past, hoping to discover that I made up every last bit of my version. But there isn't any candid documentation of my father touching me. Why can't I find it?

The movies don't count. You see, my mother always hated being in front of her little Brownie camera as it whirred away, collecting snippets of our lives in five-minute chunks that flickered later on the screen unfurled in the family room. She loved to record our lives, our outings to the park, our trips to the Shore. But she herself is barely ever there, at most convinced to wave for a second or two before she retrieves the camera from Daddy and resumes her invisible position in the background.

He only held me up for these moving pictures because I was too little to stand or even sit by myself. The films are silent, but I can almost hear her telling my father to go and hold this baby, to pose for her record.

A little over a year ago, my mother sent me my folder. This is a ritual she performs whenever one of her nine children marries. Birth certificate. First lock of hair. Old report cards. And photographs culled from her endless shoeboxes full of them.

A few months ago, I dug out my folder. I had to see something. Something nagged at me. He touched me more than twice, and somewhere there was proof.

I recalled a picture of me on the day of my First Communion, again wincing into the sun, in the lily-white dress my mother had lovingly sewn for me, with a crown of fake daisies in my hair. I never was good at posing. At pretending to enjoy the falseness of pictures, of memories staged. I remembered something else besides the statue of the Virgin behind me in the front garden.

I remember my father standing beside me. I think he is wearing a black jacket. I think he is touching me. Or maybe he's not. Maybe there is a distance between us, literally inches, metaphorically miles. I have to know for sure. I have to see this picture again. Did he actually touch me more than twice of his own accord?

When I go to my folder, I cannot locate this picture of Daddy and me. There is one of me on that day, in that dress, posed before that statue. The fake daisies are there, too. My memory is as accurate as ever. Except for one thing: no Daddy. As it is now, and was from the beginning, he lives but is not present. He is gone from me now. He was gone from me then. I am standing alone.

I know that somewhere the other picture really exists. It must be in the files still. My mother's files. Her memories. We remember things differently, she and I. She probably remembers his arm draped across my shoulders, and in her viewfinder, he is proud as can be. I am thinking, if his arm is there, it is for her sake, not mine and certainly not his. I hear him—eager to move—urging her to take the picture already.

I have spent my whole life trying to rearrange the vision of him and me in my mind. I have created fantasies in which we are hugging and laughing and he is really, truly glad to have his arm around me. And later, much later, I tried to re-create these fantasies by proxy, as I let the arms of one man or another drape around me, hold me, have me for a night, a week, sometimes years too long.

It is the simplest of psychologies. Embarrassing to me

now that I understand it. Reject the daughter and she will search for you elsewhere. She will spend forever, kill herself, if need be, looking for love.

I did not spend forever. I am not dead. I did not find that love in another man, but unbelievably I found it anyway, in a child, my son. I learned from him the greatest joy and the greatest pain. I discovered once and for all that my memory was right. Daddy did not love me. Not the right way. He did not hold me, as I hold my son. He did not listen, as I listen to my son.

He must have had his reasons. I do not know what they are. He will never say. It has been years since he has spoken to me. I am lost to him. As he is to me.

I have stumbled through a world of men, searching, searching, for thirty-four years now, trying to come up with the perfect picture. I have failed, in that regard. But somehow, oddly, surprising my own self, I have managed to create a different kind of picture. Something avant-garde? Something happy, even? It is hard to say. But I no longer wince.

I look right into the camera. Sometimes, I smile.

2

WILDWOOD, New Jersey, is a straight shot south, seventy-five miles, from Eastville—the too-tiny, too-white, too-ignorant town I grew up in. It is three miles due north of Cape May, the southernmost tip of the Garden State. Around the year I was born, 1964, my parents began a project there not unlike the one they had started ten years earlier in Eastville.

Daddy always had a gift for retrieving items discarded by others and sweating long and hard until he'd turned these things into something useful, something enjoyable. He was particularly skilled at building houses out of used scrap lumber, scavenged doors and windows, and the sundry wing or prayer he found poking from a Dumpster or the site of a demolished building.

These places he built were blueprintless wonders that seemed to grow each time my mother had yet another child. Nine of us in all. In the early sixties, with four girls already, my brother due, and four more daughters in the none-too-distant future, Daddy began to build what will always remain my favorite house in the world, the shore house.

Like the house back home in Eastville, the shore house was a rambling number. My parents eloped when my mother was nineteen and my father twenty-four, escaping from the hell of South Philly to the promise of the Jersey 'burbs. They built both houses themselves, with the help of various relatives and friends. They worked from the ground up, starting small and never stopping.

Like the house in Eastville, which was surrounded by a high, thick hedgerow to keep the neighbors out and the family in, the lot they bought in Wildwood was also surrounded, this one by water. Technically, we were not in Wildwood proper, but rather on West Wildwood, an island just off the mainland. Calling this place an island, I fear, gives the false impression of some Ricardo Montalban–inhabited paradise.

Aesthetically, the island was anything but lush and paradisaical. West Wildwood sits in a bay off of the Atlantic, so low to the ground that it's beneath the ground, if that is possible. Below sea level. A full moon or an overzealous spit out the window, and the place would flood up to here. Sometimes, even higher. Trees, grass, and any other greenery not imported and tended to scrupulously failed to thrive in the salty air, the harsh sun, the frequent brutal winds and rain tossed into this mix by Mother Nature.

In the many years before his union job would force him to work longer and odder hours and many weekends, Daddy took us every Saturday for two-day mini-vacations to West Wildwood. But the height of our pleasures there occurred each August. Two-week vacations were always scheduled then, to coincide with August 15th, the Feast of the Assumption, when it is said the body of the Mother Mary was raised intact into the heavens, when it is said the ocean is blessed by her, can heal all ills, will provide a year of peace for those who dip into the surf.

August was also the annual time for the deadly storms that would tear up and down the Atlantic coast. Being surrounded by nothing but water and sheetrock walls, we were particularly vulnerable in West Wildwood. My father didn't care. While others feared hurricanes, Daddy seemed to thrive at the man-versus-nature challenge they presented. The lone ambulance would drive around the island, the driver announcing over his bullhorn that we must evacuate immediately. Daddy, in his gruff and scoffing voice, would counter that we were going nowhere. Everyone up to the second floor. We'd ride out the storm.

These annual hurricanes necessitated tiring hours of moving furniture up onto bricks—a tactic that rarely worked. Bad years, when the floods rose high enough to conquer the raised chairs and couches and saturate the rugs, they yanked it all up, tossed it all away, and went searching the streets—the source of much of our summerhouse furnishings—to find still more Early New Jersey Castoff. To this day, I cannot pass a chair or picture frame jutting from someone's trash without at least slowing to inspect it.

And hurricane conditions or not, not one summer passed when we did not face the ocean on the Feast of the Assumption. My father was and remains the most devout man I know. Come hell, high water, lightning, or threat of imminent death, he did not care. Every August 15th he and my mother and all of us children would step into that ocean to be blessed. I remember once sitting in the family car, after my own brief salty dunk, watching Daddy swim out further and further, lightning crashing all around him.

But the Shore brought out an unexpected aspect of Daddy. During the school year, he kept each of us children on a leash so short, a choke chain looked luxurious by comparison. However, he had one odd, liberal policy. Once we hit our midteen years, we were allowed to spend summers unchaperoned (save for weekends and his annual August trip), working the boardwalk or some gift shop on the mainland.

I suppose he figured that by the time we reached sixteen his lessons had been drilled deep enough into our heads to keep us out of trouble. Besides, my grandmother and uncle had a place just around the block. Daddy counted on them to keep tabs on us. More importantly he also counted on that other tool in his belt—God—to keep us in line.

From the time I was weeks old and first dipped in the holy waters of St. Anne's church in Eastville, until I was nineteen and in college, I did not miss a single Mass. My parents did an excellent job of instilling the fear of God and the guilt of the Catholic Church in us. We knew the minute we sinned—be it by taking the Lord's name in vain or stepping barefoot on a nail when we had been ordered not to leave the house sans shoes—that God was there to punish us.

And punish us he did. No matter how hard I tried, growing up, to be the best little lamb I could be, time and again I broke one commandment or another. I was a sinner through and through. I tried so hard to compensate. I became the youngest lector in our parish. I was the kid who took herself alone, in fifth grade, to sit through the three-hour Good Friday Services, hoping beyond hope that the Holy Spirit would descend upon me in some tangible form—a bolt of lightning to my heart, the voice of God ringing loud in my ears—and would show me I was a chosen one, the good girl I tried so hard to be.

But I was never good enough. I sinned, sometimes without knowing, only to have Daddy quickly point out my wicked ways. If I shook my leg during Mass, as I did one day, so nervous was I sitting beside him, I was deemed in need of psychiatric help. If I hit my brother and turned around and stubbed my toe, it was, I was told, the wrath of the Lord coming down on me.

The sacrament of confession extended beyond the vertical coffin of the confessional box in church, to the chapel of my father. When my mother's disciplinary tactics failed, he held judgment hour in the parlor. He'd sit reading all the bad news in the papers, a dead cigar in his mouth, making whichever one of us who had sinned that day sit and wait for his command that we confess. "What did you do wrong?" he would snarl, though he knew the answer already.

After a dramatic, stuttered admission of our sins, we would be apprised of our penance, typically a tongue-lashing or an indefinite grounding. My father rarely hit us. The threat of the belt, hanging there in the closet, was more than enough. We were good kids, actually. We just didn't know it. Over and over he told us how disappointing we were to him, that there was not a lick of common sense in the lot of us.

The parlor was also the place to petition for favors. The same nervousness we approached him with during sentencing for our sins, surfaced when we came to him to timidly ask permission for this or that. "Daddy, can I go to the dance on Saturday?" I would ask on a Monday. "Daddy, may I sleep next door for my fifteenth birthday?"

Requests were met the same way as confessions; it was like Russian roulette. No outside factors could increase the chance for a positive outcome—not mowing the lawn, not cleaning the house. At most, my father would grunt at us, pausing for a good length of time, apparently to contemplate. We were subject to his whims, to his long silences, to nos rendered because he said, that's why.

"Come over here and take off my socks," he would order, sometimes, as I waited to be allowed to present a query. And I would obey, peeling back the thin nylon knee-high socks, soaked in the sweat of twelve hours of hard labor, noting the contrast between the black hairs on his feet and his fish-belly skin. "Dial me a number on the phone." "Clean my glasses."

Invariably, my requests, even when coupled with thoughtful sock-peeling, rapid phone-dialing, or flawless eyeglass-cleaning, would net the same response. After pondering our pleas with the same portentous silence that prefaced his "conversations," he would pause again, then finally proclaim "We'll see," an answer most often followed up with days of waiting for a definitive answer, of feeling total embarrassment that I could not let my girlfriends know whether or not I would be joining them that weekend.

By sixteen, I was accustomed to, if not comfortable with, my father's modus operandi. In May, weeks before the end of my sophomore year in high school, I came to him with a request I felt certainly would be shot down.

I sat in the parlor and waited for him to finish his news-papers. Finally, at the end of his cigar and reading, he put the paper down and looked up at me, over the top of his bi-focals. "What is it?" he grunted.

I stuttered, as I always did in his presence. "Um . . . Daddy? Umm . . . I was wondering if . . . ummm . . ."

"Spit it out."

"I want to go to Wildwood for the summer. With a friend. I want to get a job."

The odds against me were overwhelming. My older sis-ters, The Big Girls, as we called them, had spent many sum-mers there already. But I was different. I was four years younger than my next older sister. I had no sibling close enough in age to join me, whereas the Big Girls had had each other. My brother, two years younger, was closest in age, but too young to get a job. No one had ever been al-lowed to go to the Shore without a sibling for a roommate.

"We'll see," he grunted, as always, dismissing me with those words. I went to my room and prayed. Dear God, please. Please, please, please. Let me get the hell out of East-ville for the summer. Let me get away from the trap of this shitty town. I have already read all the books in the tiny li-brary here. Twice. I want a job. I want some freedom. I want a chance to meet boys.

I probably didn't actually admit to God that boys were on my agenda. But they most certainly were. In high school, I was the dateless wonder. Many, many years later, after I'd lived far away from home for a long time, had graduated from college even, I ran into the only boy from my high school who had ever kissed me. He told me my problem with boys was never my looks, as I'd so often suspected. He explained that everyone, including him, had been petrified of my daddy.

But I knew Wildwood would be different. Without my father to report to nightly, with only my liberal grandmother and uncle to monitor me, I would have a chance, finally, to figure out this boy-girl stuff.

For a week I sweated and worried and doubted he would let me go. Finally my father beckoned me into his parlor. "I've made a decision. You can go."

3

MORE than anything, Wildwood was a city of firsts for me. First full-time job, first kiss, first unwrapped penis encountered, and years after that grope, first fuck. Despite all my promises to my parents that I would be good and follow their strict curfew—impossible for them to enforce so far away—I was able to go out into the white-trash, carnival-like atmosphere of Wildwood and explore what I'd dreamed about forever.

Back in Eastville, I'd spent ten years longing for a boyfriend. It started in kindergarten; crush after devastating unrequited crush kept me hopeful that one day, one day I would meet the perfect mate. He would take me away from Daddy, he would recognize how hard I tried, how much I was capable of doing. He would give me the endless, unconditional love I hoped, in vain, to find at home.

This burning desire sounds so romance novel. So movie-of-the-week. And really, could a six-year-old have possibly wanted a boyfriend? I assure you, she could and she did. Time and again I eyed one boy or another and plunked him dead center into the lead role of some fantasy I created in which we ran off happily together despite the fact that we were only eight or ten years old. A few times, I was bold enough to drop hints of my plans to one or another of these boys. A note scrawled hastily and blushingly slipped to him. A word to a friend who I hoped would get word to my potential Romeo.

And each time I tried, my advances were met with devastating rejection, either total silence or in-my-face mockery. Elementary school boys did not want girl-cooties, but that factor never occurred to me. I just assumed any lack of interest meant I was the stupidest, ugliest girl in town.

Later, in junior high and then high school, the boys were less mean-spirited. By then, they were starting to acknowledge that having a girlfriend might not be so uncool and germy after all. Still, I did not rank. Surely my annoying and obvious overzealousness for their attention played a part. Too, it was due to the well-known fact that I came from a very strict family. Why bother with me when plenty of other girls had no curfew, no angry father waiting to glare at a suitor?

I overcompensated for the lack of reciprocal attention by pushing harder. I developed a wicked sense of humor, took teasing as good-naturedly as possible, and pretended to be delighted with my "special" place as one of the guys. I wonder now if any of them realized how much more I really wanted. A kiss, for starters.

Determined, at sixteen, to change my loveless status, I set to work almost immediately upon arriving at the shore. Early on, my roommate, Bette, and I unearthed two scruffy boys wandering the three-mile length of the boardwalk one night. We struck up a conversation with Chip and Dale, giddy at the attention they readily offered. We listened to their sad story: a whole weekend in front of them, no place to stay, no money to rent a room. While I had no intention of letting them into my parents' house, I saw no harm in letting them sleep in the driveway in their car.

They followed us back to West Wildwood, and, using those same heart-stopping, yo-babe, Jersey-boy skills (which is to say, none) on our naive hearts (like me, Bette had never had a boyfriend) they quickly convinced us that surely we could at least have them into the house for a little while.

Bette and Dale settled into the kitchen to talk. Chip and I sank into the soft puke-green vinyl couch in the Captain's Quarters, my father's private den. There, amidst ships in plastic bottles, rough wood carvings of raincoated fishermen, seashells-turned-ashtrays, and other sundry nautical items, I held my breath. At last, it was time.

Chip, worldly fellow that he was, deftly reached his arm across my shoulder and tugged on the pull string of the only light on in the room. "Let's save electricity," he whispered, priming me for a life full of stupid guy-lines. Let's, I thought. And finally, finally, I was transformed from the never-kissed-loser-chick into the girl-who-had-tongued-and-been-tongued-by-the-boy-with-the-peach-fuzz-mustache.

They disappeared that night, never to be heard from again. Bette's heartbreak lasted the summer. I, surprising myself, moved on quickly, replacing Chip that summer—and over the course of the following four summers spent in Wildwood—with a parade of young men, each more eager than the last to utter hollow words of love, to break me down, to somehow convince me to give up my virginity.

To facilitate my excursions into the worlds of love and lust, I learned with each passing summer to drink more and more. I had practiced a little back home, on the weekends during the school year, setting aside terrifying thoughts of what would happen if I got caught, and replacing them with notions of how much more the completely unattainable senior, Bobby O'Donnell, would be impressed by and attracted to me if I helped him guzzle the pint bottles of Jack Daniel's he carried in his jacket pocket at all times.

Now, drinking was not limited to the weekends. While Bette and I remained tame that first summer, summers two through five were far different. That second stint at the shore, my best friend, Stella, joined me. More daring than Bette, more like-minded in her quest to find a man, she made an ideal partner in crime.

I worked days that summer in a candy store run by two screaming, identical twin brothers who alternated between punching each other on the walk in front of the store, and quizzing me on my sexual exploits. It didn't matter that I had no sexual exploits.

In fact, my virginity—which I proudly acknowledged—seemed to thrill them more. Taking bets that I would never, as I swore I would, last until marriage, they would engage me in lengthy conversations that I suspect now were foreplay to their fantasies, fuel for whatever it was they did as they retreated to a backroom cot.

Stella worked nights on the shittiest amusement pier on the boardwalk, spending eight hours at a time taking tickets, jumping on and off the creaky merry-go-round. After my shifts, I'd race home, change out of the ridiculous nurse's uniform the twins insisted I wear, and arrive to keep her company, help her while away the hours until we could go out drinking, scope out men.

We quickly befriended the carnies she worked with, all of

them scruffy men, most of them illegal Irish immigrants who'd traveled to Wildwood when they'd heard, correctly, that visa-free jobs were theirs for the taking. They made at least as much money as us, but always seemed broker. Suckers for this poverty act, sucked in further by their irresistible brogues, we often had large groups of them back to my parents' house, where we'd take the little money we had and use it to prepare feasts for them. To show their appreciation, one or another would kiss me, hold me, fingerfuck me after drinking the night away at clubs with names the likes of The Bearded Clam and Woody's. I never, ever let them get to home plate—one of the endless euphemisms I used as we lay in our beds, and I described to Stella the things I had and had not done.

This was the year I consented to stick a nervous, unskilled hand down the too-tight designer jeans of an American carnie named Jimmy, a guy who proclaimed he was seventeen but appeared—save for his many tattoos—no older than ten. We stumbled out of the Garden State Bar—back then, to gain access to a club, sufficient ID consisted of little more than a three-by-five card scrawled over in crayon: I swear I am old enough to drink. The fake ID I'd sent away for from the back of a magazine was as realistic as Burt Reynolds's hair. No matter. It worked.

Jimmy and I approached the glowing foamy waves of the Atlantic, tackled each other, rolled through the wet sand. "Touch it," he ordered. Touch it? Uh-oh. Okay, maybe I'd erred and let a man's finger or two slide into my jeans before. But I had never actually come in contact with a penis. Had not the slightest idea of what to expect. My classification of sins listed being felt up as very bad, but not nearly as evil as stroking a man's dick. I was terrified. Hell doubtless awaited if I dared.

"Touch it," he urged again, then resumed chewing on my neck so hard that the next day I appeared to have been in a serious neck-on collision with a clothesline. I reached down, wriggled tentative fingers into his still-zipped jeans. I touched. I pulled. Too hard? Maybe. Probably. Because next, this man-child with the frightening blue eyes that appeared lit from behind said knowingly, "Your first one, isn't it?"

That summer ended on an awful note, also penis-related. Stella, a year my senior, had graduated the preceding June and was heading off to college. She had been my very best friend for years. One of the only companions I had daring enough to visit me at home, the place so many others avoided thanks to my father's reputation. She had listened to me cry again and again. As had I to her.

As August drew to a close, a sinking sensation filled me. I would have to head back to our horrid high school alone, without my confidante. I would have to endure being treated like a child when summers in Wildwood had taught me, at least in some capacities, that I was already grown up. I composed a long love letter of farewell to her. Took some of my meager savings and bought her the boots she had eyed, wistfully, in the shoe store window all summer. I planned to focus on her that last night.

Enter Luke. Luke was the six-foot three, blond-haired, blue-eyed bouncer at the Garden State. I flirted with him ceaselessly that summer and he flirted back, sort of. Actually, he was more like a big brother, a man too kind to flat-out reject my advances—though he never gave in, either—a man who thanked me sincerely for all the gifts of pilfered candy I brought him from my place of employ.

Perhaps because he knew I was leaving soon and posed no threat of showing up to bug him again, at last, on the eve of Stella's departure, he invited me to his boardinghouse after his shift finished at 3 A.M. Like a puppy, I followed him home, plopped into his lap, got more drunk than I already was, if that is possible. Stella joined us and was clearly outraged at my disloyalty. She hopped on her bike and stormed back to our place alone.

Hours later, after he failed to convince me to dig any further than the outer layer of his Fruit Of The Loom–clad crotch, dawn crept in. As did Stella. She found me in Luke's bed, having returned and bullied her way past his roommates, who'd tried to stop her. She demanded I get my ass up and out of there, rode her bicycle far ahead of me as we pedaled the miles back to the island.

I gave her the letter, the boots. But it was not enough to fix things, to make up for my abandoning her on what was supposed to have been our final night together. More than any gift I gave her, I gave her a message I would send to other friends again and again over the years. No matter how much I loved them, if a man stepped in, said "Come with me," ordered me to jump, I would brush off the friend and turn to the man. And all I would ask him was: How high?

4

THE first time my father ever touched me, without being prompted to do so by my camera-wielding mother, I was seventeen years old and in my senior year of high school.

A stellar student my entire time there, I'd already whizzed through all the honors English classes by my junior year, had completed an independent honors geometry course also, and managed A's easily in nearly all the other classes I took. In fact, I'd contemplated graduating a year early, joining Stella and most of my other friends who were a year ahead of me, getting the hell out of that boring prison with its bad lunches and intricate clique system.

But, thanks to a technical administrative restriction, my plans were denied. Thus I remained, stuck, stir-crazy, with only two classes, one of them PE.

To compensate for my boredom and fill my spare time, I made work for myself. Elected president of the student body, I came up with project after project. I ran dances and blood drives and flower sales. I took on duties as a teacher's aide, helping learning disabled students. At noon each day I left the building and drove my old car over to the nearby mall, where I worked thirty hours a week, sometimes more, at Macy's.

Still, there was a hole. I missed Stella terribly. The one and only boy from school who'd ever dared ask me out and kissed me a few times the year before was also gone. My status of wild-child/desired female at the shore had no impact on the slim pickings that remained—I was still just one of the guys to them. Home was a place to be avoided as much as possible. Work didn't fill up enough of my time or emptiness either. I needed something else. And so, using the skills I'd honed the summer before, I began to drink more regularly.

One night, delighted with myself for convincing a store owner to sell me an entire case of beer sans identification, I drank boldly and heartily with my friends. I still had the earliest curfew, I was still the awkward girl with the freaky father, but for those few hours I laughed with my classmates. I fit in.

So happy—and drunk—was I when I returned home, I threw caution to the wind. I let myself into the house and fumbled with the multiple locks on the front door, unfortunately located right next to my parents' bedroom. They were asleep. I marched up the stairs, decided to take a bath. Pleased with my decision, I began to sing.

Though the door was closed and my mother an entire floor removed from me, she heard. She came up after me, sleepy, knocked on the door, demanded I come out immediately.

What did I say to her then? Her face was so pained. Did I deny my drunkenness? Ignore her plea for me to hush before my father heard?

Too late. His heavy footsteps on the stairs scared us both, no doubt frightened my younger siblings, too, feigning sleep in the door-free rooms around us.

His hand crashed into my face. At least he was thoughtful enough not to ball it into a fist. No physical pain registered, thanks to the booze and the shock and the swiftness of the event. I stood there and took it. As if I had a choice.

The next morning, hungover in my bed, years of "Shhh, Daddy's home," and "Don't let Daddy find out . . ." filled my angry, humiliated, outraged ears. I was beyond sick of his shit. I had to escape.

I packed some bags, stormed down the stairs, aiming for the front door. My mother, wielding a fire poker she would never have had the heart to actually strike me with, re-strained me. I screamed. She cried. Finally, one of the Big Girls—they were all living on their own now—came and swept me away, tried to calm me.

I returned home that evening—where else could I go?—to an indefinite grounding. My first opportunity, I snuck into the liquor cabinet and stole some Scotch from the collection of bottles my father received, but never drank, every Christmas. I sat in my room, drinking some more, The Who and The Rolling Stones and Bruce Springsteen on my little clock radio, consoling me that it was only a teenage waste-land, that you can't always get what you want, that some-day we'd look back on this and it would all seem funny.

Angrily, I waded—still an outstanding student and overzealous extracurricular queen—through the remains of my senior year. In the halls of the school, I doubt anyone noticed my displeasure. I stored the rage inside while smil-ing brightly on the outside. This cheerful demeanor was the only thing that netted me the praise and love I desired. Whatever I was granted was never enough—I was insatiable. But I made do during the day with the attention of my classmates and teachers, returning to the house each night, sitting in my room, sulking, counting the days until another summer of freedom arrived.

By the time June rolled around, Daddy was fed up with me and my attitude. No way was I allowed to stay at his summerhouse again. But while he insisted he could prevent any independence on my part until I was twenty-one, for some reason he did not try to stop me from going to Wildwood anyway. I found a small basement apartment on the mainland, and Stella, home from college, joined me. Once again, all hell broke loose.

Our landlords, Jim and Jeannie McShane, lived upstairs with their six kids. Nearly all of them could, and did, drink to beat the band. I immediately developed a platonic crush on Dotty, the daughter closest to me in age. I also developed a much more agonizing crush of the romantic variety on Bugsy, the middle brother, several years my senior and old enough that even I thought of him as a man.

Stella looked on with trepidation as I overzealously sought their company, told me I was being a fool with all this infatuation. Dismissing her commentary, I trailed Dotty constantly, adopting her slang and manner of speech, emulating her punk-surfer fashions, racing out to buy and memorize the lyrics of the same new-wave music she favored.

Much more aggravating, for all involved—me, him, Dotty and Stella—was my Bugsy obsession. He was all shaggy blond hair, surfer shorts, and silence. I loved silent men. To me, it indicated that deep secrets and great thoughts were being held, locked away, waiting for me to crack the safe with the perfect combination of lust, coyness, and maniacal laughter whenever I was within earshot of the desired shy boy.

I was relentless in my quest. I studied Bugsy's schedule to use—I hoped—to my advantage. I knew the precise moment he would ride his bicycle down the driveway, past my door, on his way to work, and I made damn sure I was lying in his path, on a beach towel, in my swimsuit, appearing, I hoped, as provocative as I felt.

I'd return from days of scrubbing toilets as a chambermaid, will Dotty to come downstairs and invite me to go clubbing with her and her siblings. Dotty liked me enough to indulge me often. Early on she taught me the alleged money-saving technique of drinking before going out. More than one night, I'd pound the better part of a bottle of liquor, barely able to stand as I squeezed into the backseat of her old Maverick with a gang of surfer types, on our way out to dance until dawn to Springsteen knockoff bands and pulsating disco.

I used these opportunities, waiting until I was thoroughly saturated in beer and vodka, to sidle up to Bugsy and hang on him. Nights he was our designated drunk swerver for the trip home, I weaseled my way front seat center for the journey, pressed up close against him. When I was extra drunk and, thus, extra daring, I'd slip my hand up the leg of his baggy corduroy shorts, try to coax his whiskey dick to full attention. He hated this. Would slur-mutter for me to please stop, he was trying to concentrate.

But often enough, once the other passengers were let off, he would give in, turn to me in the car he called Anne, and kiss me sloppily. Triumphant, ecstatic, I would pet and be petted, then pass out with him amidst a pile of torn-off clothing. Each time this happened, I would wake to the glaring sun burning in my eyes, cringe at the knowledge of what was coming next.

Which was always the sound of his father's angry voice, on the upstairs porch, bitching to Jeannie about what a damn show Bugsy and I were putting on for the neighbors. Invariably, too disgusted to do so himself, he would beckon Ronny, the youngest son, to wake us, to tell us to get in the house for Chrissakes.

Though the intensity of these entanglements would wax and wane, would stretch over the next several summers, looking back I cannot recall one single conversation with this man I deemed most worthy in the world. We had only drunken make-out sessions in the car or, on a really good night, the ancient pull-out couch in my living room. We never had sex. The furthest we ever got was a nightmare attempt on my part once to render him a blow job—something I had no experience at, that he responded to by telling me to please, stop already.

Still, I hung in there. If I just tried hard enough, I reasoned—even when I wasn't drunk, even as I soberly scrubbed the bathrooms of the Premiere Hotel—one day he would come around and love me as I did him. Time and again I confused the physical need that drove him to cave in to me for something more. Time and again I would think of "real" in-love couples—the kind on TV, the kind in books and movies—and I would juxtapose our faces on these people.

But like complicated word problems that ultimately do

not prepare you for the real world—as algebra teachers like to pretend they will—it was impossible to sort through all the factors of this nonrelationship, all the signals mixed. The word problem of Bugsy and me was this: If a boy is heading toward a girl at 10 miles per hour and drunk, and that girl is heading toward the boy at 1,000 miles per hour and even drunker, at what point will they kiss? Make love? Have children? Finally, for bonus points, what should they name these children?

I spent hours, then weeks, then full summers pining for Bugsy, but he never wanted me back. Not really. Once or twice I strayed, went out with some other guy, tried to distract myself or hope to arouse jealous interest on Bugsy's part. The furthest I ever went in these attempts was accepting a date with a huge high school football player who kissed me hard one night and got angry when I would not sacrifice my virginity to him.

In my apartment, wanting to get rid of him, I played possum on the couch, pretended to be passed out as I actually listened to him standing above me, urging me angrily to suck his cock. When I refused to respond, he jacked off on my back. So unlearned was I in matters of male genitalia, for years I thought he'd pissed on me.

His antics proved Bugsy's worth. Bugsy would never do such a thing. Bugsy, the only man I might consider offering my virginity to, would never take it. He was the most perfect man ever.

I refused, ever, to recognize his rejection for what it was. I elevated him higher and higher the further he moved from me. How incredibly noble, I thought, that he would take his time like this.

Florida

5

THE second time my father touched me, we were standing in Philadelphia International Airport, at the gate marked Tampa. It was January 1983, and I was just days shy of my nineteenth birthday. After years of dreaming of this moment, finally I was about to bid my father farewell, to strike out into the world on my own, without his daily scrutiny and criticism of my actions.

As the previous summer had drawn to a close, Dotty drunkenly uttered something to me in a bar one night that stuck. Why not join her in Florida for college? I think, now, it was the kind of suggestion made lightly, a sort of "Wouldn't it be cool if . . ." sentiment meant to be forgotten the next day.

Not by me. After I graduated from high school, my longing to break from my father's short tether intensified. He'd told me, years before, that college was for posers. My duty, in the Gospel According to Daddy, was to find a job and a husband postgraduation. But that just drove me further to defy him. Though I did not have the means or permission to leave his house, and while lack of funding prohibited my attending an exclusive college that accepted my application, I signed up for classes at the local state college. Still, to my regret, I remained under my father's roof.

Bored at this nonchallenging college as much as I had been in high school, I continued to fantasize about escape. The more I dreamed, the more Dotty's words came back to me. Secretly, I mailed off an application to the University of South Florida, knowing I could never finance such a move, knowing further that Daddy would never allow it.

When an acceptance letter arrived, I sucked in my breath, let the dream of leaving get a little bigger, though I knew that was foolish. Daddy still reminded me often enough that he was my keeper until I was twenty-one, never mind that the law stated otherwise. I knew, if he said no, I would listen. Knew odds were incredibly high that he would say no.

Still, I was so weary—of my too-easy classes, my ongoing stint at my mall job, the early curfew I still had to obey—I had to at least try. As I had so many times in my life, I approached him in his parlor one night, being certain to wait until he was through reading his papers. I begged permission to move to Florida, assured him I could finance my own way, knowing he would name this as his first reason to refuse. He looked at me over the top of his bifocals. Was silent for a few moments. Then uttered the same response he'd uttered a million times before. "We'll see," he said. Dismissed.

Weeks later, after making me wait for an answer, he finally called me back into his quarters. I nearly dropped over with shock and joy when he informed me that permission

44

was granted. Surely I was dreaming. Immediately, I called Dotty, and was not even deterred when she, whom I expected to share my enthusiasm, sounded surprised—in a nice enough way—when I told her my great news.

Now, Daddy and I stood, waiting for the boarding call. Neither of us voiced sorrow at my parting or love for the other. I doubt those thoughts even crossed his mind. They certainly didn't cross mine. Still, the elation I expected to feel upon leaving him, and the joy I expected to see in his eyes at finally being rid of me, his lifelong pain in the ass, were absent. If anything, we were awkward, unable to find even small talk to pass the time. I'd never had an actual conversation with this man whose blood ran through me. I could not think of how to start one now.

The call was made, and I stepped forward to join the line of other boarding passengers. As I did, my father reached for me, in the only gentle gesture he ever made toward his wild, angry fourth daughter. He squeezed my elbow. "Stay out of trouble," he said, his standard gruff bark toned down considerably. And then he walked away.

A couple of hours later, the plane touched down in Tampa. I found a shuttle and watched dumbstruck through the window as we whizzed by palm trees and other foreign greenery, such a far cry from the icy Jersey winter I'd left behind. Except for brief trips to Philadelphia to visit my grandmothers, I had never been out of the state I was born in. More than the emerald scenery, it was the thought of my freedom that left me awestruck.

My first semester at the University of South Florida consisted of a long series of occasions when I got lost, tried to find myself, gained a hint of confidence when I did so, and then promptly got lost again. I had no idea how to register for classes at such a huge institution. Struggled as I tried to read a map of the immense grounds. Once spent over an hour trying to find my way back from the edge of campus when I rode my bicycle a little too far out.

I was still too scared of everything in the world to think to look for landmarks. Was too embarrassed at my own naiveté to stop and ask for directions. Though I continued to excel academically, I felt thoroughly stupid on a regular basis, the only blind woman in a world where everyone else, I felt certain, had twenty-twenty vision.

Men were no exception to my floundering ways. Far from it. Lacking confidence, convinced I was fat and ugly, I fell back on my well-worn, get-real-drunk-and-throw-yourself-at-them technique when trying to meet guys at bars or parties on campus. While I'd been with plenty of men in Wildwood, at nineteen I still had never had a real boyfriend, someone to talk with intimately, someone who would give me that unconditional love I still foolishly thought was out there in the form of one other, waiting for me to find him, if only I searched hard enough.

Admittedly, part of the reason I was eager to join Dotty at USF was that Bugsy had once attended the school. This offered me the bonus of vicarious thrill. I could walk the halls he had walked, breathe the air he had breathed, somehow stay a part of him though he was hundreds of miles away. And I could look forward to the day when he might visit his sisters, allowing me an opportunity to show off how well I fit in at his old hunting grounds.

Dotty introduced me to a number of Bugsy's friends and former roommates, and I entertained myself by falling for first one and then another. Though none of them ever returned the favor, they did adopt me as a pet—again, I was one of the guys—inviting me to their dorm rooms, getting me high as a kite courtesy of their floor-to-ceiling bongs, smiling at me as I sat, too stoned to speak, Pink Floyd filling my ears while fantasies of romances with these stoners filled my mind.

Finally, a couple of months into the semester, I got a date. Brian was not a friend of Bugsy's. In fact, though the first time I spotted him was on campus, he did not attend the university. I admired all six feet, four inches of his blond-haired, blue-eyed beauty from a distance, sighed when he disappeared, chastised myself for being too timid to approach him and say hello.

When I ran into him a second time, weeks later, standing in a jam-packed bar after a college basketball game, I walked right up to him and introduced myself. That he heard or even saw me is a wonder. I was nearly a foot shorter, and the crowd was obnoxiously loud. He looked down at me, smiled, made a joke, and asked for my number.

I waited, knowing he would never call. When the phone did ring a few days later I almost jumped out of my skin. We passed a couple of weeks together, dancing around the edges of romance. Brian loved to take me all over the city— he'd grown up in Tampa and knew every little offbeat place a newcomer like me could never have found unguided. He took me thrift shopping for vintage clothes, introduced me to cutting-edge music, discussed with me the philosophy he found in classic works of literature he read not for some class requirement, but simply because he wanted to.

We were an odd Eliza Doolittle and Henry Higgins. He

was the lead singer for a punk band called the Impotent Sea Snakes, an expert on the budding punk-music scene, a man who thought for himself, someone who blatantly ignored rules he didn't care for. I was still a good little girl, continuing to attend Mass, striving to please my professors, scared to death to walk past the NO TRESPASSING signs and join him skateboarding in drained swimming pools.

But his impact was undeniable. I cut my long, straight, Breck-girl hair into a spiky mess and then a flattop. I listened to the music he recommended, embraced the antiestablishment messages I found there. I ditched my mall clothes in favor of vintage until, at least outwardly, I gave off the tough air of a street kid.

Not long into our adventures, we decided to spend a night alone, drinking in my dorm. Armed with a bottle of booze and a bag of ice, we headed up the three flights of stairs. Many drinks and a few kisses later, Brian made a move for more. Still a virgin, I awkwardly summoned aloud the unspoken no that had worked with all those boys back in Jersey. Brian sat up and looked at me, puzzled. Wasn't my invitation to be alone with him on my bed an obvious request for sex?

After a moment, in a mock movie-hero voice, he said, "Only two things to do on a rainy night, and I didn't come here to play cards."

I smiled, weakly, at his attempt to make light of this misunderstanding. He hugged me hard, sincere as ever, and stood to leave. Seeing the sadness on my face, he consoled me. "Don't worry. I'll call you. I promise."

Right, I thought, and monkeys will fly out of my ass on the first ring. Damn him for being so typical after all. I would never see him again, this promise of a call clearly an excuse to slip away quickly, before I started crying or begging.

For a second time, though, Brian stunned me. He rang me up the Monday morning following our fiasco. Could he take me to breakfast? That call placed him on a pedestal still intact now, fifteen years later. Unlike all those boys I'd messed with at the Shore, Brian did not mock me with lies and promises broken.

Nearly every Monday, for the next four years, he called to take me to breakfast and spend the day with me. No matter what I was doing—including having the sex I finally decided wasn't such a sin—I rushed to finish, to rush off with Brian, jealous boyfriend be damned.

Somehow, I managed to get past my crush and accept that Brian was my friend. No bitterness. No fear. This was one of the best moves in my life. Brian continued to dote on me, to teach me things from common sense to the works of Italo Calvino to Volkswagen repair. For the first time, I had a man around I wasn't hell-bent on making fall in love with me. I was at ease around him. I didn't try to hide my ignorance, my fears, my giddiness. Brian, in turn, showed me that these things did not make me bad or unattractive. In fact, he taught me that so many of the things I loathed about myself were actually attractive assets.

It was a lot to learn in one semester. I can't recall the details of a single class I took that year, but I can still see Brian and me bouncing along in his VW bus to a cheap Mexican restaurant. Or Brian explaining the ways of the world to me. Or reaching out to touch me, to encourage me to grow into the woman he seemed clearly to see, while I still looked into a mirror that reflected an awkward girl.

Brian's influence inspired me to question many of my beliefs, particularly my Catholicism. One Sunday, late in the semester, I sat in Mass and several people turned and openly gawked at my haircut, ridiculed me with their stares. Something clicked. I was tired of following blindly, of being part of a group that included such idiots. I left that day and never went back. Granted, I never fully overcame the guilty trappings pounded into me by that institution for two decades. Still, at least I escaped the weekly sexist, didactic rituals.

I did not realize then how strongly I associated the Church with my father, though I see now, easily, that the two were inseparable in my mind. Both stunted my growth, both tried to control me, both filled me with fear and insisted upon self-flagellation. Too scared to flat-out thumb my nose at either, I believe I embraced a lifestyle that I subconsciously knew would get me kicked out of both the Daddy club and the Pope club.

And the job I did was efficient. I went back to Wildwood at the end of the semester, for another summer in Chateau McShane. Daddy came by once to see me, took one look at my radical new haircut, and attacked me. This wouldn't have happened if I had stayed at home and been a good girl. See? College was for idiots. I was despicable. He did not visit me again that summer.

6

MY final two summers in Wildwood were a blur of waiting on tables, drinking away the nights, napping for what seemed like mere minutes, only to head back to work and do it all again. The only real sleep I ever got came on my rare days off or for a few hours in the afternoons, after work, as I lay crashed on a towel by the ocean.

Both years, I returned to the Premiere Hotel, where I had cut my teeth changing sheets and sanitizing toilets the preceding summer. Rewarding me for my cheerful attitude toward cleaning up the shit of others, Rhonda, the owner, promoted me to a coveted food-service position.

Rhonda was a four-star bitch, a former minor beauty queen, who had blown up to over two hundred pounds, married the prick son of another rich hotel family for property purposes (South Jersey's answer to a royal wedding), and proceeded to take out the misery these things caused her on her lowly employees.

Mornings, we reported in at 5:30 A.M., and often we did not clock out again until fourteen hours later, sometimes longer. Respite came in the form of intense bonding among her small, disgruntled staff. En masse, we smiled to Rhonda's face, ran at her heels like pedigreed poodles, nipping to answer her sharp commands.

"Detail! Detail!" she would snap, clapping her hands and pointing to a mis-set table or some speck on the floor. Behind her back, during short breaks between banquet meals for hundreds upon hundreds of senior citizens, we'd sneak off to a pub up the road. There, we'd pound a few drafts and have a field day of mean-spirited commentary at her expense.

Of all my fellow waiters, I grew closest, fastest, to Jonathan, a smart-ass with a spiky haircut and cynical attitude nearly identical to my own. Never tiring of each other, even with eighty-hour work weeks spent side by side, we often shared our days off together, too.

Like Brian, Jonathan saw in me things I would not notice in myself for years. When he pointed out something he admired in me, I found it nearly impossible to believe him. Except for one very brief, very drunken make-out session up against a cigarette machine in a bar one night, Jonny and I had no physical interest in each other. We were kindred spirits, confidants, each the voice that egged the other on when one of us grew upset over some outrageous injustice—like a bartender with a bad attitude and poor mixing skills.

We didn't just catch each other's attention. Together, we made a scene for the city wherever we went to drink and dance through the night. Everyone paid attention. The old people we served in the banquet room were the most delighted by us. They gushed about our wacky haircuts, the way Jonathan managed to somehow make his required black-and-white uniform look uniquely "punky," our faux-irreverent service. Many of them insisted on taking our picture together to show the folks back home "those punk-rock kids we met down at the shore."

Best of all, in Jonathan I found someone whose ears perked up when I told my Daddy stories. He listened, outraged at my childhood tales. Much as I despised the way my father treated me, I also had grown to accept it as the norm. Jonathan pointed out how warped this thinking was, insisted Daddy's behavior was inexcusable. To underscore his point, he introduced me to his own parents, buoyant people who enjoyed my company, laughed at my jokes, and didn't treat me like I was five. These people were parents?

Jonathan showered me with vintage clothes, odd earrings, tapes he made for me, and other funny little gifts. But the best thing he ever gave me was a sentence. "I love you," he said one night as the summer grew to a close and we faced our imminent separation. I squirmed. I was twenty years old and no one had ever, ever said those words to me. I'd waited forever to hear this sentiment, but now, as I did, I had no idea how to respond.

I returned to Florida for my sophomore year of college, remained boyfriend-free, though I did manage a couple of drunken one-night dry-hump stands. Mostly, I relied on letters and calls to Jonathan, and breakfasts with Brian, to fill my need for intimacy.

The less attention guys—potential boyfriends all of them—gave me, the more I went out of my way to get some. I kept cutting my hair, started piercing my ear until I looked like the goalie for a dart team, and my choice in clothes grew odder still. At parties, I danced wildly, laughed loudest of all. If being chosen as a partner was out, being noticed would have to do.

When spring semester ended, I went back to Wildwood for my final summer. Unbelievably, Daddy, who had started speaking to me again, offered the West Wildwood house, cheap, to me and two friends. That lasted about two weeks, ending when he came to check up on me. We had another one of our stupid fights, this time facing off in the driveway, screaming at each other. Screw him, I decided. My friends, not nearly as enticed by my beloved shore as I was, left town immediately. I set off to find a room in a boardinghouse.

Jonathan arrived around this time with a schoolmate. Stan, too, needed housing, so we decided to room together. We found an ancient house by the sea, and chatted up the white-trash proprietress. We assured her we were brother and sister and that one room would do just fine.

She gave us a tour of the place, yapping in her thick Jersey brogue as she led us up to the third floor, her burning cigarette clenched between her lips, bouncing bouncing, the ash growing longer and longer until finally she cupped one hand and used it for an ashtray without missing a beat. "This room," she said, making a game-show-hostess wave to show off a ten-by-twenty-foot cell with two beds and one small dresser, "is sixty dollars a week." We took it.

Our very first night together, Stan and I went out and got plowed. Despite the fact I found myself attracted to him, I knew he had a girlfriend, making him strictly off limits. Therefore, I had no need to impress and woo him by feigning coyness. Ironically, the real, loud, outspoken me excited him. He clung to my every word. With this sort of attention, as the night wore on and the drinks sank in, my morals wore off. By the time we stumbled back up to our garret, I was pretty sure I had misplaced the will to resist the pass he wasted no time in making.

He pinned me to the bed, tore off his clothes and most of mine. Still a virgin, I panicked. But again, the booze took over. I lay there as he mounted me, and had a conversation in my head. I was getting so sick of this virgin shit. I had already let so many men touch me in so many ways. Why not just go for it?

Because I couldn't. I just could not. This was wrong for too many reasons. My panic grew. I tried to push him away. He held me down more firmly, spread my legs wider, moved to make his grand entrance.

Somehow, I stopped him, kept him from entering me, though it literally took me years to figure out I had not given up my virginity that night. He had come so close. I did not know the "symptoms" of lost virginity, my parents had breathed not one word about sex to me, and I hadn't thought to ask my girlfriends what, precisely, first-time penetration entailed. This ignorance beyond ignorance led me, then, to believe he had done the deed.

The next morning, my eyes glued tight from hangover and humiliation, I tried to piece together the preceding night's events. Slowly, I willed my eyelids open and saw I was still lying beside him. I had another conversation in my head. This was all my fault. I had led him on. Worse, I had let him down. Even if I had—as I believed I had—given in to him, I had not done so agreeably. How awful of me. Figuring he must be mad and determining he deserved some reward for how I had treated him, I decided penance was in order.

I crawled under the blankets, inched my way down, examined his flaccid penis, weighed the benefits of attempting an apologetic blow job. He stirred in his sleep, irritated to discover me anywhere near him, and swatted me away. Maybe he was mad at me for not yielding to him the night before. Maybe he was mad at himself for cheating on his jealous girlfriend. Either way, he was clearly annoyed which, to me, translated to rejection. Without saying a word (certainly not the most appropriate word—"Sorry"), he invoked in me, with his sullen, angry stare, a horrid guilt that I had not pleased him. Mea culpa, mea culpa.

We spent a month after that, living in awkward silences followed by loud arguments. Finally he moved out, took a room across the hall. Jonathan's girlfriend took Stan's place. I tried to put the whole thing out of my mind.

And how better to erase the troubles of the mind than by drinking even more heavily? Wildwood being a town of hundreds of bars, there was no trouble finding a fun place, and fun people, to help me drink away my anger and sorrows any hour, day or night. It was at one of my many "bars away from home" that I finally met the man who would eventually do me the dubious honor of deflowering me.

Tom—all bulging eyes, oily skin, and cheesy mustache— worked the door at this bar. He was several years my senior and used his older-man charm, drinks on the house, blatant flirting, and failure to mention his girlfriend, as tactics to seduce me.

After a few weeks of this—my trust built, my defenses down, my vodka-to-corpuscle ratio at a sufficient level—he took me to his house one night after work. I wish I could say that what he did to me, what I allowed him to do to me, was a one-time affair. It was not. From the first time to the last—and so drunk was I each time that I cannot recall the numbers—he flat-out fucked me, no foreplay, no petting, no sentiments of love.

I reflect on these memories of Tom through a shattered looking glass in my otherwise crystal-clear memory, because I cannot bear to look clearly at who I was then and what drove me to do what I did. Without asking for or demanding the things I truly desired—to be held gently, loved freely, talked to softly—I let this man strip me first of my clothes, second of my virginity, and finally of any shred of self-esteem I had garnered by hanging out with men like Jonny and Brian.

How I hated what happened between us. And how I went back for more. Once, in the middle of one of these "sessions"—I can see my bathing suit pulled down around my knees, my body on the hard floor beneath him—I am so drunk and angry that booze and bile rise in my throat. I get up, midthrust, run for the toilet, puke. Tom doesn't seem to mind this brief interruption. He follows me into the bathroom, hands me a toothbrush shaped like a naked lady, tells me to brush, and waits for me to return so he can finish off the job.

Jonathan was there for me after each of these penetration parties, usually visiting his girlfriend in the room I shared with her. Each time I cried to him. And he cried with me. Only to Jonny could I reveal, out loud, how disappointed I was in myself.

After he consoled me, I would leave him to wander for miles along the boardwalk alone, silently screaming at myself for not using birth control, convincing myself I was pregnant, visualizing myself dropping out of college to raise the child of this greasy man on my own. I am so ugly. I am so stupid. My father is right. I am an idiot.

I left that godforsaken town for the final time that August, summer of '84, a bundle of nerves and mixed emotions. I would miss Jonathan so much. I would not miss Tom. My father was still not talking to me—in fact I had not heard at all from my family the whole summer. I was not a virgin anymore, but this left me far from feeling triumphant or freed. I was a mess. I was ready to get back to Florida, to try, impossibly, to get back to some sort of square one.

7

A MONTH into the first semester of my junior year, Matt arrived at my first-floor dorm room one night, banged on the window, beckoned me to buzz him in. I'd met him once before, at the campus bar. That night, I shook his hand, chatted momentarily. He asked if he could see me sometime. I said sure and then forgot about him. He was not particularly memorable, did not match my fantasy of tall, odd, and charismatic.

At this same time in my life, I was gaining a peculiar sort of popularity on campus, one that was equal parts love and hate. For one, I was the resident assistant with the modified mohawk, fully half my head shaved down to the skin, something that initially frightened the parents of the freshmen left in my care.

For another, and due in great part to this same haircut, I was becoming the star reporter for the college's daily newspaper. A letter I'd written bitching about frat daddies' verbal abuse of me, based on my looks, caught the admiring eye of an editor, and the hateful response of countless frat boys when it was published. Having proved my ability to provoke, I was hired as a weekly columnist. My picture accompanied my writing, and I was stopped often by people who either agreed enthusiastically with me or else wanted me dead.

Matt, a huge fan of Hunter Thompson, was drawn to my popularity as a reporter, my oddball appearance, my outspokenness. I suppose I was the closest he'd ever come to meeting a gonzo journalist.

The first night he came to my room, we talked a long time. I looked into his sad, droopy green eyes and decided I liked him more than I'd first realized. Within a month we were dating, an official item, and at last, at age twenty, I had what I had wanted forever: my first real boyfriend, someone who belonged exclusively to me. For my final two years at USF, my life revolved around him completely.

In the beginning of our affair, I refused to sleep with him. What I'd done with Tom the summer before had been horrible and traumatizing and filled me with more guilt than I could gauge. I was not eager to revisit such territory. But Matt coaxed, pleaded, convinced me to at last, at least, shower with him. We did this in the dark—I was so ashamed of my body, always had been.

Finally, I gave in, went on the pill, slowly let him move closer and closer until suddenly, we were fucking like bunnies. Almost overnight I went from being shy and nervous to trying anything Matt requested. Though my preferred sleeping attire leaned toward boxer shorts and men's undershirts, Matt had a thing for cheap, flimsy lingerie. I obliged. Frilly nighties, butt-floss thongs, strategically cut T-shirts—if it got him off, then I was doing my job as good girlfriend. Whatever Matt wanted, I gave him.

A pattern developed quickly in my relationship with Matt, one I repeated with nearly every ensuing man. Despite my independence of two years, my loudmouthed newspaper columns, my radical appearance, my love for the feminism I was learning and embracing in my Women's Studies classes, and my advice to my girlfriends to NEVER put up with shit from men, I gave myself over fully to Matt. I handed him control of the relationship, and he took it without question. Whatever strong-woman image I presented outwardly, when I was with him, I was at his beck and call. The smart-ass, joking, confident, star reporter turned into the humble, obedient little woman behind closed doors.

Matt was the jealous type, and not just jealous of men. Anything that took away from our time together infuriated him. The same journalist's popularity that had drawn him to me quickly turned into a source of anger for him.

People loved to stop and chat with me around campus or in bars at night. Matt would watch from the sidelines when this happened, fuming that I dare turn away from him. Invariably, I wound up apologizing, making it up to him with strokes both emotional and physical back in his room.

As our relationship wore on, he developed a habit of bowing out just before we were scheduled to go somewhere. Worse, he would convince me to stay with him. If I didn't, that meant I did not love him. We withdrew from everything and everyone. Breakfasts with Brian were pretty much the only times I went out without Matt regularly anymore. And he hated this too, but it was the one place where I stood my ground.

I never dreamed of looking for another, more suitable

man. Matt wanted me, which meant Matt was the one for me. I was fully dedicated to him, inspired no doubt by watching my mother's dedication to my father, regardless of his behavior. My mother had very few adult friends and saw her siblings only on holidays. Unwittingly, and though I disliked how she seemed to cater solely to Daddy, I was emulating her, cutting off everyone else in my life, limiting my own world to Matt.

My friends—and when this relationship started I had had many—resented Matt and how I changed myself on his account. Elaine, who lived next door to me in the dorm, had been my partying partner for nearly a year when I began neglecting our friendship, when I deserted her for Matt. I tried, sometimes, to show her I was still dedicated to her, but my efforts were shallow. She grew thoroughly disgusted one night when, to show her I was "allowed" to still be friends with her, I invited her to join Matt and me at his best friend's apartment to watch a movie.

The best friend was a true freak, a recluse obsessed with two things: anything NASA-related and his beloved black cats. He wore only black, and bleached his cropped, thinning hair nearly white. The night of our "party," he showed us a horrid Nazi porno film, *Illsa, She-Wolf of the SS*. We could have walked out on this trash, but I refused to leave my boyfriend's side. Elaine stayed, but the damage was done.

I refused to let anyone tell me that Matt was a domineering loser. By our second semester together, I quit my dorm job—which paid for my room and board—to move across campus into the apartment-style housing he lived in, courtesy of his parents' bankroll. This allowed me to spend as many nights as I cared to with him (or, more accurately, as he would have me) without getting written up by my supervisor back in the dorm.

This new arrangement cost me at least as much emotionally as it did financially. Two weeks after I moved in, across the quad from him, my effervescent roommate, Jean, threw a wild party to celebrate my twenty-first birthday. I was less than enthusiastic. Matt had called that morning to announce he was tired of me, needed some space. He didn't care that I had sacrificed my job to be with him. And he didn't care that it was my birthday. He wanted to deliver the message right then, and so he did.

I spent the day crying, pleading with him for one more chance. Please, I begged, wasn't I worthy? He caved in to the guilt trip, much to my relief, and so, tentatively at first, I started to loosen up at my party, pounding drinks, waiting for him to ceremoniously emerge from his room twenty feet across the quad, join me in my celebration.

When at last he deigned to honor me, the birthday princess, he greeted me with a frown. He "caught" me dancing, happily and platonically, with a male friend. He exploded, stormed back over to his quarters, waited for me to follow. I did.

Only this time, fueled by booze, I was angry, in no mood to beg forgiveness. I barged into his room, marched over to where he lay pouting and prone on the bottom bunk. Drunk as shit and mad as hell, I rushed at him, knelt on his chest, pounding him with my index finger, screaming at him for wrecking my party.

Which was when, infuriated, he reached up with both hands and shoved me across the room. Crying, wanting him—of all people—to hold me, console me, I got up from the floor and climbed up to the vacant top bunk of his absent roommate, curling into the fetal position that had become as much a part of our relationship as sex or fighting. So many times I had done this—withdrawn to a corner of the bed, made myself as small as possible, banged my head against the wall crying, in hope that he would offer me some sign that I was loved.

All that night Matt refused to come near me. I wept in my bunk while he slept soundly on the bed beneath me. I cried myself to sleep. I woke up crying, willing him to come to me. Finally, after what he considered proper punishment, he did join me, fucked me, held me.

Relieved that I was still loved, I tried not to think about the pain I still felt. Later, in the shower alone, I examined the black-and-purple work of violent art that covered my ass, a precise imprint of the bicycle derailer that had broken my fall the night before.

But I had no intention of leaving my alleged true love. The spring semester ended and I decided to stay in Tampa. The temptation of Jonathan and Wildwood was gone. Elaine stayed, too, and after a disastrous attempt on my part at being a live-in nanny for a family of wackos, I moved to an off-campus apartment with her.

My old friend Dotty took an apartment in the same complex, as did a number of other wild friends. Before long, we were like a seedier, drunker version of some twenty-something TV show—a cast of college coeds drinking our way through school and summer, laboring at shitty jobs, and dealing with what invariably turned out for all of us to be horrible, destructive relationships.

Matt was scheduled to move to St. Petersburg for his final

semester in the fall, to take classes unavailable in Tampa. Rather than find an apartment for two months while he waited, I decided—and convinced a very hesitant Elaine—to let him live with us in the interim.

He and I continued to withdraw together, locking ourselves in my room while Elaine and our friends partied in the living room. The cage grew smaller still when he did depart for St. Pete. I spent most of my money then—loans earmarked for tuition and books—procuring an aesthetically perfect, mechanically doomed, gas-sucking '63 Galaxy 500, which I drove, often, across the long bridge to see my man.

He was constantly moping—poor, poor Matt. Stuck in a beach town, living on his parents' money, getting laid by me before he could even ask. I did everything I could to cheer him up—bought him an expensive camera, enhanced my ridiculous lingerie collection, cooked him wonderful meals, sucked his stupid cock on demand. Nothing, none of these things, was ever enough.

Until he spotted a FOR SALE sign on a '67 VW camper. At last, something excited him. We fantasized together about buying it, traversing the country, neo-hippies free and in love. He took his savings and I tossed in mine and we had just enough to buy it together, though submissive girlfriend that I was, I did not protest when only his name appeared on the title. I could not see how this might present a problem. In my family, it was standard operating procedure to marry one's first serious beau. Matt and I were destined, I knew, for a life together. Forever.

8

I DROPPED out of school to travel with Matt when he graduated in December. I had only one semester left myself, but I put off my own plans to appease him. I could finish up my coursework in the summer.

Unfortunately shortsighted, when our departure date arrived we had no money to fund this great adventure. Reluctantly, Matt's parents agreed to let us stay with them while we worked temporary jobs to save enough for gas, food, and lodging.

I'd met May and Bill on a number of occasions, and while they were civil to me, it wasn't too hard to discern that they—May especially—did not particularly care for me. Magnifying this problem was the fact that Matt was a mama's boy, something May cultivated at every turn. It was a wonder she wasn't still breast-feeding him—she did just about everything else she could to keep her apron-string noose tight around his neck. Time Matt spent with me was moments stolen from May. This, she made very clear, did not please her.

May could've been Nancy Reagan's twin sister—painfully

thin, hair a helmet over bulging eyes, with a gratingly self-righteous personality that softened only in its robotic worship of her husband. Each night, just after five, she responded to the sound of the garage door opening—"Bill's home!!"—by dropping whatever gourmet meal she was in the midst of preparing to bustle her tennis-skirted self off to the liquor cabinet. There, she deftly whipped up two martinis—one with a twist, one with an olive!!—for their ritualistic happy hour.

Bill, invariably, would walk in the door, give a paternal grunt in a fashion that echoed my own father's preferred form of communication, accept a peck from May, and head straight for the La-Z-Boy, clutching his beverage. Once there, he engrossed himself in a twenty-gazillion-piece jigsaw puzzle, stopping only to yell at the dogs, tamp his pipe, or begrudgingly join us at the dinner table.

I was a vegetarian, so May went into a carnivorous frenzy. Rare steaks, roasted quail—if it had fur or feathers, she served it. And at every meal May prattled on shrilly, either touting her own fabulousness or bitching about Matt's black-sheep sister "who will *never* amount to anything." The steady gush of twist-top white wine over ice was the only thing that kept these meals from seeming as horrible as they actually were.

We were supposed to be working and saving, but Matt just couldn't seem to find a job. Now that he had a degree, he refused to settle for minimum-wage work, no matter how badly we needed money. I, having been steadily employed at crappy jobs since I was fifteen, had no trouble accepting a low-wage gig. I quickly found work at the local grocery store, working my ass off overtime to make our plan viable.

Naturally, Matt and I were not allowed to sleep together in the house of May, so sex had to be planned carefully for days when I was off and May was out doing whatever bullshit it was she did to keep herself entertained until cocktail hour.

Once, she "caught" us together in Matt's room, fully dressed, him lying on the bed, me sitting innocently on the edge. Later, she lectured her son on our totally inappropriate behavior. She surely would've dropped dead on the spot had she known that just days before we'd fucked in every imaginable position on that very same bed, all the while Matt's rented video camera capturing each thrust and grunt, close-up.

When finally we (read: I) had saved up a significant amount of cash, I put in my notice and we prepared to embark, at last, on our fantasy trip, which was turning into a nightmare before we could even pull out of the driveway. The arguing about the trip began long before the trip itself.

Come to think of it, we realized, we were both bad drivers, both afraid of unfamiliar highways and parts unknown. So, rather than go see the Wild West, as planned, suddenly we were looking at driving north on the incredibly boring, indescribably bland I-95 to see, of all places, New Jersey. Whatever. At least we were getting the hell out of May's house.

We arrived at my parents' house after two solid weeks of fighting at every scenic overlook, campground, and historic site along the way. Daddy took one look at Matt—their first meeting—and growled, "Get in da truck." Matt looked confused, a little frightened.

I hadn't told Matt about the way my father immediately tested any men his daughters brought home. Typically, he liked to stick a hammer in their hands and have them add a room or two onto the house. On this day, Daddy had spotted an old stove in the trash somewhere over in Philly. If he hurried, it might still be there, could be of some possible use. But he couldn't lift it alone.

Much as I hated Daddy's need to test everyone and everything, I have to admit, in this case, it was amusing to see my boyfriend—who did not have the strength to fill out a job application—get sucked into hard labor. Better still, it meant a break from him.

Of all the plans I had for the trip, I never fulfilled the one that meant the most to me. I wanted desperately to see Jonathan. I hadn't seen him for a year or so and I missed him terribly. But as Matt and I drove to see him, we got in yet another huge verbal brawl. Just miles from Jonathan's place in Atlantic City, we aborted the mission, turned around, and drove back to my parents' house.

Something tells me, looking back, that perhaps I subconsciously instigated this particular fight to keep my boyfriend and my best friend from ever meeting. Introducing a man I liked to Jonathan was worse than introducing that same man to my father. Because actually having my Jonny meet some guy I had spent hours on the phone bragging about meant having to face the music, admitting Mr. Wonderful was anything but.

Somewhere inside, I knew Matt was nothing like the man I described to Jonny. And there was no way—absolutely not a Popsicle's chance in hell—that he could live up to Jonathan's standards. Or for that matter, live up to Jonathan himself, the unconditional love he gave me, the affection he freely offered.

When the trip was finally over, I wrote my friend a letter

of apology. While I admitted that a fight had curtailed our trip to see him, I quickly glossed over that, said my brother's wedding just days later—and my consequential need to help out—had caused the most interference. I didn't detail the awful things Matt and I screamed at each other. Didn't mention the time he abandoned me in a large mall in Philadelphia with no way back to Jersey.

In the same letter, I dropped a bomb on my oldest friend. Matt and I had finally discussed our troubles, our inability to get along for more than two hours at a time, our never-ending battles. After serious contemplation, we decided there was only one solution. We would move in together.

Really.

When we returned to Tampa, we found a cramped du-plex reminiscent of the amount of space we had in the camper. Nights we drank five-dollar half gallons of sticky red wine and smoked bong hit after bong hit of the cheap-est skunk weed just to be able to tolerate each other. I had a few weeks before my final summer semester commenced, and so, to finance our pitiful vices and keep that tiny roof over our heads, I worked full-time and then some.

Once again, I was in a grocery store, now slicing pound upon pound of water-bloated boiled ham—"Very thin, please. No—thinner than that!"—for an endless stream of cranky housewives. Once again, Matt just couldn't seem to find a job worthy of his skills. In fact, he could barely bring himself to look at the want ads. He sat home and sulked while I paid for everything.

Finally, when my classes began and I was strapped with a twenty-two-hour course load packed into ten weeks, he condescended to take a part-time position at a bookstore in the mall. I kept working as many hours as I could. Somehow, between homework and boiled ham, I still found myself cooking all the meals. I even made Matt's lunch every day. I thought I was just being funny packing his sandwiches in a child's lunchbox. It never occurred to me that I was playing mommy to this tantrum-throwing overgrown child who could not let go of his own.

With August came my graduation and a revelation. I could not stand Matt one minute longer. We had reached the point of no return, that stage where all you can think is, "I hate you so much all I can bear to do is fuck you. With my eyes shut tight."

This angry, loveless sex led, in no time, to a shock-inducing missed period. I was off the pill by now, was an idiot about remembering to use my diaphragm, and so God stepped in and punished me yet again. Panicking when the pregnancy was confirmed, I made an immediate appointment for an abortion and Matt made an immediate appointment with a friend, to borrow the necessary money.

There was only one problem. From the time I was very little, Daddy banged into my head that abortion was the biggest, fastest, first-class ticket to hell. It was murder. It was unthinkable.

How he conveyed this information was quite interesting. Like anything else related to sex, actually mentioning words associated with or potentially resulting from that act was strictly verboten. My mother never even told me about my period—leaving that up to a vague film shown in fifth grade, followed up by a little pamphlet left on my bed when I was twelve, a booklet that talked more about blooming flowers than ripe ovaries.

But my father had his ways. Before the ink had dried on *Roe v. Wade*, he formed a one-man picket line down at the local hospital when they began performing abortions there. Rather than spend Sunday, his only day off, with the nine children he spawned, he chose to use this time focusing on all the unborn children of the world.

Further, he carted us around in an old-style airport limousine—a sort of double-length station wagon—the only car big enough to hold us all at once. On the tailgate of this vehicle was painted the message, in huge, bold, fluorescent letters: ABORTION IS KILLING YOUR OWN CHILD.

All the years I rode in that car, I had no idea what the words meant—somehow it was made silently clear that we were not to ask. Still, we ascertained from the context that whatever ABORTION was, it was awful. When people honked at us, it never occurred to me they might be responding to my father's message. I always waved happily, glad for the attention, figured it was the unique car, remained ignorant that I was part of Daddy's rolling performance-art piece decrying the rights of women. (Actually, in his world, women only had one right: the right to remain silent.)

Now I stood, all those years later, accidentally pregnant and fully aware of what abortion was. Knowing further that to have one meant I could go out into the world, as planned, use my brand-new degree to get a job, and figure out in my own time what I wanted from life. But Daddy's message was embedded far too deeply. By then I was politically pro-choice, thanks to all the Women's Studies courses I'd taken. Personally, though, I couldn't get past the idea that that was a real baby growing in me. I simply could not bring myself to kill it.

My sister Bridget, as if I needed further encouragement, adamantly responded to my long-distance confession of pregnancy. She herself was pregnant at the time and, like a street-corner preacher, read to me over the phone from her prenatal books. After some quick math, she said, "You are eight weeks pregnant. At eight weeks, the fetus has a heartbeat and is a child." She went on and on. Freaked out completely, I bid her a hasty good-bye. I picked up the phone again, called the clinic, canceled my appointment.

Matt responded with absolute shock. He consulted his parents, and I can only surmise what May had to say about that damn slut trapping her poor, sweet, innocent little baby. Regardless, he returned with a proposal. Mumbling nearly inaudibly and looking straight at the floor, he asked, "You don't want to get married, do you?"

In all of my confusion and sorrow, here was one thing I was clear on. I did NOT want to get married. Did not want to be near him. The sight of him repelled me. I hated him. I would have the baby, yes. But on my own.

Daddy picked me up in that same airport he'd dropped me off in, three years before. There was no touching this time, not even a squeeze on the elbow. He looked at me somberly, his silence deafening as we retrieved my luggage. On the way across the Walt Whitman Bridge for the millionth time in my life, back to Jersey, back to all I thought I had escaped at nineteen, I waited for something, anything. A grunt. An explosion.

Nothing.

Finally, he turned to me. "For starters," he said, "you're going to have to change your hair and the way you dress."

9

DESPITE how much we clearly disliked each other, despite the fact that my condition must have shamed him, and despite the fact that he'd said if any of his eight daughters ever got pregnant without the benefit of marriage we could consider ourselves forever on our own, Daddy pulled through for me then. He'd insisted, when I stuttered, crying, the news to him over the phone, that I come back to where he could take care of me.

He and my mother set me up in the downstairs apartment of one of two side-by-side houses they owned. They lived next door, with my youngest two sisters. Two other sisters lived in the apartment above me. My place was wonderful, filled with all sorts of mismatched used furniture and oddities my parents had collected at auctions and estate sales.

I was still a wreck over my condition and what it meant, but the coziness of my surroundings offered a little nest of hope. Bridget loaned me a typewriter, and I set up shop at the kitchen table, determined to spend the next six months improving my writing, perhaps even selling some.

Daddy, as was most often the case—except for moments of explosion following cumulative months of angry silence—had little to say to me. This time around his lack of words was a blessing. He did not pick on me. Kept his distance. Things remained at a tense but tolerable level.

Like some awful déjà-vu play, co-scripted by Sartre and Springsteen—to be titled *Which Exit? No Exit*—I returned to the same mall job I'd worked throughout high school. It was as if my years away had never happened. Except for the fact that my parents lived in a different house (same town, though), I was driving the same route to work, returning nights to my father's overwatchful eye, destined to a fate I could not, as I had foolishly dreamed, escape after all.

In mid-November, though, I hit a certain rhythm. I actually began to look forward to my child, due in May. I was completely sober for the first time in years. And without incessant fights with Matt—whom I no longer spoke to at all—I was growing increasingly optimistic, contemplating going back to school for a teaching certificate so I could get a solid job to support my baby.

The bleeding began on the cusp of my fourth month. Frightened, I whispered the news to my mother, who tried unsuccessfully to calm me. "This sort of thing happens a lot," she reassured me. "Get some sleep. It's probably nothing to worry about. We'll see what tomorrow brings."

Tomorrow, as it turned out, brought more blood. Seemingly buckets of it. I sat in the office of an unfamiliar gynecologist, a man at least as cold in manner as the instruments of his trade. Without a trace of emotion he informed me I was in the middle of a miscarriage.

Rendering neither advice about what to expect, nor painkillers to ease the agony that lay ahead, he sent me home and told me to come back when it was over. I suppose now it doesn't really matter that he did not hint at what was to come. Nothing could have prepared me for the anguish of the next twenty-four hours.

I cramped and I bled, mini-contractions—agonizing nonetheless—for my mini-baby. Egg—that was my nickname for the fetus—exited my body one crimson clot at a time, aching cramp upon aching cramp squeezing this potential life out of me.

My mother stayed with me through the night, holding a heating pad to my back, stroking my hair. Finally, the contractions stopped, and I slept a miserable sleep, waiting for my second trip to the awful doctor.

At last, morning came. Overwhelmed with grief, completely in shock, I shuffled out to the driveway, my head hung in deep, deep sorrow. My father was in the car already, prepared to drive me to the doctor's office. I climbed in the back, sat directly behind him, silent, nervous, distraught.

Without turning to me, he finally spoke, directing his words at the windshield rather than turning to look at the mess of me slumped and weeping. "Your mother got you through it, didn't she?" he asked. The end. No "How do you feel?" No "Honey I'm sorry." No "One day you will get past this, I promise." Just the insinuation that I had disappointed him after he had found a way to accept me and my sinful pregnancy.

The gynecologist, tying my father for first place in the compassion category, swiftly examined me and scheduled me for a very ironic D&C. I would have my abortion after all, to ensure I was fully cleaned out.

I hid in my bedroom for days after that, insisted to my mother that I would never go back to work, would never get out of bed for that matter. She insisted otherwise, explaining the more I kept busy, the less I would have time to get depressed. I did not want to believe her, but finally made a halfhearted attempt at her recommended denial technique. Turns out she was right. Before long, I was working doubles as often as I could. I would've worked triples if that were possible.

When shifts weren't available to keep my mind from thoughts of my loss, I drank. Anything to block out the words both inside and outside me. When I allowed myself to think about the whole thing, I could not help but believe that my initial ambivalence had caused the death of this child. When I allowed myself to listen to those around me, I wanted to strangle everyone who said, "Oh, it was all for the best."

The best what? The best way to quickly lose my mind at an early age? Giving birth to death filled me with a grief so intense that I would not match it again for another ten years. The best?

Matt called one night, only making things worse. Just as I was starting to feel a tiny bit like myself again, he decided he had to discuss certain matters with me. A friend had informed him of the miscarriage. Now he wept, telling me that he was so so so sorry. Wanting to believe him, I foolishly slipped momentarily back into mothering mode, soothing him when I was the one who really needed consoling.

Once he had me there, in that forgiving position, he decided to test me further. He just could not hold the truth back anymore. That woman at work I'd accused him of having an affair with at the end of our relationship? Well, um, actually, I had been right.

I screamed. I slammed down the phone. I fell to the floor,

still bundled in my heavy winter coat. I shook, outraged at his rotten news, his hideous timing, his childish manipulation of me at this most vulnerable time.

For weeks I spent every night alone, drunk or stoned, scribbling hateful thoughts in my journal about all men. Occasionally, I'd call an old friend back in Florida, or be cheered when one thought to call me. One night, I picked up the ringing phone, surprised and delighted to hear the voice of Kevin on the other end.

Once, years before, Kevin had been the object of one of my obsessive crushes, a man who had literally fled from me and my refusal to take no for an answer. Somehow, miraculously, we had managed over the years—thanks in part to inadvertently finding ourselves co-workers in the dorms—to salvage a mature, platonic relationship.

I cried to him and he listened. Inspired, lonely, craving the company of a loving man, and knowing he loved architecture, I invited him to fly to Jersey, to join me for a trip into New York City to walk the streets and look at buildings. He accepted.

My father, upon being informed of this plan, blew up. I was not, he said, to have male visitors staying in my apartment. He claimed this command came directly from the Bible. He seemed to have forgotten the year before when he allowed Matt and me to stay together. We were now, officially, back to the days of high school. Under his roof I was to follow his rules.

Filled with rage at this ridiculous proclamation, with the wounds of all our fights over the years gapingly reopened by this latest argument, I fumed. As I had experienced my father's fury unfurling without warning my whole life, I now felt an unstoppable bitterness of my own burst forth.

78

Returning from work late one December afternoon, lit to the gills thanks to an all-day, on-the-clock, toxic-strength holiday cocktail fest, I sought out my father. Too drunk to be scared of him once I located him, I hurled a steady stream of profanity his way, swore a blue streak at his denying me a visit from my friend. Blind with vodka and hatred, I felt damn near ready to kill him.

This is the third time my father reached out to touch me. How I wish my mother had been there this time with her little whirring movie camera wound up and ready to go. How I would love to show the world—to see for myself—a slow-motion replay of us, a two-human tornado spinning through my apartment, winding up, ultimately, in a corner of the kitchen, my back against the stove, he inches from my face.

I spewed a little more venom then, as I stood trapped by his short, stocky mass. Glaring, completely out of control, he pulled back his arm, balled his fist, and swung. Half ducking, half slumping, I denied him contact.

This outrageous moment was not enough to stop us, though. We had been saving up twenty-three years for this big event. Though three inches shorter and a good thirty pounds lighter, I leaped up for round two. Barreling toward him, I lashed out blindly, grabbed for his shirt. Instead, my fingers wrapped around the chain he always wore, various religious medals dangling from it, hanging there on his chest like some sort of superhero icon.

The chain broke. The medals clattered to the floor. This was what broke the spell, finally. We stopped. He glared once more, bent down to retrieve the things that were his, and walked away from the daughter who made it clear, once and for all, that she was not one of those things.

A pall fell over the family. My mother retreated into silence. My father and I avoided each other at all costs. I felt guilty living in his place, knew I should have been more grateful for his support, no matter the emotional cost. I knew I was breaking one of the Ten Commandments in my failure to honor him.

I did not cancel my plans with Kevin. In fact, I called again to tell him I would be going back to Florida with him after our visit together. I was no longer potentially redeemable in my father's eyes now that I was no longer pregnant. I reverted back to horrid-child status in his eyes, sinner extraordinaire, the slut daughter heading straight for hell. I had to get out of his house, his state, his constant and overbearing presence.

Kevin and I spent five days in the city, walking miles and miles every day in the bitter cold. By the end of our stay, after listening to my story over and over, he convinced me to try to talk to my father, to apologize for the fight, to calm the family.

Just before I'd left for New York, my mother had broken her silence to inform me Daddy had gone out and bought me a car. He still wasn't speaking to me. I knew he would never utter the word "sorry." But using his lifelong tactic of matching every overzealous mean gesture with an overzealous kind one, he had gone out and dropped a couple of hundred bucks on a '67 Valiant for me.

At first, I'd told my mother—in the kindest words I could think of—that Daddy could shove the vehicle up his ass. Now, a week later, I creaked down the stairs to look for him in the sanctuary of his basement conclave. There he sat, amidst stacks of old LPs, musical instruments, statues of saints and the Virgin, crucifixes on the walls. "Daddy," I stuttered, "I'm sorry."

The brief exchange that followed was the closest we ever came to a real conversation. He asked me my plans, and I told him I was leaving, that if it was still being offered, I would accept the car and drive with Kevin back to Florida. He said he wanted me to consider reconciling with Matt— no doubt because he wanted me to marry this man I had slept with. Stunned, I told him this was not an option.

The conversation ended abruptly after that. A few days later, Kevin and I drove that old car to Tampa. I moved back to the house with the four friends who'd taken me in during my monthlong post-Matt, pre–New Jersey interim. We lived in a huge, decrepit house, in the dead center of a crack neighborhood.

That very first night, at a party in my honor, someone stole a hundred dollars—my only money in the world— from my luggage. Back to ground zero, I went out and found another waitressing job. I continued to grieve the loss of my child. And I continued to drink as much as I could, as often as I could, in a vain attempt to wash that grief away.

10

TWO months later, I left Tampa—packed the car with my few belongings, turned it around, and headed to Tennessee. Before the whole pregnancy/miscarriage mishap, I had applied for an internship with Whittle Communications, a magazine company in Knoxville. Now an offer came in— would I be interested in spending three months getting paid to learn the ins and outs of print media?

As much as I looked forward to escaping the destructive get-drunk-and-fuck-whoever-would-have-me phase I had fallen into in Tampa, I still cried as I bid my friends farewell. They were more family to me than my blood relatives. The thought of moving, completely on my own, to a city where I knew no one, in a state with a reputation for being totally backwoods, scared the hell out of me.

But Tennessee turned out to be a far cry from what I'd imagined in the panicky, worst-case, *Hee-Haw* scenarios that flickered through my mind as I drove north on the highway. Knoxville had a big town/small city feel that offered the best of both worlds.

It was not unusual (or unnerving) for strangers to greet you with a sincere hello. Shop owners ended each transaction with a peculiar imperative: "Come back!" And the mix of people included representatives from all, and I mean all, walks: stereotypical bumpkins, loud street-corner preachers prophesying sure and certain doom, intellectuals—real and pseudo—students, UT football zealots decked out head to toe in orange, and countless young hipsters. Many members of this latter group had been recruited from larger cities by Whittle, a company that thrived as much on its happy, shiny image as it did on its exploding business.

Housing was provided blocks away from the University of Tennessee, the tiny rent lowered further by a company subsidy. My assigned roommate was Anne, a graphic illustrator slightly older than me. Whip smart and deeply cynical, Anne was world wise and happy to share her insights on every topic from freelancing to men.

Before we could even unpack our things, a flasher appeared at the open, waist-high window of our ground-floor apartment. Calmly, he beat off while we watched, more stunned at his boldness than his wares, flapping in the wind at us.

Anne, demonstrating her life skills, announced that we were not going to put up with this sort of thing. When this man returned a second time, she did not wait for a third visit. Dragging me with her, she literally went to the top, taking the elevator to the CEO's office, demanding something be done. Immediately.

Perhaps fearing a lawsuit, top officials did not attempt to placate her with a condescending "Now hush; you're being hysterical." Instead, within the week they had moved us out

of our shitty little apartment and into one of the nicest ho-
tels in downtown Knoxville, picking up 100 percent of the
tab for us to each have our own private room for the dura-
tion of our internships. Suddenly, I was the recipient of
maid service, free continental breakfasts, and complimen-
tary daily national and local newspapers. The other interns
took all this in with amused envy.

The job proved far less glamorous than our new accom-
modations. I spent my time writing peppy copy for *Veteri-
nary Practice Management Magazine*, standing for hours at
the copy machine, and cold-calling people to survey them
about their pets. ("Hi, you don't know me, but I was wondering if I could ask you about your dog. . . .")

Needless to say, I figured out pretty quickly that whatever intellectual skills I had were not going to be necessary.
For me to keep my job, the biggest requirement was that I
show up on time, and even that—in keeping with the
young, hip feel Whittle aimed for—was flexible. Not having
to use my mind for work meant I could continue to a) kill
my brain cells nightly at bars and b) use my mind to obsess
over one man or another, to plot procuring one to test out
that nice big bed in my hotel.

First came Ted, the art director who hummed while he
ate and favored a teeny purple Speedo for our lunchtime
tanning sessions on the roof of headquarters. I tailed him
like a badly trained spy, plied him with postwork drinks,
and convinced him as often as possible to visit my room,
where he had no choice but to sit on the bed, my none-too-
subtle way of hinting I wanted to fuck him.

Fuck him I did, finally, one night at his house. Afterward,
he pretended it had never happened. When I confronted

him on this, he admitted that during the night we'd spent together he felt as if his mother was in the room with us, which made him too uncomfortable to do it again. I certainly knew how to pick them.

By the time I left that town, three years later, I had more notches on my belt than a man with a fifty-inch waist. There was not a party or bar I could go to without running into at least two lovers in the same night. But the most transformative relationship I had during this period did not come courtesy of any of these fellows. Rather, it was brought on by a woman named Mel.

Though I never stopped being hard on myself, thinking myself too fat, too ugly, too whatever, somehow I continued to project this image of fun-loving wild thing. The loud-mouthed, untameable chick with the wacky haircut, ready to party or drive to the Smokies in a heartbeat, had no trouble enticing all sorts of men for a little fun of the one-night variety. Little Miss Fun, Fun, Fun—that was me.

I suppose it was this mythical image that I put forth that also attracted Mel, a full-time editor. I pegged her as a bitch from the get-go, hated how she crucified my work with the collection of purple pens she kept handy at all times, despised the condescending tone she took with me in meetings.

And so I was shocked when one day, in early spring, she popped by my cubby to announce that she was orchestrating a boat trip that weekend, and I was invited. Or was I commanded? Too stunned to say no, flattered that somebody I couldn't stand was acting interested in me, I agreed, showing up promptly at the appointed time.

That trip touched off an unlikely friendship that ignited

quickly, a far blacker version of what I had had with Dotty back in Wildwood all those years before. I was drawn to her like a magnet, wanted to exude the same kind of confidence and don't-give-a-shit attitude she pulled off so well. She was not particularly stunning, in fact she was rather plain, but I could clearly see that when she flirted, men paid attention. I needed to acquire such skills from her far more than I needed to learn journalism techniques.

She took me under her wing after that first excursion, and by late fall we were inseparable. Whittle had renewed my internship and then, after that, offered me a full-time editing job. Having made, at this point, as many friends as I'd left in Tampa, I jumped at both chances. Mel and I shared our lunch hours regularly, met several times a week for happy hour.

We confided our deepest secrets in each other. Like giddy seventh graders we pledged to never reveal to others the things we said about them, the way we judged them. As cynical as I had been most of my life, I'd also maintained a broad nice streak; now that narrowed. If Mel said someone was a loser, that person was banished from our little two-woman clique.

Mel had a boyfriend, Patrick, who was her polar opposite. Incredibly handsome and genuinely good-hearted, he was kind to me from our first hello. Here was the kind of man I hoped to one day meet, to call soul mate, to have forever. I suppressed my attraction to him, though, kept it all on the up-and-up. Not only was he another woman's man, he was Mel's man. Doubly off limits.

Patrick laughed, sympathetically, when one day I revealed that I had not been laid in forever, that I had an itch, that I wanted a fuck-buddy to satisfy my needs. A week later, the phone rang: Vince, friend of Patrick, a man I had met a few times. He asked me out. Temporarily forgetting what I'd told Patrick, not realizing he'd passed the information on, I was a little taken aback to have Vince, someone I barely knew, be so out-of-the-blue forward.

The picture cleared up quickly though. Realizing he was offering to scratch my proclaimed itch, I accepted his invitation. We got stoned on his balcony while he played his guitar and sang to me with the gravelly voice of a rebel angel. This serenade session was followed up with unnecessary—and far too many—drinks at the Long Branch Saloon. Not one to waste time, when we were sufficiently drunk I brought him back to the house I now lived in, laughed at his puzzled look when he noted I slept on a blanket on the floor.

The next morning, more than a little hungover, I woke up beside myself, and better yet, beside this beautiful man. I refused to recall one thing he'd mentioned the night before: In three weeks he was moving, permanently, to West Virginia to take a job. I also blocked out what I knew had brought him to me—my proclamation to Patrick that I was looking to get laid, no strings attached. The moment Vince kissed me, my plans changed. I had to have him.

Thus began yet another of my no-holds-barred campaigns to win yet another unattainable man, a man who guaranteed, on the first date, that he was going to leave me. The challenge made him irresistible. I would make him love me, I would make him need me. Hell, maybe I could make him ask me to move with him.

I spent much of my time at work writing him funny

notes, photocopying interesting articles I thought he might like, and leaving these things—along with gifts of wildflowers and pretty rocks—on his back step for him to discover in the evenings. Except fucking me whenever he felt like it—thankfully this was at least fairly often—he did not respond to my gestures, or to me, as I wished. He remained mysterious, laconic, dispassionate.

There was little intimacy in the things we did, only an animalist rhythm and release of loveless sex, followed immediately by a return to stoicism on his part once we'd finished. The less he spoke, the more I did, trying to fill all the blank spaces left by his silence with my rapid-fire giddy words. The curious looks he gave me after these outbursts filled me with shame. Could I not ever shut up?

Our three weeks together flew by, and every day I came up with a new, even-more-harebrained scheme to capture his attention. My most intricate plan involved a long-distance trip to Jersey. Whittle had offered to pay to move my possessions to Tennessee. Would Vince help me go and retrieve them?

The truth was that I had no possessions other than the few things I'd brought from Tampa. But my parents had offered to supply me with the used furniture necessary to fill the apartment next to Mel and Patrick, which I had recently rented. More than desiring these gifts, I leaped at the opportunity because, the way I saw it, it gave me one long, last, chance to win Vince over. Company financed, no less. What better way to win a man than take him up the Jersey Turnpike to meet Daddy?

The trip was far longer than it was romantic. So many men have mean streaks. Vince had a nice streak, which

slipped behind clouds of irritation often. When I lit a cigarette in our rental truck, or accidentally smeared mayon-
naise on the bread bag while making us sandwiches, he shot
me an Archie-to-Edith look. I had three standard responses:
act hurt, attempt to overcompensate and wind up making
things worse, or hide my annoyance behind a gosh-I-really-
am-dumb-huh? grin.

Once again, Daddy unintentionally came to the rescue,
offering Vince the same sort of comeuppance he'd given
Matt on the day of the stove in the trash in Philly. Vince
was an environmentalist by trade, a man who worshipped
the earth, who liked to sleep outside whenever possible. So
he was speechless when my father showed him to his
"room," a windowless corner of the basement that held a
mildewed, lumpy mattress.

Stunning Vince further, Daddy beckoned him to the
backyard, to discuss with him the removal of a huge, ancient black walnut tree, one of the only really magnificent
trees in our neighborhood. It seemed Daddy wanted to get
rid of that tree because the squirrels were spitting walnut
juice on his fleet of rusted-out old cars, allegedly wrecking
what paint remained on these vehicles.

My father wouldn't consider moving the cars. Clearly, it
was the tree's fault for growing in his way. As he relayed
this information to Vince, a squirrel, on cue, spit a wad of
juice directly at my father's head. It hit the brim of his hat,
rolled over that, and slid down the front of his glasses.
"See?!" he said to Vince.

Vince told me this story, both of us laughing uncontrollably, as we sat in the beach house in West Wildwood,
where we escaped for a couple of days before the return

trip south. It was his first glimpse, ever, of an ocean, and I was proud to be doing the showing, acted as if I had created the Atlantic with my own hands.

Sitting in this house that I still loved most in the world, in the upstairs kitchen overlooking the bay, we toasted each other with Jack Daniel's—Tennessee champagne—and chased these shots with beer after beer. We stuffed ourselves with crabs and then stepped out on the porch to better enjoy the salty breeze.

"You look pretty," Vince said softly, sincerely, as my skirt blew around my legs. So infrequently in my life had I had such a compliment, I blushed and gave the words too much weight. I recorded that moment, as well as the rest of our short time together at the Shore, with that movie camera in my mind, the one like my mother's, the one that saved the good parts and never seemed to capture the bad. Better than my mother's, though, in its ability to collect smells and sounds and textures.

There we are, moving closer on the porch, kissing. There we are, later that night, lying in my parents' very off-limits bed. There we are, by the dawn's early light, Vince's eyes changed overnight from precisely the green of the beer bottles we sucked on at dinner, to the bright blue of the shirt I have pulled back on in the morning chill. I hear his breathing, I feel his skin. And the salty smell—of sex and sweat and bay—fills my nostrils.

I am so in love with you, don't ever leave me—this is the voice-over accompanying these images, spoken so quietly, it is subliminal. Never, ever would I have dreamed of saying such a thing out loud. That would make Vince unhappy. That would make Vince frown. We couldn't have that. I had to be a good girl. I had to shut my mouth. I had to do just the right dance and invoke just the right saints to keep him, keep him.

He left me. I whined and cried to Mel and Patrick, and they listened, tolerated my rants as we sat drinking together nights at the Long Branch. Once, Patrick drove with me to West Virginia, so I could deliver gifts and myself to Vince, who accepted the trinkets but rejected, once again, the woman.

Privately, back at home, I cried over this abandonment. Publicly, I continued my boisterous front, frequenting bars with the ever-confident Mel, intensifying our relationship now that Vince was gone.

11

WHEN Whittle Communications hired Rufus Standy, it marked the beginning of a very long, very dragged-out ending for Mel and me. Rufus was clever, handsome, and studious. The first day I met him, I scrutinized him, noting immediately his most outstanding feature: that telltale gold band flashing, like a warning signal, on his left ring finger.

This embellishment, and all it stood for, did not deter Mel, however. Patrick had left her the month before, after seven years together, to return to their hometown of St. Louis. Their relationship had run its course, and concluded mutually, without hostility. I missed Patrick far more than Mel did, continued to adore him even from afar. She seemed nothing but relieved, eager for a chance to get out there and sow some wild eggs.

I did not catch on to Mel and Rufus's illicit affair for quite some time. Because, for the first time in nearly a year, Mel—who had previously appointed me guardian of so many of her secrets—chose now to keep pertinent information from me.

I befriended Rufus immediately, and took to his wife, Karen, as well when we met at a company party. I began baby-sitting for their son, Max. Some nights, they'd have informal parties of the salon variety. These times, Rufus and Karen, any number of their artist friends, and Mel and I, stayed up late in their living room drinking, smoking, discussing the works of James Agee, the eccentric Pulitzer Prize winner who'd once lived in Knoxville.

When I finally did learn that Rufus and Mel were sleeping together, I was mortified, felt like some unwitting accomplice in their sleazy disrespect for Karen. How dare Mel still socialize with them as a couple while she simultaneously threatened their marriage?

I was too close to Mel, and not close enough to Karen, to tell the latter this awful information I had uncovered. And so, abruptly, with the lamest of excuses, I began to decline Rufus and Karen's invitations, apologized for not being able to baby-sit anymore, tried to shut the whole situation out of my mind.

As I withdrew from them, Mel withdrew from me, caught further and further in the clandestine fantasy world she created with Rufus, mostly during long lunch hours when they snuck off to her place to fuck. Now, feeling rejected by my alleged best girlfriend, and noting that this rejection felt somehow deeper, somehow worse than any man's rejection, I set out defiantly to prove I was just fine without her.

This basically entailed me hoofing it down the six blocks from my apartment to the Long Branch alone, nightly, seeking solace in several rounds of longnecks with the lone-wolf regulars and pool sharks. Sufficiently drunk, I often concluded these evenings seducing some man, dragging him back to my apartment, introducing him to the excitement of sex on the floor—I still had no mattress—and waking up to wish either that I hadn't done what I'd done, or else that I had at least had the common sense to insert my diaphragm.

Common sense, however, was not my forte. I had one goal, and one goal only: I had to have attention. I had to overcome the sting I still felt at Vince's dumping me, the open wound I was nursing thanks to Mel's withdrawal.

Artists, musicians, co-workers, barflies—I fucked anyone with whom I shared the faintest mutual interest. Any attention was, after all, better than no attention at all. Inside, my self-esteem continued to shrink. Outside, I just kept getting louder and more daring.

In the midst of all this sex and pain, I decided to head to Jersey for Christmas. I hated the holiday, but had no invitations to go elsewhere, preferring to be miserable in the company of my family than alone in my apartment. Pointing that old Valiant north yet again, I drove and drove, arriving exhausted at my parents' home a few days before the dreaded holiday.

Daddy wasted no time starting in on me. Not five minutes after I'd dropped my bags on the floor and hugged my mother, he came barging into the house. "Get that thing off your car or leave!" he barked.

Confusion took over momentarily, until it dawned on me what the hell he was talking about. The bumper sticker. My father, who found and displayed most of his life philosophies via bumper stickers, had seen my own latest addition and was not amused. SHIT HAPPENS, it said. This was before shit started happening to every bumper in America, and Daddy, seeing the sentiment for the first time, was outraged.

"I'm not taking it off," I said, standing my ground.

My mother, across the room and talking on the phone, now got a frantic look on her face. Daddy and I were at it again, and she could tell. She gestured for me to wait, hold on for one minute. I refused. I picked up my bag and stormed out. Getting into the car, I noticed the bumper sticker, all scrawled over in that same famous black marker he'd used in Wildwood to count down, on the refrigerator, days until the end of vacations. I slammed the door, started the engine, and aimed for Atlantic City, to Jonathan, the one man in my life I could consistently count on.

I drank for days, Jonathan trying to console me, the various siblings I called to consult yelling at me for being an idiot. "I'll dance on his grave!" I screamed back. "I hate him!"

Christmas Eve, I drove back to Eastville, snuck into my parents' house to find my mother, apologize, and say goodbye. My father caught me, eyed me hatefully, said nothing. Ah, the old wall of silence.

I spent that night with one of my sisters, waking up at dawn Christmas morning to drive the thirteen hours my old car required to get back to Knoxville. Midway there, I discovered a gift of crabs bestowed upon me by one of my many lovers, a gift that would keep me wide awake with itch and anger the entire drive, knowing there was not one drugstore with the available cure open on this holy day.

Distraught over my family and my crotch, I gave up that year on ever counting Christmas as a possible time of happiness, on Daddy as a man capable of redemption. I stumbled, bleary-eyed, into my dirty apartment late that night and collapsed on the floor, curling into a miserable ball on the blanket I called bed, eager for the next day to arrive so I could buy something to kill the damn bugs eating away at my groin.

A month later, fed up with editing, tired of seeing writers get paid three times my weekly salary for pieces I had to rewrite for them, I quit, determined to freelance. Until I could generate enough writing to sustain me, I took a job waitressing, and was happy for my decision. The hours were much shorter, the pay almost identical to that of my professional gig, the thinking required even less. This all fit in very nicely with my continuing quest to drink myself silly every night. Now, I had time to sleep in late in the mornings, nap away my hangovers in the afternoon, to insure that I would be fresh for the next night's booze and fuckfest.

I began to write and read angry poetry at open-mike nights then, and the small crowds that gathered ate up my sardonic musings, applauded loudly, encouraged me to delve deeper into the bitterness raging inside. My popularity as a "local character" grew. If I was not beautiful, petite, demure, I was nonetheless desired for my talents and boldness. I grew confident in my growing ability to sleep with the men I chose, to act like I didn't care, to behave like a stereotypical man. Finally, I stopped confusing—or so I told myself—nakedness with love. I was, I pretended, a guilt-free, take-no-prisoners sex machine.

Really, though, I never stopped craving the intimacy I lost when Mel left me for Rufus. And so, for my emotional needs, I turned to Craig, the roommate of my most steady fuck-buddy, Thad. Almost instantly, we became so close that everyone, including me and excepting him, mistook us for a couple.

Craig did little to push me away, smiled kindly at my drunken confessions that I loved him. Still, he refused to get as close as I desired. He would go out with me seven nights a week, stay up with me until all hours, discuss any topic, but he would not sleep with me. And so, in earnest, I began to pursue him like a greyhound chasing a mechanical rabbit.

Sometime during the course of this, my latest crush, Rufus began to back off from Mel, to cave in to the guilt of his marital betrayal. Mel, trying to act unaffected, attempted to slip right back into her place in my life. She quickly moved in on me and my newest crowd of men friends, flirting unabashedly, reveling in their blatant adoration of her.

I could not, absolutely refused to, fully acknowledge Craig's attraction to Mel. Even more, would not admit the way she reciprocated, the way she toyed with him, clearly and cruelly using his affection to soothe the ego left damaged by Rufus.

So naive was I, so ill versed in the practice of girlfriend betraying girlfriend (no other woman had ever done such a thing to me), that I ignored their mutual flirtation, sought counsel from Mel on ways to win Craig as a lover. Mel, playing innocence personified, listened intently to my deepest confidences, my sacred details, encouraged me to tell her more and more, offered tips on improving my odds with Craig.

And then, she turned around and fucked him. Right under my nose. After tagging along with us on a night I had planned for just Craig and me, she edged her bar stool closer and closer to his until she was nearly in his lap. It was clear beyond any doubt that before the night was over they would consummate this ongoing flirtation of theirs. Unable to watch for another agonizing second, I stumbled home, crying bitterly, and vowed never to speak to either of them again.

The next day, bolder than ever before, Mel sought me out. Giddy at her exploits, she giggled, "I bet you're mad." I said nothing. Stared darkly. "Don't be angry. Come ON! I just did that for fun." As if that would make me, who sincerely wanted a real relationship with Craig, feel any better, knowing she had simply used him. Still, like a beaten wife accepting the apology bouquet, I consented to join her for the afternoon, tried with all my might to hide my anger.

With Mel, Craig, and my sundry collection of boys, I continued to hang out, drink, laugh. But the dynamic was never the same. I drank more. I slept around more. Discrimination of any sort no longer part of my criteria, I stormed around my town and my life, basking in anger and hatred. I blamed Mel. I blamed Craig. And, most often, I blamed my father for setting me up for a lifetime of rejection and its painful fallout.

Which is why I nearly shit my pants one Saturday night when I answered the door to find him standing there. With Mel and my dear friend John as my witnesses, I shut the door in Daddy's face, convinced I must be hallucinating, turned ashen at the specter of him.

But whoever or whatever I had seen looked precisely like my father. Same sleeveless undershirt topped with same flannel workshirt. Same khaki pants. Same cigar stub clenched between same toothless gums. And this thing, this person at the door, had said, in his same gruff voice, "Your mother's in da car."

No. Had that really been my father? Had I really shut the door in his face? I opened it again. No one was there. Of course I had imagined it. Daddy was eight hundred miles away in New Jersey. He hadn't spoken to me in months. Had no idea where I lived. Surely, if he *was* going to drop by, he would have called first.

Tentatively, I stepped out onto the porch. Sure enough, there was his station wagon parked in the street. More sure enough still, there was my mother, in da car. Once again, my father, unable to simply apologize, made a grand gesture instead. He decided to fix his most recent damage— the Christmas fiasco—by toting my mother all that way to see me.

Funny, I actually understood this maneuver. The biggest thing Daddy and I had in common was our love of my mother. Our fights distressed her endlessly, and the only times we ever feigned getting along were times when we both wanted to give her the gift of peace.

I approached the car, embraced my mother as she stepped out to the curb, held her tight. I spent so much of my life resenting my father, blaming him for the mistakes I made. But my mother . . .

There were times over the years when I got angry with her. Rarely did I scrutinize these feelings. It was so much easier to forgive her than Daddy, to blame what I saw as her failure to defend me on "the way things were." Now and then I'd think her complicitous because I'd never heard her take up for me when my daddy criticized my actions— surely that must have meant she agreed with him.

But somewhere deep inside, I felt differently. Yes, I'd

watched her kow-tow to his demands. No, I had not witnessed her speak up on my part. Still—and I hold this true to this day—she must have argued with him behind closed doors, called him on his harsh ways. This belief is underscored by memories of her telling me, again and again, that I could do anything I wanted when I grew up, and by her gentle and proud teasing each time I brought home another flawless report card. My mother's encouragement, rendered while my father was off at work, tempered his predictions that I would fail and fail again.

I imagine my mother's subtle, behind-the-scenes influence affected him similarly. Though Daddy and I loathed each other, this woman who connected us inspired us both. We adored her, each growing embarrassed, I believe, when our immature bickering manifested itself in the sad silence with which she always responded to our fights.

I insisted they stay at my place. Daddy, at first, refused, then relented, agreeing to sleep on the pile of mattresses I had by now accumulated from pitying friends who just did not believe me when I insisted that I liked sleeping on the floor.

Once they were settled in, I went out for my previously planned night of drinking. It wasn't like my parents and I had much to say to each other, or that they were interested in staying up late, hearing about my life. They retired early, and I went out and learned, unintentionally and precisely, how my father had located me.

As if he had some homing device, he wandered into the Vatican Pizza, the place where I read so many angry poems about him. There, of all the people he could stop and ask about my whereabouts, he managed to approach the very last man I had slept with. Denny, not thinking twice—after all, this was my father—gave Daddy directions to my apartment.

It was an odd visit with minimal conversation. Daddy and I were on our best behavior, which is to say our silence was less bitter than usual. We loathed the thought of giving in to the other, but more than that, we both ached to ease my mother's pain at our mutual disparagement.

On their last night in town, we decided to go to a nice restaurant. Dining out with my parents was not a common experience for me. Growing up, we children only ate out when my mother gave birth. Those times, my father would drive all of us kids to the fast-food place across from the hospital, buy a bag of burgers, and let us eat silently in the car as my mother waved down to us from the maternity ward window, far above.

This night, they wanted steak. We sat, and I was amazed as my nearly teetotaling parents ordered a round of Melonballs—fluorescent green, sticky-sweet teenager drinks they had recently discovered. The food arrived at last, and, just before my father slathered his steak teriyaki with ketchup, my shy mother proposed a toast.

They lifted their glowing drinks and clanked them against my pilsner glass. "To new beginnings," my mother said softly. It was one of her favorite sentiments.

12

MEL and I still hung out sometimes—quite the masochistic endeavor on my part. Like Stepford wives, we maintained a pleasant outward appearance of close friendship when we were together, continued laughing at those she deemed unworthy. But these occasions had a hollow ring to them now. I sensed I was being classified more and more as one no longer up to her haughty standards. We were drifting, our inevitable demise further hastened as she continued to sabotage me at random intervals.

Once, she set me up on a blind date with a man she assured me was perfect. Not only did she "forget" to tell the man that this outing was to be of the romantic variety, she also came along, allegedly to offer moral support. Then she went home with him that night. I didn't care about the potential love lost—the guy was nice enough but not my type. I just grew more and more stunned at the competitive things she did to show me how much more fabulous she was than me.

Another time, I learned that she handled my request for a recommendation letter in her own unique style. I had hoped to join a good friend of mine who was doing mission-ary work on a reservation in New Mexico, and I needed ref-erences to round out my application. Rather than tell me she did not feel comfortable with the task, my "friend" agreed to "help." She then went on to write to the priest in charge informing him what a poor, immature candidate I was. Position denied.

Even I could not close my eyes to this betrayal. I shut her out then, finally, only to hear the resulting rumors she her-self circulated. She informed our mutual friends that I was angry because I was in love with her and she wouldn't have me. She pointed to the gifts I brought her—flowers to cheer her when Rufus dumped her, expensive paints for her birthday—as false evidence of this alleged unrequited love.

Whatever happiness, independence, and fledgling success as a writer I enjoyed in Knoxville over the preceding years was now darkly overshadowed, blanked out completely at times, by these events. A deep sadness, a bottomless loneli-ness, took over.

Fortunately, a bit of respite and inspiration came my way, albeit fleetingly, via a traveling street musician named Johnny, whom I met outside the Long Branch one night. He was planning to head west the next day. I convinced him to stay the night in my apartment, rather than in his cramped van.

Surprising myself, when I got him home I did not make a move to bed him down, though we were clearly attracted to each other. There was something so kindred in him, so sincere, that for once I could foresee how sex might cheapen an experience, would definitely take away from the hours we spent talking.

He decided to stay a second day, and we went to a party

out in the country that night. There, we got drunk and stoned and lay beneath a blanket of brilliant stars, stars made brighter by the absence of city lights.

We summarized our lives and outlined our plans as we listened to bongo drums banging from within a teepee set up in the distance. He turned to me after a pause, and kissed me in a very nonawkward, very meant-to-be sort of way. An hour later, I woke up naked in the tall grass, having drifted off after genuine lovemaking, so different from the wham-bam technique I had perfected back in town.

He handed me my clothes, led me back to his van, tucked me in on the tiny cot, and did not mock me when, in my exhaustion and inebriation, I let out a little too much of my insecurity. "Promise me," I said, and stumbled on the words. "Promise me you'll come back." He promised—well, of course, it was his van—and headed back to the party. I woke up in the morning to find him wrapped around me—a nearly impossible feat given the size of that bed.

That was to be the end of it. He would leave and I would let him. There would be no obsessing with this one. I would simply keep a little movie of our fun two-night stand in my heart and head forever. Wax nostalgic at the mystery man who made me smile momentarily and then drove off into the sunset. He dropped me off at work that morning and we agreed to say good-bye that afternoon.

Instead, I returned to find his departure plans drastically changed by the fact that we had unwittingly rolled through not a field of grass, but one of poison ivy. He was a bright red rash from head to toe.

By midnight, frighteningly swollen and hardly able to move, he needed immediate medical attention. In the emergency room, the staff eyed me suspiciously: This was the second time in as many weeks I'd shown up with a different man in the middle of the night. (Thad was the other, having fallen on a dead bush as we'd staggered home one night, impaling his butt so deeply that the doctor at first refused to believe his wound was not a gunshot.)

My own poison ivy—declared "the worst ever seen" by more than one medical professional—appeared the following day. My turn to go to the hospital. Consequently, Johnny and I spent the next week drifting in and out of antihistamine hazes and itch-inhibited naps, unable to touch ourselves, let alone each other. Overcompensating for a lack of physical intimacy, we spent our odd waking hours talking softly and ceaselessly, discussing our many common interests.

Johnny was so free with his love and attention, such a non-game player, that now the thought of his leaving made my heart want to crack, split, ooze, and turn black as the wounds on my legs. But I knew, from our conversations, that with no offense intended, nothing could convince him to stay once he'd healed. And nothing could convince him to invite me to join him—something I would've done in a heartbeat. He was determined to take his long trip alone.

Had he left quickly, as originally planned, I could have kept him on a little shelf in my mind, in the room reserved for pleasant memories. But each day that he lingered, my attachment grew. When he finally did sing me one last sad song, kiss me one last time, I choked back tears. God, I was so tired of being lonely, of being left.

It was the final sad straw for me. I had to get out of that town. For the first time in my life, I had a little money saved. So I called Elaine, my old college roommate, still in Florida. Elaine was always game for an adventure. And she had a decent car, too. "Could I," I inquired, "possibly convince you to travel the country with me for a couple of months?" Elaine, in desperate need of an escape from her crazy, alcoholic boyfriend, Chris, jumped at the offer.

I took a Greyhound down to Tampa to meet her. We loaded up with camping gear and followed a path first north, back to Tennessee, then through the Southwest, finally reaching L.A. By then, Elaine missed Chris terribly. After yet another long-distance call to him, she hung up and announced, "He's flying out to drive back with us."

Annoyed initially, fearing I would be relegated to third-wheel status, I was quickly won over—as most of the world was upon encountering him—by Chris's lilting brogue, wild streak, and undeniable charisma. We got good and drunk in L.A., impulsively getting tattooed one day and heading for San Francisco the next. The still-drunk Chris insisted on steering us up the treacherous Pacific Coast Highway, a can of warm beer in his hand, Elaine and I too frightened to talk him out of driving.

We made it as far as Victoria, British Columbia, before it occurred to me that our money situation was more dire than I had allowed myself to believe. We had burned through my stash, stopping at every bar and junk store on the way. I had about enough cash to get us halfway back to Tennessee, provided we ate sparingly. I also had a corporate check that I had been unable to cash anywhere—no bank, not even a casino in Vegas would take it.

I suddenly thought of Patrick, Mel's ex, in St. Louis. I would love to see him, and a phone call revealed the feeling to be mutual. Plus, he would be glad to help with my check. The closer we got to Missouri, the more my imagination went into overdrive. The feelings I'd once had—and repressed—for Patrick returned. I would confess my old crush, I decided, and try to seduce him. The gesture would be sincere, but I have to admit I also enjoyed the thought of Mel fuming, if only she knew.

Patrick and I did share a drunken, sloppy kiss or three, and I slept beside him that first night. But when I tried to turn push to love, he declined. "You mean so much to me," he said, "but this just can't happen." Then he added: "I really think you should meet my brother."

His brother? It was a bizarre suggestion, I suppose, one that could be considered an offering of the sloppy-seconds variety. But I was on a roll, still high from all that traveling and drinking and thinking and blocking thoughts out for the preceding six weeks. His brother? What the hell?

And so it was that I met James Neil O'Reilley, first glimpsing him through the window of his parents' kitchen, where he was living and recovering from an accident that had left him in a wheelchair and then on crutches the entire summer. He was standing on his own for only the second day in months when I walked in the backdoor and shook his hand. He was six feet tall, paler than Wonder Bread, skinnier than an anorexic toothpick, and crowned with enough thick, curly red hair to provide sweaters for the entire IRA. Ah, quirky, just my type.

That particular weekend, the parents O'Reilley were out of town, so all of their six children, each bringing a friend or two, gathered in the backyard of headquarters for an impromptu party. We sat and joked and swilled warm cans of

Schaeffer pilfered when the guys lifted the locked booze closet door from its hinges.

James and I sat side by side, joining in the larger conversation, and swapping intimate, silly asides. I had to hand it to Patrick: James and I were like cynical peas in a sarcastic pod. We spent much of the rest of the weekend together, promising, as I left to finish the last leg of my trip, to write each other soon.

As it happened, Knoxville would not be the last stop after all. The sadness that had driven me from there again filled me, almost immediately, upon my return. For starters, I had nowhere to live, and my temporary stay with friends wore on all of our nerves quickly. So, in a move that appealed to me in some warped Bukowskian manner, I took a room at the decrepit YWCA downtown, noting with irony that I was just a stone's throw from the Blakely House, that fabulous hotel I had inhabited when I first came to Knoxville.

I floundered around for a month or so, picking up waitressing shifts and writing gigs by day, returning at night to my hell-hot room when the filthy shotgun tavern across the street closed and there was nowhere else left to go. I composed still more angry poetry, flipped through recently acquired Tarot cards trying to come up with a plan. Delved further still into the mystical when I was assigned to interview a number of psychics, asking them for personal help in addition to quotes for my article.

Nothing, no one, seemed able to offer solid advice on how or where I would find happiness. My patience spent, I headed once again to New Jersey for what I hoped to be some cleansing time at the beach.

Two weeks of solitude in Wildwood—it was the off-season and all the loud tourists were gone—calmed me. I walked ten miles a day, wrote essays at night, stayed sober, plunked out tunes on a recently purchased guitar. All the while I waited for a call from Daddy. I'd given him the last of my money and asked him to find me a VW camper to replace that one I'd left behind in Tampa years before.

While my father expected precise adherence to any instructions he rendered, he himself had no trouble ignoring my specifications. "I gotcha a truck," he said, when I picked up the ringing phone. It was a monster, a '67 Chevy pickup that, despite its age, miraculously had only twenty-five thousand miles on it.

With terror in my heart—I'd always considered myself less than a great driver—I steered that beast with its three-on-the-tree gearshift and toe-numbing, too-taut clutch back to Tennessee. Unbelievably, I did not cause death or destruction on the way. Back in the town I once loved dearly and now seemed unable to escape, I settled into the shittiest apartment I'd ever lived in—which is saying quite a lot—and found yet another waitressing job, this time in a new nightclub owned by an old friend.

That was the good part. The club was a haven for me, filled with a group of co-workers who were smart, funny, artist types and, better still, had no connection to Mel. I continued to see my old friends—our old friends—somewhat regularly, but our entire group had been splintered when Mel and I went our angry, separate ways. Mostly I focused on my new circle, on trying to start over again after feeling so lost for so long.

From time to time, Mel popped up, acting, it seemed, as

if nothing had gone wrong between us. Though I could barely stand the sight of her, I could not resist one invitation she extended. She was going to St. Louis for a weekend; did I care to join?

I drove, hurtled us west in that huge pickup with visions of James in my head. We had kept in touch, sporadically, but I wanted more. On this trip, though we were still far too shy with each other to make a physical move, we were completely inseparable, staying up into the wee hours, making up stories, fantasizing about great writing projects we would one day collaborate on.

This touched off an exchange of letters that filled my spare time. I would work in the club until two, drink till four, wake up at noon, and head off to the post office to either send or retrieve another long missive. It was a great game for us, a challenge to one-up the other, to evoke the hardest laughter possible. I fell in love with him through these letters and the elaborate cartoon series of my life he created.

In January, James came east for my twenty-fifth birthday, agreed to be my date for a huge bash held in the club on an off night. He had arrived just that morning, and, both of us nervous beyond nervous, we had decided the only logical thing to do was start drinking. Never mind that it was only nine in the morning. We pounded a half a case of beer and when that was through, we got some more. Drunk, giddy, still nervous, we finally kissed that night in the little room reserved for the band.

He stayed for a week, far longer than planned, and except for the hours I was away at work, we spent every single minute drinking, having sex, or walking for hours through

Knoxville holding hands. He was, I felt certain, my soul mate. I flew three feet above the ground when we were together. And when he left, I fell hard, the wings on my ankles clipped, replaced by the heavy black scabs of loneliness returned.

In April of that year, my grandmother—my father's mother—died, after longing to do so for nearly a decade. Because of this wish, her demise was neither shocking nor too terribly sad. Nonetheless, I took an entire week off "for grieving." I would spend two days in Jersey, then race over to spend the remainder in St. Louis, with my new official boyfriend.

Back in Jersey, I traded Daddy the truck for an old station wagon. I told him and myself I was doing this because the truck was just too hard to drive. Really, I think I wanted somehow to cheer my father, who had loved his mother, now lying before us in a coffin. Also, I believe I wanted to try, once again, to show him what a very good girl I was. I had known, from the first moment he showed me the Chevy, that he'd wished he had one to match it.

The trade-off had an unforeseen benefit. As I shuffled past my grandmother's corpse for the last time—actually, an unrecognizable figure, overstuffed with embalming fluid, not my grandmother at all but rather some huge, wickless candle—I noted my father standing solemnly, unavoidably, at the head of the coffin. I stopped. I did not know what to say to him as he mourned the loss of his mother, had not known what to say to him my whole life, even in situations far less intense. Consoling words failed me. I looked at him. He at me. Finally, he broke the silence. "How'd the station wagon run on the way over?"

"Fine," I answered.

Saved, once again, by the topic of automobiles.

I left immediately after the burial, drove sixteen hours straight to Missouri to spend the rest of my vacation drinking, laughing, and rolling naked with James across the basement floor of his parents' house. We decided then that we could not go on living so far apart.

Four weeks later, I crammed that station wagon full of everything I could fit, left what I couldn't for my landlord along with a broken lease, and moved once again, this time heading for the redhead at the end of the line.

St. Louis, Cleveland, St. Louis

13

A LARGE party, hosted this time by James's parents, was in full swing when I pulled up to Headquarters O'Reilley. Not in my honor—Neil and Maureen had no idea I was moving to their city to live with their son. In fact, if they had, they would have marked the occasion with whatever is the opposite of party. They were practical people. James and I, despite our cynical streaks, were hopeless romantics.

Telling his parents what we had in mind would have presented immediate obstacles we did not care to face just then. Neil, as devout a Catholic as my father, would have condemned our plan to live in sin. Far more problematic was the fact that there actually was no "plan." James still lived with his parents, and neither of us had any money. An apartment together was out of the question.

But we had convinced ourselves that if we just found a way to live in the same city, then soon enough—without seriously considering or discussing how—we would find a way to share the same bed. Admitting out loud the impossibility of this would have destroyed the fantasy we had created in our many letters and long-distance calls.

And so, unsuspecting, my boyfriend's parents greeted me warmly. They were curious people. Neil was an odd mixture of stoicism and Irish sparkle. He could put his arm around you and hand you a drink and tell you a bad joke one minute, and then, without warning, he could switch gears, tell you to put on your work clothes and mow the lawn the next. Maureen, as I knew from my handful of prior visits, brooded and complained fairly often, but only in private. When guests came in the door, she was all smiles.

Together, Neil and Maureen were odder still. If you didn't know them well, they appeared the perfect hosts, a handsome couple married for nearly thirty years. But I knew better. Rumor had it this marriage had unraveled at least a decade before. Conversation between them was short, not very sweet, and rare. Their best talks were a sort of pleasant, cocktail party repartee.

Tension surfaced when Neil finally noticed my beat-up, crap-packed car parked in front of his toney house in his toney neighborhood. He told James to tell me to move the vehicle to a less conspicuous place. And, after a week of finding me camped out in his basement every morning as he descended to retrieve his laundry, his unease mounted. It was clear I needed to find an alternative floor to sleep on.

James's sister, Molly, and her roommate took me in until James and I could raise the necessary funds from our pathetic restaurant jobs—I could not find a waitressing gig and had to settle for bussing tables—to secure a cellblock-sized efficiency apartment, with a two-by-three-foot "kitchen area," a bathroom the size of a closet, and no second room into which we might escape from each other should need for time alone arise. We spread blankets on the floor to symbolize the bed we did not have, borrowed our only furniture—a table and two chairs—and began to play house.

James worked just blocks away, at Memo's Pizza. My days off were frequent—I simply could not find enough work—and so I joined him most afternoons at the end of his shift. We'd stand at the counter and toss back free drafts, then pick up a six-pack or two to take home with us. Ah, romance.

In the face of too much beer and too little room, we managed to have fun anyway, at least for the first few months. St. Louis was new territory for me to explore, a city of contrasts. I wandered through the old-money neighborhoods of three-story, single-family mansions, and made up tales in my head about what went on behind those heavy doors. Or, more often, I drank heavily in the abundant blue-collar pubs, where flashing neon signs proudly proclaimed that Busch on tap—America's worst beer—was served on the premises.

I tried, now and then, to put some of my stories on paper and sell them. But there were few places to get published in St. Louis, and my work was by no means ready for prime time. I sat around and accumulated well-deserved rejection letters, cursing the various editors who dared send them, refusing to acknowledge that my stories had been slapped sloppily, hastily together and were basically getting what they deserved.

To kill time and bring in a little more money, I began picking up shifts with James. We spent more and more time together, and this, combined with daily drinking and my sense of frustration with my writing, led to an increase in spats. By Christmas of our first year together, I had exploded at him on numerous occasions, though what resolution I was hoping for I could not say then or now.

I suppose I wanted, impossibly, to hang on to the same excitement and challenge we faced when we had blindly decided to live together. But there was no challenge in our jobs or our rituals. Every day was the same: wake up hungover, go to a mindless job, drink, fuck, and on a really ambitious day, read a little. I was bored. And though I never, ever stopped loving him, or the idea that I was loved by one man—such a lifelong goal—inside, I had to admit I missed Knoxville, the friends and independence I'd had there, and the audiences that had come to hear me read my poetry.

St. Patrick's Day, our second together, rolled around. This was the highest of holy days for the O'Reilleys, and the whole family joined drinking forces at a bar downtown. Neil, his Irish pride visibly bursting from within, was in an atypically light mood, buying round after round of drinks for us all, recounting tales of his children's youth with the bragging force of a man announcing the birth of his first son.

Maureen arrived a little late, having just flown in that day from Cleveland where she was visiting her sister Colleen and their ailing mother, Nell. Despite her second-generation Irish blood, and her devotion to any holiday—but St. Pat's most of all—she was surprisingly withdrawn. She gathered us together and told us sorrowfully that her mother was sick, and that Colleen was having a hard time doing all the caregiving. Perhaps, she suggested, one of the O'Reilley children might go to Cleveland for a spell and help?

Here, admittedly, my recollection goes a bit exaggerated. I see us standing there, the six children O'Reilley and me, lined up drunk against the bar. I'm a little less drunk than the rest, thanks to the fact I have just returned from puking in the ladies' room. I'm also a little more eager, always wanting to earn the one extra brownie point that might push me over the edge into Maureen's Permanent Good Graces.

I hear her voice, clear as a bell, cutting through the drunken cacophony surrounding us. She is asking for help. I see the other children appear to take a step backward, in unison—as if in an old Warner Brothers cartoon—giving the distinct impression that I have stepped forward to volunteer. Further compelling me to respond is the little martyr that lives on my shoulder, whispering loudly in my ear, "You HAVE to do it."

"I can go!" I shout. Stunned looks of disbelief on James' and his siblings' faces. A sweet eyeful of gratitude from Maureen who thanks me kindly but says, no, really, her mother hardly knows me. Ta-da. Mission accomplished. Points gained without having to actually work for them.

Not so fast. Within a few days, Maureen rethinks my offer, consults her sister and her mother, and calls me. Come to think of it, they have decided I would be ideal for the situation. When can I leave?

Which is how I found myself driving yet again, my things packed into that station wagon yet again, heading off for an unpredictable adventure yet again. Kara, James's oldest sister, was my happy, chattering copilot, joining me ostensibly to help me settle in, but really to escape her miserable marriage for a few days and drink in peace.

Kara used the excuse of a light snowfall to cajole me into pulling over to pound a few too many brews in a bar designed to resemble a medieval castle. Admittedly, I needed little prompting, my own drinking having escalated exponentially in both quantity and regularity since I'd moved in with James. I do believe that, from the moment I set permanent foot in St. Louis, not one single day passed in which I was sober, my boozefests almost invariably beginning long before sunset.

We sat there, in that silly bar, and I listened to Kara shred the various people she disliked. Nearly everyone and everything provoked her. And I knew, from having observed her, that when she got drunk enough, it was not beyond her reach to switch from verbal brawling to flat-out fisticuffs. I made a mental note then to never, ever get on her bad side. Reluctantly, finally saying no to the bartender's ongoing inquiry—"Another round?"—we set sail for the last hundred miles.

We arrived in Cleveland sufficiently tipsy. Aunt Colleen greeted us warmly, a cold beer in either hand to reward us for our troubles. I was so happy as they gushed over me, my willingness to sacrifice and help Grandmother Nell. I was endearing myself. I was a good girl, a useful girl. I was becoming a part of James's family more and more.

We went to Nell's house the next day, and I noted immediately that my new charge was, beyond a doubt, the genetic source of Kara's fierce temper. Nell had come over from County Cork over half a century before, though the thickness of her brogue suggested this arrival had occurred no earlier than last week.

She sat in her La-Z-Boy, listening to hate radio most of the day, having discovered and sainted Rush Limbaugh long before he ever had mass appeal. Whenever anything remotely British was mentioned, she would scowl. The announcement of a tragedy would be a call for her to fish her rosary beads out of her housedress pocket and begin immediately to pray for the victims.

Nell was not the only one under my care. They waited until I had arrived to spring on me news of Fritzy, the hellion feline. Fritzy had nothing but evil intentions. He also, according to Nell and Colleen, had very specific daily rituals that were not to be toyed with. For example, each night at precisely eight o'clock, I was to throw exactly four kitty treats down the basement stairs and, as he ran to fetch them, lock the door behind him. I have no idea how the number four was chosen, or if the cat could count. But I knew better than to break the rules and upset the old lady.

The walls of my assigned bedroom sagged inward slightly, so weighed down were they with religious icons. Lying down in my twin bed at night, I felt like I was back in Daddy's house. Particularly disconcerting was a print on the wall, one that, in fact, *had* been in Daddy's collection. Titled *The Handkerchief of Veronica*, it was said to be a replica of the imprint left by Jesus as Veronica reached up to mop his brow, to provide a little comfort as he dragged that cross through the streets, heading toward his death. In the sepia-toned portrait, he is wearing a bloody crown of thorns and an agonized expression. His eyelids droop with pain.

As if the sight of this twisted face was not unnerving enough, an inscription offered further creepy potential. It suggested that he who stares hard enough will be honored with seeing Christ's eyelids flip open and stare back. I couldn't stand it, was horrified thoroughly by it, took it down immediately, and placed it facedown on the dresser.

On my fourth day in Cleveland, a growing nag in the back of my mind gave way to the unavoidable truth. My period, typically regular as a Swiss timepiece, was quite late. I'd mentioned this to James before my departure, but assured us both it was just due to my nerves, my reluctance to leave him. Now, worried, I snuck out and bought a pregnancy test. At 4 A.M. the following morning, unable to wait any longer, I tiptoed down the hall to the bathroom. taking great care not to disturb Kara, sleeping on the twin bed across from mine.

I pissed on the white plastic stick and watched for an eternal ten minutes as, like the ghost of some future present, the oh-shit-blue line materialized. I had fucked recklessly and randomly for three years in Knoxville, had managed somehow all that time to avoid this situation, and now, in this house of holy, I discovered myself to be carrying the bastard great-grandchild of the old woman snoring a floor beneath me.

In shock, I crept back to the room and balled up on my little bed, looked at Kara sleeping against the other wall. I thought of Christ, facedown on the dresser. I tried to smile. I had sworn to myself, after the miscarriage, that if I ever got pregnant again, I would not, WOULD NOT, think one negative or even vaguely ambivalent thought. Would not risk losing another child due to a bad attitude, something I still sometimes blamed for the loss of that other pregnancy.

At 6 A.M., still wide awake, I got up again. This time, I left the house, headed out in a bizarre April snowstorm to search for a pay phone. A sharp wind whipped my face and blinded me as I headed straight up the main road, panicking nonetheless that in these severe conditions and given my hideous sense of direction, I would get lost in this blizzard.

A mile up the line, I spotted a convenience store with a phone outside. I called James first, though I knew he would not be awake yet, let alone sober enough, to hear the news. "James . . ."—long pause—"I'm pregnant." He responded with a pause of his own, finally coming back with his unfiltered thoughts. "I can't talk about this now." That was it. We hung up.

I tried again. This time, I called Jonathan. "I'm pregnant." By now, Jonny had been with me for ten years, ever supportive, ever encouraging, even in my most screwed-up moments. He had seen what the miscarriage had done to me. Like James, he paused, too. Not the pause of denial though. The pause of tears. Finally, he said, "It's going to be okay." Upon hearing this, I tried unsuccessfully to hold back my own tears, freezing against my cheeks in that icy wind.

I knew exactly why I had called Jonathan. Sometimes, many months passed between our letters or calls. Still, I always knew right where to find him when I needed him, knew I could count implicitly on his support without endless interrogation. He never let me down. I carried his voice in my head at all times, he my invisible safety net catching me over and over again through the years. "It is going to be okay," he said. And I made myself believe him.

14

A FEW others feigned support over the course of the next week or two. But overall, things turned pretty ugly, pretty quickly, as I began the task of sharing my news.

I called James again, and told him I understood fatherhood was not something he had planned for. Further, I informed him that, if he wanted, he could bail now, obligation-free, with my blessings.

Perhaps I was being too easy on him, but a number of factors shaped my generous offer. For starters, I had no interest in sharing parenting with a resentful partner. And I knew, without question, that I would indeed be raising a child, with or without James. I'd already figured out with the earlier pregnancy that, though I remained a staunch pro-choice supporter, abortion was not a choice I could consider personally.

On the other hand—technically, legally—I did have the option to terminate. I thought it only fair that James have some sort of choice, too. No, he couldn't demand an actual abortion. But he could try, if he so desired, to obtain an emotional one.

A level of guilt also led me to offer him an easy out. I could clearly remember certain times, during arguments, fuming around, thinking I should just get pregnant and leave him, perhaps even voicing this to him. I still sometimes felt a sense of failure from my miscarriage and was occasionally visited with a strong desire to "make up" for that loss. That I actually was now pregnant sent my mea-culpa complex into overdrive. I was responsible for this, my subconscious yearnings turned concrete, threatening poor, poor James's carefree existence.

But I was not solely responsible. Not only was I as surprised as James, he clearly had more than a hand in matters. We both were aware of the day, time, and place of conception. We both also were aware that on that occasion, my diaphragm was not in place. We opted to do what we did anyway, using the it-won't-happen-just-this-once method of birth control (one that had worked a number of times before). Despite these truths, I greatly feared being labeled the cliché man-trapper, the woman so insecure that she purposefully, stealthily gets knocked up to insure that her partner will stay.

James considered my offer only briefly, almost immediately promising to stick with me through whatever the future held, though there were hints of reluctance and fear in his voice. Neither of us thought marriage necessary, so that was out. But I was relieved that he loved me enough to stay with me.

There was no way I could remain with Nell past my first trimester once I started showing—it wouldn't do to be an unmarried pending-mother caring for a traditional, ancient Catholic. Besides, they only paid me seventy-five dollars a week. Also, given this new twist, I no longer had it in me to care for someone else. I had too much to sort through, too much to plan. We decided James would join me as soon as his semester ended, in six weeks. From there we would head off to raise money, to do whatever we had to do, to prepare.

That decision made, I confided in James's sister and aunt, begging them to tell no one else until James and I could plan how to best inform our parents. Though I was twenty-six and James was twenty-four, we both still feared our parents.

Kara and Colleen hugged me when I finally told them what was going on. I felt relieved and supported.

Fortified by their favorable response, I told my parents next. They did not lecture, just let forth a sigh of resignation over the phone from across the miles that separated us. Two pregnancies, two different men, no marriage certificate either time. What could be worse? Easy: an abortion. The fact that I did not choose to have one (as if I would tell them if I had) tipped the scales in my favor. They, too, were supportive, and I told them I would come for a visit soon.

The first serious opposition I encountered came from Aunt Sarah, another sister of James's mother. I do not know if she knew I was pregnant, but the hostile way she treated me when she came to visit Nell certainly suggested there was something—bastard in the belly, anybody?—that fired her dislike of me.

Sarah was the holy-rolling, dickless twin of my father, and she immediately beckoned me to join her upstairs. We stood in the doorway of a bedroom, confusion registering on my face. Reaching into her purse, she extracted a holy card—sort of the Catholic version of baseball cards, each featuring a different saint—and handed it to me. "I want you to meet someone special," she said through a false, taut smile.

I looked down at the picture of St. Teresa, Little Flower, she pressed into my hand, and I cut her off at the pass. "I am already familiar," I countered. "Teresa is my patron saint, my confirmation name is hers."

Click. Off went the switch of kindness. The next second, she snapped at me, her true colors blazing. "Mother doesn't like when you put your feet on the couch. And stop using the phone. It disturbs her."

Now, there I was, twenty-four hours a day, taking care of this bitch's mother, a woman with such poor vision she could not see her own feet at the end of her legs, let alone mine on the sofa, and deaf enough that she'd never heard me on the phone. I had to wonder why Sarah was spending her brief visit picking on me when she could have been downstairs loving her mother.

Next outburst: Neil. James had been too nervous to tell his parents, and so I asked Colleen to break the news to Maureen. Maureen told Neil, and Neil spewed forth. It was wrong for me to want to have and keep this child of sin. On the other hand, the damage was done, and abortion was out of the question. He informed James that I should carry the baby, bear the baby, and give the baby up for adoption.

I have had little luck forgiving Neil this, even now, nearly ten years later. I try to understand, in retrospect, that he was simply worried sick about our potential—or lack thereof— to be parents. In his picture of us, we had less than nothing to offer. In fact, we had every conceivable hurdle firmly planted in our path.

Between us we made less than two hundred dollars a week. We had no insurance. We had an apartment that did not fit two people and could never accommodate a third. We drank all the time (though I stopped as soon as I knew I was pregnant). What he did not know, could not know, was that deep inside the confused, oft-drunk, loudmouthed pregnant girlfriend of his middle son, there remained the overachieving, straight-A, Goody Two-shoes, ready to prove I could follow through on and excel at any project I decided to pursue.

At least Neil was back in St. Louis, easy enough to put out of my mind for the time being. Right then, I had my hands full with my immediate circumstances. Nell liked me well enough, but she hated my cooking. I hated her ongoing racist comments. And both of us, I'm sure, hated being cooped up in the house so much. On top of all this, Colleen was beginning to act very strange, her loving-aunt routine giving way to a palpable chill.

When at last James arrived in mid-May, the storm that had been brewing within Colleen came to a head of frightening proportions. Nell's house was full—many of James's out-of-state cousins and his sister Kara were in for a visit, a scaled-down family reunion of sorts. Bolstered by the presence of so many relatives, Colleen attacked from a position of strength. If blood was thicker than water, angry Irish blood was thicker than a prison wall.

The day before James and I were scheduled to leave town, visit my parents, and then head to Tennessee, where I knew I could find lucrative work for the summer, I finally learned the source of Colleen's ire. Unbeknownst to me, on my one day off per week, she had been sneaking into my room, rifling through my writings, while I was out running errands.

I didn't exactly keep a journal, but I did keep sundry written accounts of my experiences in Cleveland, as well as photocopies of letters I'd sent to cheer and encourage James. Hard to say which offended her more.

In my writings, I complained of Nell's racism and crankiness, bemoaned the fact that pride drove her to try to empty her own bedpan in the mornings, before I came downstairs. But successfully balancing a bedpan while shuffling with the aid of a walker proved impossible for the ninety-two-year-old. Time and again she spilled, and time and again—my olfactory nerve in high gear thanks to pregnancy—I grew nauseated at the stench of the urine-soaked carpet.

The letters to James were downright pornographic, though amusingly so. Hoping to prove life did not have to change drastically, I fell back to our original method of courtship. I created hysterical scenarios, detailed ridiculous things I would do to his body when I finally saw him after such a long break.

And finally, there was the comedy routine. I'd dabbled in one-woman shows in Knoxville and now, armed with a whole new set of material, I sat down to write a monologue. It was dumb, granted. More important, though, it was painfully obviously a *joke*. But Colleen didn't get it. She read where I explained how I got pregnant: Following the doctor's advice that a diaphragm is in the right place if you can't feel it, I left it in my dresser.

This was the "proof" she used to drag me down. I found her in the basement, standing before a very pale James, who was squirming on the couch. She spun around, saw me, and spat venom. "We are trying to have a discussion here!" I took the hint, hightailed it back up the stairs, and—still not realizing she had invaded my privacy—sat down next to Nell and tried to figure out what the hell was going on.

Finally, James emerged. Sheepish, verbally beaten, he answered the question in my eyes. "My aunt doesn't like you very much," he whispered.

Stunned, stupefied, still absolutely clueless, I did not stop to interrogate him. "I'm leaving. Now. Come with me if you want." I ran up the stairs, dragged down my belongings in heavy boxes and trashbags. I was petrified this lifting might induce a miscarriage, but not one of the many cousins or the glaring Kara made a move to help. Everyone but me, it seemed, was in on Colleen's big, ugly secret.

Once I'd shoved everything in the car, I wiped away my tears and confronted Colleen.

"I want my money. You owe me for two weeks," I said.

"You owe it to me for the phone bill," she hissed. "You're not getting anything."

I stormed to the car, crying until I shook, waiting for James to hurry the hell up. Finally, one cousin emerged, approached me, apologized and thanked me for caring for her grandmother. "Please, my grandmother loves you. Come in and tell her good-bye." I could not.

James finally joined me, having taken so long because the others insisted he stop and pose for some family pictures. He had not known how to refuse. As soon as he shut his door, I hit reverse, peeled out of that driveway, and drove all night, fueled by rage and needing no caffeine, across the Pennsylvania Turnpike to New Jersey.

I had to do all of the driving; James had never had a license, would not get one until I was too pregnant to fit behind the wheel. I cried and he talked. I asked and he answered. Colleen, he told me, had photocopied my writing to distribute among her siblings—including James's mother. She had also stressed to him what a horrible woman I was, and how I was clearly trying to trap him. I was the evil slut come to steal the seed of James Neil O'Reilley and put a black mark on his family.

Part of me wanted to spit. To turn around, hunt her down, and scream in her face. But another part of me knew I would get my revenge another way. I would show them what a good mother I could be.

After a brief stay in Wildwood, we spent three months in Knoxville. I held down an editing job by day and waited tables at night, squirreling away money to pay for the delivery of the child now kicking inside me. James earned little more than beer money at his part-time dishwashing job, which he swore was the only work he could find.

I tried not to push the issue. Already, more than once, he had broken down, confessed that he could not go through with this. Each time, after yelling at him to grow up, I apologized, backed off, tried to think of a new way to make things better, to show him there was nothing to worry about.

No luck. He grew increasingly reluctant and I grew increasingly enthusiastic. He grew increasingly withdrawn and drunk. I grew increasingly, period, eventually ballooning up to over two hundred pounds by the end of my third trimester, which we spent in St. Louis. Rarely did James's family ask how I felt, what my plans were.

Perhaps they thought ignoring my pregnancy would make it, or me, go away. Perhaps they were just so worried they were dumbfounded. Sometimes I think I got so big in an effort to make them see me, to see this thing, their very own blood, I carried inside. My plan hardly worked. Patrick was kind. James's sister Maggie threw a big shower. But Neil said nothing. And Kara just stared at me hostilely the rare occasions when I was forced to be in the same room with her.

Dear Henry,

On December 1, 1990, your daddy and I were sitting on the old sofa in the living room of our new place, an old duplex in a poor neighborhood in St. Louis. We were watching a staticy picture on the big, old, fake-wood console TV your grandpa gave us. The pictures were mostly red and green, but it was better than nothing. It was eleven o'clock at night and I felt this thing inside of me and I turned to your daddy and I said, "I think this is it."

We had decided—well, I had decided—to have your birth at home. Because that's how so many of my friends in Tennessee had their babies. And my friends in Tennessee were so wonderful the whole summer I was living there, carrying you inside. They were full of smart advice and generous with their good food and had given me comfortable places to sleep and any support I needed. I liked how they lived their lives. I wanted the same thing for us.

As soon as I knew it really was time, we called the midwife. She told us to get some sleep, because it was going to be a while before you came and I would need to be well rested for the hard work ahead of me. Your daddy fell right off— he'd had some beers to help and besides, he never had much trouble sleeping. Me, I lay there, thinking a million things. Wondering what you would be like. Scared and excited and nervous and happy. I could not sleep. The harder I tried, the more awake I became.

I finally got up, sat in the kitchen all night trying to read, my mind too preoccupied to concentrate on anything long. Read a passage. Feel a contraction. Look at your daddy sleeping in the other room. This went on until 7 A.M. when, annoyed at him for being able to sleep, I finally woke him. I told him to call the midwife again; the pains were getting closer.

The midwife assured him that she would be there soon. Meanwhile, we called up Lisa, a nurse friend of ours who wanted to help. Lisa showed up right away, and started to boil water, which is sort of a joke, but you know, they actually do that in real life.

About twelve hours into it, the midwife finally came, and the four of us just waited for you. I was in so much pain by then. Worse, I was angry that I was in so much pain. I walked around that apartment a thousand times looking for a place to stand where it wouldn't hurt, like looking for a warm spot in a cold ocean. That didn't help much, so I began to search for circles.

I looked at light fixtures and earrings. Looked for the letter "O" printed somewhere. Anything round and open to make me think of a fully dilated cervix, to encourage my mind to tell my body to make like that circle, to open up, to let you out.

Afternoon came but you did not. My feet by now were so entirely swollen, my legs too, that the midwife said it wasn't up to me anymore, that I had to quit standing and lie down. I waddled over to the bed and situated myself on top of a beanbag chair she had put there, supposedly to make me more comfortable. It was something new to be mad about. I hated that beanbag. The pain just got worse.

Your daddy kneeled on the bed, near my head, and said over and over, "You're doing a great job, babe, a great job." More than one time I thought, If he says that one more time I'm going to have to punch him. That's what it's like when a baby is about to come—the mother's mind gets to this place where she just wants everyone to shut up and leave her alone so she can concentrate.

But I couldn't concentrate. Because down at my other end, the midwife and Lisa had set up camp and were pushing my legs up in the air, then back, over my shoulders, trying to fold me in half, pushing my ankles to my ears, me hollering the whole time.

The midwife started to get a little nervous by this point so she and your daddy went and had a smoke. I lay there with Lisa, crying. I wanted to leave, wanted them to find a way to finish the job without me. It had been fifteen hours and I was scared and tired.

The midwife came back and said we had to make a choice. You were being stubborn and we needed to decide if you could make it out here, in the house, or if we should get the whole show on the road and head on over to the hospital. I didn't want to go—I hate hospitals. And she didn't want to send me.

They folded me in half again. I screamed some more. I wanted you out and I was tired of trying to act sane. I was not sane. I was crazy with the pain of it.

And then, her voice like mission control, the midwife said, "We have a problem." The technical term for it was "shoulder dystosia," which means your shoulders were too broad to fit past my pelvis. Not only that, but when she reached up inside of me to grab your arm and turn you to an easier position, it turns out your arms were wrapped up funny behind you. Which is to say you were stuck. She could not get ahold of you.

For a split second we had relief. Your head showed a little, *and we thought maybe this would be it. Maybe you would come. But then you slipped right back in. We didn't know what to do. She could break your collarbone and sort of fold you up and pull you out. Or she could pull on your head, but that could mean brain damage. It was too late to take me in for a C-section. You were stuck. We were all stuck. And we panicked.*

The midwife began to shout. She told me if I didn't find a way to push you out you were going to die, right there inside of me. That is exactly what she said, and I hated her with all my heart for saying it. And I hated myself, too. Because my brain said to my muscles PUSH PUSH PUSH, but my muscles wouldn't listen.

This was not the groovy, whale-music scenario described by my friends back in Tennessee. This was a circle of hell Dante could not have fathomed—me pushing out a dead baby or her pulling out a brain-damaged one. Then something happened and I pushed and you turned and then, there you were.

Here is where, in the old movies, they slap the baby and the baby screams and someone says, "It's a boy!" or "It's a girl!" But none of those things happened. No one had time to tell me what I had delivered because you were already onto scary trick number two. Seems you decided, on the way out, to breathe in your own amniotic fluid. You were drowning in yourself, not breathing, just grunting and grunting, trying to live, your little body all bluish black.

"Breathe dammit!" the midwife yelled at you as she flicked the bottoms of your tiny feet over and over, trying to get a response, anything. And she started saying things to Lisa, all kinds of medical jargon, and Lisa—I tell you that

woman saved your life, son—Lisa had the oxygen tank running and all this equipment prepped in two seconds flat.

As for me, well, I just laid there, quiet and stunned. I had fucked up so many things in my life and now, there you lay, my project of faith, my baby in the face of two families thinking your daddy and me crazy, my proof to the world I was somebody and I could do something right—there you lay near dead. Or maybe you were dead. I couldn't tell.

Your daddy called 911 and said, "Help! We need help!" And they sent help, but the wrong kind. These ambulance guys weren't trained to deal with newborn babies. And so they had to call different help. Meanwhile, it was a freezing day, ice everywhere, and every time one of them would run in or out of the door the midwife yelled some more. "Shut the door! Shut the door; you're going to kill him!" And I just kept lying there, still as I could be.

We waited some more for the right guys, and finally, in they raced, along with the wind. There I was, surrounded by blood-spattered walls and too too many uniformed men when all I had wanted was to have you away from such a fuss.

Some cops drove by, saw the flashing lights of the ambulances parked out front, and considered it like an invitation to a grand ball. They popped in, uninvited, and now the room was crawling like a cocktail-party fund-raiser for public servants. None of them had any idea what was going on—that we had planned this birth in this house—and all of them looked shocked. I began to groan and someone said, "Does she need to be transported?" and the midwife said, "No."

The pain that had exited my body along with you had

suddenly returned. Jesus, not more. I moaned, again, this time louder. The midwife barely glanced at me, she was too busy with you. "Push," she said. Push? Again? And so I did. Then this thing, this thing I had forgotten about—the placenta—came shooting out of my body looking like some big bloody pudding product, some marketing fiasco by Jell-O. Everyone stopped. And all those cops and ambulance drivers, so unprepared for what they were seeing, just looked at me like I had given birth to your evil twin, to the Antichrist.

Jesus, how many minutes passed? I still didn't know if you were alive. And then you were gone. They took your little body, all hooked up to the oxygen, you barely breathing, and they loaded you and your daddy into the ambulance, and they sped away as fast as they safely could on those icy roads. And your daddy told me later he remembered two things.

First, no one would pull over and let the ambulance pass.

Second, he said, the driver of the ambulance turned to him. And he said to your daddy, "Is this your first baby?" like nothing was wrong. And your daddy said, "Yes."

And the ambulance driver said, "Well, congratulations!"

Austin

15

ELAINE and I embraced in the Austin airport, September 1991, then stood back and took inventory of each other. I was forty pounds heavier than the last time we'd met. And slung on my hip was Henry, now nine months old. Elaine, impossibly, was thinner and paler and more drawn than I had ever seen her in our near-decade of friendship.

In the two years since our wild-ass jaunt across the country, much had happened. For starters, Chris, that crazy boyfriend of hers, had killed himself. She'd called me on New Year's Day, 1990, to tell me she'd found him hanging in his studio. I had been more fortunate, suffering only through Henry's near-death crisis. It had passed, and we'd gotten away with no further medical complications.

Sometimes our letters were sporadic, but Elaine and I always stayed in touch. She'd moved to Austin, choosing the city on a whim—we'd only visited it once together, for three days—to try to escape the ghosts of Chris and her life on the edge with him in Florida. Time and again, she'd urged me to join her. Finally, sick of St. Louis and funded by the check for an extremely lucrative writing assignment that had fallen, accidentally, into my lap, I agreed.

I gave James little say in the matter, telling him, more than asking him, about relocating. He did not argue. He'd never had much interest in control. And what minimal grasp he did have on the reins of our family, I'd wrested from him months before, when I left him for three days because his drinking had become a serious problem for both of us.

Though he clearly adored Henry, James was, at best, more like a fun uncle than a responsible father. And though he was living in the same house as us, he stayed later and later after work, drinking, coming in drunk, leaving most of the parenting to me. No amount of yelling or tears on my part ever convinced him to change his behavior. My moving out, however, scared him enough—induced a big enough measure of guilt—to at least evoke a promise that he would drink less, try harder.

He didn't, not really, but I was too scared of being alone, and too in love with him—despite our problems, our increasing arguments, I was still convinced he was my soul mate—to leave again. Promise in hand, I resumed overcompensating for his lack of responsibility, went back to overlooking his drunkenness.

Not that I was exactly Miss Clean and Sober. I'd quit drinking during my pregnancy—save for an occasional, single, post-twelve-hour-shift draft beer late in the game—but resumed when Henry was barely a month old. I started slowly at first, but it wasn't slow enough. Using James as my foil, I determined that the six-packs I often indulged in, once the baby was asleep for the night, were really no big deal. James was outdrinking me at least two to one on most occasions, thereby making him, in my eyes, the one with the real problem.

We were in such a damn rut, with Henry my only consistent, daily joy, that I had no reason to want to stay in St. Louis. I wasn't ready to claim personal responsibility for the mess I was in. It was far easier to blame my growing unhappiness on the city, and the things there I did not like, the things I wished to escape.

Yes, the parents O'Reilley, having the change of heart a new grandchild often brings, initially went overboard to help us when Henry was born. Maureen insisted we stay at Headquarters O'Reilley that first week after the hospital nightmare. She and Neil gave us money for food, and then a large check—a graduation gift when James finished college that winter—to help us out until I could resume working. They doted on the baby. But our relationship, which started out decidedly civil and went downhill from there, was never really close.

Also, the splinter of Cleveland never stopped festering in my heart. Distrustful of more than one member of James's family, I was less than motivated to try to bridge the distance that had opened so wide between us during my gloomily received pregnancy.

Finally, nothing of significance was happening for me in St. Louis. Yes, there was an occasional writing assignment, but most of these were for magazines or papers far away. It felt good that I had finally found the discipline to fashion acceptable pieces. But, realistically, I could continue to write such pieces anywhere. Ditto my day job. It wasn't like St. Louis had cornered the market on restaurants.

So, I opted for the old history-repeats routine: When in

need of a change, I always had to make it a big one, preferably moving a thousand miles or further. I knew better than to think I could run away from problems and unhappiness, but I'd also learned that starting over offers certain clean-slate benefits.

I'd spent a total of forty-eight hours in the capital city of Texas and had almost no memory of the place, but fueled by conversations with Elaine and a desire to go somewhere, anywhere new, I created a fantasy. No job, no apartment, no plan: no problem. Austin would be my Promised Land.

I would find a stunning place to live, and learn to miraculously budget myself. The two thousand I had left after moving expenses would last indefinitely. James would spend the month finishing out our lease in St. Louis, tidying up the place, getting a grip on his drinking, and realizing how much he missed Henry and me, how much he wanted to be a dedicated partner and father. Thus inspired, he would drive our latest ancient car to Austin, where we would all embrace happily, and forge ahead successfully, soberly, and without any further obstacles in our lives.

Okay, so what if Elaine insisted we pick up a twelve-pack on the way back to her place that first afternoon in my new town? No big deal, just a little celebration. Henry crawled around her very non-baby-proofed apartment, reaching for electrical outlets, terrified cats, and fragile knickknacks, while my friend and I put on a good midday buzz and eagerly discussed how different things were going to be from now on.

Within the week, noting rental prices (which I had failed to research), I gave up the first dream of a wonderful, sunny little cottage. Instead, I took the two-window cave of an apartment next door to Elaine, in a hellish, motel-style complex. Never mind the darkness and the shit-brown carpeting. We would be outside most of the time anyway, I rationalized.

Within a month, panic and disappointment set in. James arrived, but was far from the newly enthusiastic man I hoped for. He was having a hard time finding work, and I recoiled at the thought of taking on yet another restaurant gig to support us. I wanted to stay home with Henry, to work on my writing, which I had finally proved was worth something. Depressed to the point that I actually started to miss St. Louis, I drank more and more, James and Elaine eager to join me or, more likely, to initiate happy hour in the late afternoon.

Eventually, I hit upon a plan. To augment the pittance James began to bring in when he picked up a part-time graveyard shift at a newspaper plant, I would tap into a guaranteed source of income. Austin is home to numerous colleges, and more than a hundred thousand students. I would tutor.

The ad I placed in the University of Texas student newspaper did, in fact, net me a few calls. But I quickly learned that most students who contacted me had no interest in tutoring. Once they scrutinized me and determined I wasn't a narc, they laid it flat out: Here is some cash; write me a paper.

I was so good, so fast, and so stupid—having no idea how much to charge, I charged far too little—that word spread quickly. Soon, I was buried under a heap of assignments. The ethics may have stunk, but the results were undeniable.

Not only did I bring in enough to support us, as I toiled

through the nights writing freshman-level theses on John Locke, William Shakespeare, and Dante, I was drinking less. I had no choice. I bought fewer six-packs of beer and more six-packs of Diet Coke to provide caffeine-induced semi-alertness (all that was really necessary for my trade).

Better, because I worked mostly at night, I could spend my days strolling with Henry over to the little park nearby, situated in the heart of yuppieville. Compared to the vast majority of the other mothers—with their snappy diaper bags, clean clothes, and healthy snacks—I felt like an alien. I was disheveled at all times, hungover often enough, my son rarely clad in more than a drooping diaper.

I didn't necessarily dislike these other women I encountered. I just had so little to say to them. I simply did not find discussions on parenting techniques and sundry baby products engaging. I needed more. I needed Grace.

The first day we met, Grace was pushing her baby in a swing. I placed Henry in the next swing over. We got to talking and I was delighted to learn we had more to discuss than functioning reproductive systems, seemingly my only common denominator with the other mothers. The conversation revealed a number of similarities between us. She was unmarried, politically liberal, a home-birther, and my age. Unbelievably, her son's name was JohnHenry. Further beyond belief was this: The babies shared a birthday, her son just hours older than mine.

Finally, a new friend in my new city. She came at the most perfect time. Elaine and James were pairing off more and more as drinking partners, and I had been feeling left out. Even if I'd wanted to stay up all night and get drunk and watch TV with them, I had far less opportunity to do so. I had papers to write and a child to deal with.

Slowly, I began to confide in Grace. Scared of being judged for my filthy apartment, my alcoholic partner, and my own still-too-frequent excessive-drinking episodes, I preferred to paint a prettier picture for her, opted to meet her at the park or a restaurant rather than invite her over to the reality of my life.

But as things deteriorated between James and me, as Elaine grew moodier, I revealed more and more to Grace. Trained extensively in social work—in fact, just mere credits shy of a Ph.D.—she offered support and insights. I appreciated the advice, but within my own limits. Sometimes, what felt like psychobabble annoyed me. If I allowed myself to listen too intently to her, then I would be forced to admit my life was more than just a little fucked up. And I was not yet ready—not even close—to face the steady deterioration of my relationship with James, not ready to acknowledge the injustices I knew, in my heart, I was doing my son.

Even when I did begin to flirt with the idea that I needed to make some serious changes, I ignored obvious signs of the true problem (a trash can ever overflowing with beer cans), deciding something else was at the root of our unhappiness. First, I blamed James, almost exclusively, for all that was wrong. I chastised him for sleeping all day and neglecting Henry and me. But he was so passive, his lack of response was maddening. He could look at me, agree things were his fault, then walk over to the fridge and extract another tallboy.

Needing another, more responsive culprit—one I could change on my own—I next decided my business was the real source of aggravation. Writing all those term papers, staying up late so many nights—that must be what was getting to me.

Ditching all but the smallest handful of steady clients, I leaped back into the world of waitressing. I got a job at the Old Oak Cafe, where I moved quickly up the ranks from hostess to waitress to assistant manager. James and Elaine, on my recommendation, soon came on board. And when a house opened for rent around the block, despite the fact it was a bona fide piece of shit, a hazard to human occupants, and run by landlords Hitler would have loved, I convinced them that we should all move in together.

Forgetting my months-before vow to never work in restaurants again, I was ecstatic to be back to slinging hash and all that food service entailed. No longer isolated for days alone with a one-year-old and nights alone with either a stack of papers to write or a quiet, drunk man, I thrived on the camaraderie of my new cohorts. They were smart, funny, irreverent, and eager to befriend.

Given our close proximity to the Old Oak, and the fact that the place was open twenty-four hours a day, our house became party central. Someone was always just getting off a shift, always popping by with a six-pack or a twelve-pack, to add to whatever was already in the fridge. Convincing myself I was disciplined and responsible, I usually waited until after Henry was sound asleep before indulging in the final fifth or sixth beer, the one that sent me from buzzed to drunk.

I thrived on the chaos at first, glad for the distraction of so many people to block out the ongoing deterioration of James and me. But a summer trip with Henry and sans James back to Jersey was a catalyst. A week of sobriety, of being able to actually focus 100 percent on this funny little child was like getting poked with a cattle prod. Henry, so even-keeled and good-natured, adored me. He had no idea how confused I was; he just loved me.

I took him to the beach, the boardwalk, wore him out with my enthusiasm. Then, I would lie beside this boy, all pink from the sun, and watch him sleep hard and peaceful. Wildwood was far, far away from the turmoil back in Texas and Henry made it further still.

I returned to Austin and resumed my crazy, booze-filled life, but I could not shake the thing I had felt that summer. I was evidently a good mother—my child was thriving and people stopped me all the time to compliment both of us. But I was not the best mother I could be. Not even close.

By November, I could no longer bear the sight of James. He would return home from work and retreat to a corner of the living room with a book and a beer, and then another beer, and then another. We no longer argued much anymore. In fact, we barely spoke at all.

One night, my stomach twisted, I sat down across from him as he prepared, once again, to undertake his evening ritual. "James," I said, "I think you need to move out."

He didn't protest, as part of me hoped he would. He never exploded with fury or refused to leave his son or even insisted that he would make everything all better. That was not who James was. He was nonconfrontational. And he was vanishing, a sweet, loving man lost in alcoholism. A week later, one month shy of Henry's second birthday, he moved into a place up the street, and continued drinking quietly, usually alone.

16

BLACK turmoil, splashed with unexpected, unpredictable flashes of blinding light and optimism, made the next year a psychedelic journey of toddling forward, being jerked backward twice as far, and then toddling forward a little more.

The little money James contributed was now gone. He needed his tiny salary to afford separate quarters. Despite my anger and deep sadness at losing him, or perhaps driven by it, I decided I would quit screwing around with my writing. I would make time to work on it, find places to sell it. Which meant I needed time, outside of my restaurant shifts, away from Henry.

I enrolled my son, part-time (even that was more than I could really afford), in a little Montessori school two blocks from home. The guilt I felt at "abandoning" him, rather than staying with him constantly as my mother had with me, fast gave way to the realization that these people knew a hell of a lot more about children than I. I came to rely heavily on them for advice on how to be a better parent. They were delighted to help.

Another blessing came in the form of Marty, a smartass, fast-talking, archetypal New York Jew, who had arrived in Austin via New Orleans, fresh out of law school and looking for work and friends. Introduced by a mutual friend, we drank together one night. Days later, unannounced, he came by the house. I decided to have a crush on him. He decided to have a crush on Henry.

I was thankful that my crush didn't work out. For some reason—I guess I realized that as a fat, depressed, neurotic, newly single mother I just wasn't Marty's type—I quickly gave up romantic designs on him. But after one hour of playing with Henry, Marty decided that was it; he was part of the family, no further questions, your honor.

He visited often, assuming first the role of brother and then adopted extra father for Henry. Tirelessly, he played Henry's favorite game, Bounce on Bed, again and again. Henry still clung to James when they were together, but those times were too sad for me to relax and laugh as I did when Marty was around. Marty's willingness to get down on all fours and be an overgrown two-year-old gave Henry and me both fits of giggles.

Sometimes, my James-sadness gave way to out-and-out terror, as it did the night I left Henry in his charge, while I slipped out for a quick dinner to celebrate my twenty-ninth birthday. I did not leave them alone together often, and when I did it was for short periods, usually so I could work. This particular night, I was in too much of a hurry—and James was too good at hiding the level of his inebriation—to realize he was thoroughly drunk when he arrived.

I returned, cold sober and as scheduled, before ten

o'clock, to find Henry asleep alone on the couch, a book spread across his chest as if he had dozed off entertaining himself. James was nowhere in sight.

Panicked, I looked around the room. There, three feet away from the couch and facing my son, was a stack of newspapers next to a space heater. Nearby was an open pack of matches, begging for the curious fingers of a toddler to play with. Rage filled me.

I stormed through the house. Dining room. No. Kitchen. No. Elaine's room. No. Finally, in the back room, the one I shared with Henry, the one all three of us used to share, I found James passed out on the bed. Screaming, I shook him awake, a task that required several tries.

He came to, exited quickly and in a daze, all confusion and regret. I cried, scooped my baby into my arms, rocked him, cursed his father. I could not count on James. Why had I even tried? Goddamn him. Goddamn his fucking drinking. Goddamn his refusal to be a good father. And goddamn me, most of all, for thinking I could leave him in charge for even five minutes.

My anger and frustration with James seeped into other areas of my life. I hated my job more and more. Worse, I pined for Peter, the extremely unavailable, extremely inappropriate cook I worked with on Tuesday nights. Peter was a goofy Midwesterner, as sober as James was drunk and thus my momentary, rebound idea of the perfect man. He was translucently white, wore his pressed Levi's way too tight, and for reasons unknown, kept an Afro comb crammed deeply in one of his back pockets. We had absolutely nothing in common.

He was a goofus supreme, but he was a flirt supreme, too.

Night after night he came on to me. Night after night I responded like a schoolgirl, giddily eating up his empty praise, the dinner specials he created for me and named in my honor. We both knew he was engaged, but unfortunately only he used that information to end the game at the end of our shifts together.

I was lonely, desperate to feel wanted, and he was on my mind constantly. I was the stupid girl once again thinking she could prove her worth through her ability to attract a man. When he said no to my demand that he meet me privately, discuss the romantic tension, come to some resolution, it was one more reason to be angry. Men sucked. They could all go to hell.

But again, there was a yin to this yang. In addition to Peter, I also worked with the very French, very passionate Parisian hostess, Elisabeth. Elisabeth adopted me as her pet project, determined to turn my caterpillar into a butterfly. Against loud protests on my part, she demanded I accompany her on her daily four-mile walks. On the hiking trail, she commanded me to hup-hup in an irresistible accent.

After a few months, even I could see that her efforts were paying off. Not only did I manage to ditch the forty extra pounds I had been hauling around since Henry's birth, I also started to toy with the idea of self-esteem. While we were walking we were talking about everything from food to philosophy, from metaphysics to men. Especially me. Elisabeth's advice on men was classically French. She explained how to lure them, how to eradicate them, how to make them give you what you wanted, and it might have sounded like a long series of *Cosmo* articles, but for me, it was a revelation. I needed to start thinking of myself in terms other than as a poor, pitiful, eternally rejected woman, and Elisabeth showed me—in a hundred ways—that I could take as much control of my life as I wanted to.

It must have taken us, literally, six hundred miles of walking and talking for her to convince me Peter was not worthy, to make me acknowledge his insincere ways. But that she did so at all was a small miracle, a sign of great progress for my must-have-a-crush-at-all-times heart. And I wasn't merely learning about men from Elisabeth, I was learning about women, too.

Grace and I had continued our friendship. In fact, our boys were now good friends too. But I didn't see her often, due to our conflicting work schedules. Before Elisabeth imposed herself, happily, in my life, I was left with only Elaine as a steady female companion. And more and more, things with Elaine were just not working out.

Upon James's departure, I cut back further on my drinking. While I did continue to occasionally overindulge, those episodes were less frequent. Elaine never slowed down for a second. Defensively, she viewed my fledgling attempts at sobriety as some sort of superiority trip on my part. The tension grew until we decided we could no longer live together. Now I had something new to worry about—there was no way I could afford an apartment on my own.

If not for Elisabeth and Grace, I would have felt totally defeated by this point. But with their encouragement, I set out to find a place. Marking this bold step forward came those ten unavoidable steps backward. Rather than acknowledge that I simply could not afford the duplex I decided was perfect, I fell back upon my need to try to force impossible solutions.

With a roommate, I *could* afford this clean, pleasant apartment. And what better roommate than James? He could have his own room, we could skip the romance, and Henry would have the benefit of both parents under one roof. It was all so simple.

James, at least as delusional as I, accepted the plan because he was as broke as I was. A solemn pact of platonic living was made and broken, night one, by a rousing round of sex on the furniture-free kitchen floor. Not only did we have sex, we accentuated this stupidity with plenty of cheap beer. Drinking with the drunk, getting drunk myself, made me far more forgiving of his addiction. And so we were right back to where we'd left off. Well, at least it was familiar.

We continued this foolishness for several months while I rationalized: Hey, we weren't sleeping together, we were just relieving some sexual tension. I refused to acknowledge the sick hope lurking inside that maybe we could one day salvage a family out of the stew of unspoken broken emotions that filled the house and the river of booze in which we tried to drown them.

A condom catastrophe was jolt number one on the reunion tour. When it broke, I immediately began to do the math. I was ovulating. Oh, sweet Jesus, I thought, and my anger at the world hurtled to new heights. James's response was worse. He left the house, stumbling back many hours later, thoroughly wasted.

At 2 A.M., I wandered downstairs to find the front door not simply unlocked, but wide open. Our neighborhood was not exactly Sesame Street. Hookers worked nearby corners, and homeless drunks lived in the dry creek bed that ran along our front yard. Anyone could've walked in, robbed us, hurt the baby. Fear accented rage.

Never mind that the pregnancy test read negative. That relief was not relief enough. We needed, once and for all, to end this mess. Again I told him to leave. Again, without protest, he obliged. Again he moved into a hovel blocks away.

Daddy called in the thick of all this and for once, so distraught was I, I did not limit our conversation to car talk. He wanted to know why I was upset. I told him. "It's time for you to come home," he said. "Time for you to be where we can take care of you. You can't do it on your own. Something bad will happen to that baby. He'll get kidnapped or something."

Well, thank you, Mr. Supportive. Like I needed any more fears to feed the paranoid scenarios already dancing through my brain. There he was, as always, assuming I was a helpless little girl who would die without him even though I'd left him more than a decade before. And if I could believe what I heard in his voice, every time I stumbled like this seemed to be a triumph for him.

I did not go back to New Jersey. Instead, I avoided further phone calls with my father, who despite this latest spat, insisted on sending Henry a check every month to cover part of his day-care expenses. I protested loudly to my mother— taking his money meant admitting defeat—and she responded, not realizing the hurtful implications, by saying that my father did what he did because I wasn't getting child support. Read: Unlike my sisters, I couldn't snag a responsible man to save my life.

Though I cursed those checks and the guilt I felt, I cashed them. And when he offered to drive that old Chevy pickup down to Texas, to give it back to me, I did not try to stop him. Not that I could have. But I gave up even arguing.

Because Daddy was right: I couldn't do it on my own. I was broke, I wasn't getting child support, and the credit cards I was relying on to fill in the increasing gaps were maxing out fast. At least Elaine and I patched things up, to a degree, and she moved in to help with the rent and Henry. She agreed to watch him weekend nights, allowing me to take on a second job bartending. This, in turn, netted me enough in tips to allow me to cut back hours at the cafe and focus more on both Henry and my writing.

Okay, then, move forward again. And then—unbelievably—move forward still more, this time several steps. The phone rang one day: *Playboy.* A writing query I'd sent paid off. Could I write a big piece for them?

The price the editor named was so high, I nearly fainted. Had he requested, I would've dyed my hair plaid and fucked monkeys to get the gig. Instead, all I had to do was review forty "instructional sex videos"—schlocky soft-porn, barely disguised as educational material with the addition of authoritarian voice-overs and allegedly highly trained "sexperts."

Marty and I had a huge, delighted laugh over this assignment. He offered to help with my "research." While the whole thing did seem rather silly, I had to admit I felt a flash of pride. I was an unknown writer working for a prominent national magazine. Marty was proud of me, too, and that bolstered me further. I wanted, so much, the positive attention of a man. And he stood by, waiting to give this approval.

More and more, I relied on Marty's moral support. To further validate myself as a writer, I'd begun reading poetry in public again, and he often accompanied me. The stage fright I'd developed in St. Louis melted away as the audiences in Austin embraced me in the same manner I had grown accustomed to in Knoxville. Things were looking up for me and my career and my creativity. Now I toyed with the idea of using the payment from the sex article to quit the restaurant and push for a full-time writing career.

I did quit, but sooner than I planned to, and months before the money arrived. One day, I called in sick—a rarity. My manager, Carla, took the call, showing little interest in my health. She had more important things to discuss. "I'm firing James at the end of his shift. Guess you won't be getting money from him anymore."

This sent my head, already swimming with fever, spinning in several directions. First, I could not believe my boss would say such a shitty, callous thing. I'd worked in that stupid restaurant on holidays. I'd come in in emergencies to work with Henry strapped to my back. As a manager myself, and privy to how things worked, I knew the firing was merely a symbolic gesture to put the fear of God in other workers. James might have been a drunk, but he was a hard, quiet worker, sober on the job. She was just being a flat-out bitch.

And why was she telling me, anyway? She knew James gave me little, if any, money. She knew James and I had broken up. Her news put me in the position of having to make a choice I didn't care to make. I could call him, warn him, tell him to walk. Or I could back off, recognize we were no longer a couple, and let him deal with the firing on his own.

I made the wrong choice, electing to be silent. The phone rang a little while later. My co-worker, Magan, with bad news. Upon being fired, James had had a grand mal seizure. Terrified, I raced to the restaurant and arrived to find him sprawled on the floor, surrounded by paramedics, Elaine cradling his head.

James was not an epileptic, had not had seizures before. The doctors could not pinpoint a definitive cause, though I suspected it was the alcohol. I shared this theory with Maureen, when I called from the hospital to break the news to her in St. Louis. She angrily denied what I felt certain to be the truth. Could not bear to acknowledge her son was an alcoholic, and a very sick one at that.

When I was through with Maureen, I picked up the pay phone again. I called the restaurant, demanded to speak to Carla. I was so mad at her. So mad at James. So mad at everyone who seemed to keep sticking their feet out to trip me just as I started to make a little progress. "Carla? I want you to know, I hate your stupid restaurant. And I am never coming back."

Next on my hit list: James. At first, I was kind, loving, and concerned as I would be for any sick friend. I offered to take care of a few errands for him while he was in the hospital, an offer that necessitated a trip to his apartment.

I walked in. The place stank—a deep, penetrating, months-accumulated smell of spilled beer, dirty sneakers, stale cigarette smoke. It was filthier than any place I'd ever seen. There was no furniture, just stacks and stacks of crumpled, empty beer cans, overflowing ashtrays, a few to-go containers from the restaurant, some books. The refrigerator held nothing but the lightbulb that lit it. Apparently, James had spent the little he made on a liquid diet.

I waited for him to get out of the hospital, get settled in. I bought him two weeks' worth of groceries. And then, I blew up. He had brought Henry into this filth? Jesus, when was he going to do something about his problem, this awful self-destruction?

I stormed away and did not see him for weeks. One night, after a particularly cathartic and successful poetry reading, Marty was dropping me off at home when we spotted someone breaking into my truck. We looked closer. James. He was drunker than I had ever, ever seen him, could barely stand up. I sent the furious Marty away, led the staggering James into my apartment, laid him down on the couch.

Upstairs, I held my son—our son. Beneath us, his father, so sad about something I never could figure out, had once again medicated himself into oblivion. I tried to think of words to say to James the next day, but when I woke, he was gone again, somehow managing to rouse himself from his stupor and slip out silently. He disappeared for weeks. A friend told me he had been evicted, was homeless.

When he finally did turn up, to see the baby, I yanked hard, once again, on the reins of control. "I think you should go back to St. Louis," I informed him, flatly. I could not bear to have him in the same town any longer. The more he stayed, the more I clung to some stupid false hope that he would get sober, if not for himself, for Henry. At least, if he were far away, I would not have to face the truth with my eyes every day.

As always, he did not protest. Another week passed and he showed up to kiss Henry good-bye and ask for a ride to the bus station. I did not have the emotional strength to take him. He held Henry tightly for a few minutes, told him he loved him, told him good-bye.

Then he got in Elaine's car, and she drove him away. Inside the apartment, I held my son, trying hard not to let him see my tears.

17

ANY mother who claims to have the best child ever is, I suppose, a typical mother. Okay then, I was a typical mother. But—not that it was a contest, not that I kept score—I had more than a few people to back me up in my high opinion of Henry.

Friends, and even total strangers, often approached us, beaming, eager to say hello to my sparkling baby, to remark on his amazing disposition, to compliment the way we interacted with each other. In spite of shuffling from apartment to apartment, having a father leave, return, and then leave again, Henry remained remarkably adaptable, happy. No matter how much our world went TILT, Henry maintained an even keel.

Now three, he was funnier than ever, with the added bonus of being able to speak long, articulate sentences. He brought me joy daily, and I disregarded, with no uncertain skepticism, the occasional naysayer who warned me that, soon enough, he would turn into a holy terror, that all children do so eventually. Maybe their kids did. Not mine.

Which is not to say he was perfect or tantrum-free. But the overwhelming majority of the time, he was little Mr. Pleasant.

So many people—Marty, Grace, Elaine, the Montessori teachers—helped me with my son, encouraged both of us. Henry basked in the attention, smiled easily, giggled often, and asked me about everything from God to tattoos to Santa Claus. Always I answered honestly, even if the answer was an admission that I didn't have an answer.

To me, that was the secret of the success of our relationship. I did not coo baby talk at my child. If he was aware enough to ask me about something, I reasoned, then he was entitled to whatever truth I could offer, on his level. When he wanted to know about James, about why he left, I explained calmly that his daddy loved us and that we loved him, but, I would add, he had a problem, a sickness, he drank too many beers.

Not one for discretion, Henry would take information he extracted from me, and use it in conversations with others. After our talk about James's departure, he flat-out asked during a phone call, "So, Dad, how come you drink too many beers?" This made me wince at first, but I did not try to hush him. He was not accusing James, just trying to understand. If I was going to be open with Henry, I realized, I could not expect him to do less.

When he asked to switch from part-time to full-time at his day care, the same guilt I'd fought upon enrolling him half days returned, though to a lesser degree. Didn't it make me a bad mom if I wasn't spending every free moment with him? I asked him what he thought, whether he would miss me too much.

Henry assured me he knew what he wanted, and he wanted to stay later so he could participate in the afternoon cooking and art classes. How blessed I was.

I sometimes encountered cynics who thought I projected words into my son's mouth and thoughts into his mind as I recounted things he had said. Never. Though a part of him was very much a wide-eyed toddler, he has always had a serious, determined side that set him apart from other children.

And while I read media reports that assumed the superiority of two-parent families, Henry and I were both thriving. Without the triangle of a child plus two parents in love (or, worse, two parents at war)—all three competing for one another's attention—we could focus on each other. Henry and I were one part mother/son, one part freewheeling roommates.

We took trips together, ate what we wanted when we wanted, had no one to answer to but ourselves. As sole parent/instructor/disciplinarian, I could instill my own value system in my child. As my anger at James subsided, I had to admit that more peace than pain came from his departure. Without having to deal with his drinking, I could work on building a more stable life for Henry, a solid writing career for myself.

I wanted to date again, but I wanted to be careful. I determined that any future men I got involved with would be strictly for my own pleasure. I did not need a father for my son. Nor did I want to parade one man after another before my child, announce that I was in love, and then have the relationship fall apart, leaving him confused and feeling abandoned by yet another disappearing man. Given my track

160

record, the odds of my staying with a man for any substantial amount of time seemed slim. Maybe one day we would try to fully incorporate a new adult male into our family. But not now.

Besides, we had Marty to play the part of consistent, responsible male role model. He ate dinner with us several times a week. And he took Henry out one-on-one on Friday evenings to get ice cream, shop for records, have boy talk, and belch loudly. That Marty and I were not romantically involved helped tremendously. Because I had no fear of being rejected by him, I could fully be myself around him. Times when I needed a date for a social event, Marty filled in as surrogate boyfriend.

I always needed someone to attach my romantic fantasies to, though, some man to seek approval from, if only in my imagination. When Peter, the flirtatious cook, denied that all those backrubs in the walk-in had been anything but totally innocent, I moved on to Jerry, a co-worker at a club where I bartended.

Jerry, I decided, fit the bill of man-for-me-but-not-my-son perfectly. That he was ten years my senior, never married, no children and unattached made him, in my mind, an excellent start as I dipped my toes back in the ocean of men. I was drawn to his quietness, telling myself I could bring him out of his shell.

Had Sigmund Freud happened upon us one night, having postshift cocktails with a crowd of co-workers, me yammering away while Jerry stood silently, he would no doubt have pissed his pants laughing at my pathetic, transparent self. I swear I never consciously noticed that this latest object of my desire was the precise height and build as my father, had the same gray hair, the same hazel eyes, wore the same khaki work pants, the same soft black shoes.

Odder still, there were similarities between the two I could not have known. As I got to know him a little better I discovered that, like Daddy, he had a huge, eclectic collection of music. Like Daddy, though in a very different, very let's-get-stoned-in-the-garden-and-praise-God way, he was also a religious nut. And like Daddy, he drove a twenty-year-old piece of crap car because he had no use for new cars.

I convinced him to attend a concert with me in June. When he agreed, I viewed it as a date. He didn't. I tried another tactic, sent him a flirtatious letter, challenged him to a game of pen-pal madness. Knowing film was his passion, I also went overboard making a video "movie" for his birthday, featuring his friends.

To these overtures, he responded frankly. Also using the postal system to convey his message, he informed me that my crush was painfully obvious, and that while he liked me just fine "as a friend" (how many times had I heard *that* line?), I should give up immediately.

Naturally, I read nonexistent messages between his lines and took this rejection as a cue that he just needed a little more time, a little more prompting. I wrote him another letter, this one twenty pages long. He responded with his own lengthy missive. This went on for months until, finally, he caved in and asked me to attend a wedding with him.

What ensued was a most bizarre one-year relationship. Jerry was shy, had lived the past decade in near-cloister conditions, interacting with others—particularly women—almost exclusively at work. When he condescended to date me, he made it clear the relationship would be on his terms.

162

First, I had to accept that he'd had a years-long, unrequited crush on another co-worker, and that nothing I could ever do would make me as desirable to him as she was. Second, we would not have sex until he decided he was ready, a process that took over a month. Third, under no circumstances would we engage in public displays of affection around our co-workers. This relationship was our secret.

Since even after Elisabeth's walking therapy my self-esteem rarely emerged from negative readings on the love barometer anyway, I was happy to comply. It didn't matter how he wanted me as long as he wanted me. He wasn't particularly mean about his criteria, and when we were together alone in his house, he was happy to show signs of affection. He slipped me little gifts, silly love notes, mixed tapes of music that were quite good—at least we had similar tastes in that area.

When he visited with both Henry and me, he usually cooked us wonderful meals and brought Henry videotaped cartoons. Jerry could be incredibly sweet and generous. But like me, he had a whole lot of issues yet to work out regarding romantic love.

Immersing himself fully in a committed relationship was beyond his reach. While he went overboard working to help me as I undertook pet projects (such as the two benefits I orchestrated during our affair), and while I went overboard helping him make videos, we never fell into that relaxed, comfortable intimacy that lovers have. Jerry told me that he loved me, yes, but was very quick to clarify that he loved everyone, just as Jesus had.

I classified every odd quirk of his as parts whose sum total equalled a unique, desirable man. Told myself that in due time he would get past his insistence that we be secretive. I refused to acknowledge that he felt some shame at what we were doing, and that by giving in to his demands, I was buying into the notion that I was someone to be ashamed of. He was just timid. Really, any day now, he would come around and proclaim our love to the world, would "allow" me to do the same.

Instead, he continued to refuse to hold my hand on the street after work, unless I agreed to walk several blocks away from the club first. And he just would not stop bringing up references to Jennifer, the woman he couldn't shake from his heart and mind. He would borrow my video camera one week, and I'd arrive at his house the next to discover he had taped her goofing off, and was watching the footage. I tried not to be hurt.

Sex, once we did get around to it, was not spectacular, though we both had a better-than-nothing attitude toward it. We each had an awful lot of catching up to do; both of us had been sexless for long enough that we were like starving people suddenly standing before an endless buffet. His initial reluctance—he was almost superstitious about wanting to wait—gave way, at long last, to curious abandon. What we lacked in chemistry and/or skill we made up for in quantity.

By the second month of our affair, we went from near-chaste kisses to experimenting with sundry positions. And locations. Because we were often the last ones to leave the club, we fell into a pattern of screwing all over the cavernous building. On the stage. On a sticky, beer-stained love seat in the main room. On a couch in the women's rest room.

There was only one place Jerry did not like to have sex: my bed. Just as he continued insisting we not reveal our affair to others, he was also adamant that we meet on his turf the one or two nonwork nights a week he deigned to see me. This wasn't too upsetting. I liked keeping him separate from my real life as a mother. Except for the implication that he wanted total control, I actually enjoyed going to his place, escaping my own apartment once in a while. And Elaine was perfectly willing to take care of Henry, eliminating guilt on my part that I might be neglecting him.

That summer, Elaine and I took Henry on a trip east, across the southern states, then up to New Jersey. It was a strange trip. Elaine, who had recently gone sober, was focusing hard on all the issues such a disciplined undertaking requires. Her task was made much more difficult by the fact that all the friends we stopped to see along the way, friends who remembered us as party animals, were eager to throw boozy parties in our honor. Elaine showed amazing restraint. I did not, though I at least paced myself. Still, hungover in the car, I would feel as if I'd let her down somehow.

I spent the many hours on the road alternately entertaining Henry—who grew quite bored, quite often in the backseat—and contemplating Jerry. Did I love him? What did I want from him? Some days I missed him terribly. Other days I was relieved to the point of sheer joy at not having to deal with him and his rules and rituals.

On our way back to Texas, we took a detour so Henry could visit James. It had been eight months since they'd seen each other, and watching them together was agonizing. Henry worshipped James as one does an unrequited love. I watched him follow his father around like a baby duck imprinting on its mother. Breaking up with James had been the best thing for all of us, but I missed him, too. Unlike Jerry, he had had no rules, no secrets. In the beginning, before his drinking became uncontrollable, he had been more than happy to openly show his love for me. Even as I grew nostalgic, I knew enough to start the car and keep moving.

Back home, tired of our stillwater relationship, but with no better prospects on the horizon, I continued to see Jerry. But little by little, I pulled away from him, suggested a breakup, followed this with reconciliation.

The dismantling of the whole affair took nearly as long as it had for me to woo him. Fortunately, my writing career continued to move closer and closer to a place where I could rely on it for my entire income. I used my magazine assignments increasingly as an excuse to break away from both the bartending job and the man I'd met there. Rather than be forthright with myself or him, to say I was sick of how he treated me, I eased myself away.

The less time I spent with Jerry, the less I felt like I needed him. Also, I drank less. When we were together, we always needed to put on a good buzz to enjoy ourselves. And working in a bar certainly facilitated such overindulgence. But more and more I was going to bed sober, waking up delighted to not have a hangover. In fact, the only times I really drank anymore were when I was with him.

I was especially inspired to lay off the sauce by Elaine's continuing success with sobriety. After wallowing in the depths of serious alcoholism for years, she was moving fast toward a full year of abstaining. Wanting to both emulate and encourage her, I rarely, if ever, drank at home. So it was odd for me to come downstairs one evening as I finished up an essay and prepared to head to Jerry's for the night, to find a twelve-pack in the refrigerator. I knew I hadn't put it there.

I heard laughter on the back porch and looked out. Elaine was sitting with an ex-boyfriend, an Old Oak Cafe cook and bona fide loser. Apparently, he'd come by and enticed her—how, I have no idea; she had been so disciplined for so long now—to get loaded. Though I was alarmed, I figured there was nothing I could do. So I joined them in a drink, then left for the night, leaving Henry in the care of Grace.

The next day, I found Elaine sleeping hard, though it was late in the morning and she had become an early riser. I wrote this off as a very bad hangover, ran some errands, returned much later to find her still passed out. I shook her. Groggily she mumbled something. It took a little while, but finally, I got it out of her. After her ex had left, she got upset, ate a bottle of sleeping pills.

The drama lasted for days. It was too late for a stomach pumping, so we waited for the toxins to be flushed from her system naturally. Depressed and frightened, she apologized over and over, said she knew I was pissed. Actually, I wasn't. Not at first. I treated her as I had James after his seizure. I was loving, kind, and nurturing. And then, a week later, the event's impact hit me full force. Yes, I loved her. But I could not live with the specter of suicide hanging over my house, the threat that Henry might one day find her dead.

A month of awkward silence ended when I returned from a trip with Henry to Manhattan, where I went to visit Jonathan and meet with editors. I returned to find she had meticulously cleaned the house, yet again, this time going so far as to rearrange my bedroom. Wishing she would work on her inside instead of on the things outside of her, I confronted her. "Elaine, I think we should live apart. And I want to keep the apartment."

It was a move that shocked us both. She felt betrayed. I was scared shitless, with no idea how I would pay rent on my own, how I would manage Henry without the help she had so generously given. But we could not go on like this. For ten years we had helped each other maintain almost entirely static existences. We both needed to grow up.

For my next act in moving forward, in trying to figure out what the hell I was going to do with my life—for Christ's sake, I was about to turn thirty-one, and I was still tending bar—I quit my night job and dumped Jerry for good. And I vowed that, until I could figure out what I wanted from my life and from men, I would not date again.

18

I LEANED across the table, looked at Nick, and asked, as if he were Bachelor Number Two on the *Dating Game,* "So, what do you think about Noam Chomsky?"

"Who's Noam Chomsky?"

I blushed as red as the Keds I'd slipped on to wear to our very clichéd, post-one-night-stand breakfast. "Um, I don't know."

He laughed. I blushed a few shades deeper and tried to change the subject. Marty, tired of hearing me talk year after year about crush after crush, had compiled Marty's Criteria—a list of questions, including the Chomsky one—for me to ask the next Mr. Perfect. If the candidate could answer them thoughtfully and correctly, then, Marty said—only half joking—he would finally believe I'd landed a decent one.

My swearing off men was like Bukowski swearing off booze. Three weeks into my grand proclamation that there would be no more liaisons for a *long, long* time, I'd grown—if it is conceivable—more smitten with Nick than I had been with any man before him.

He was in town from L.A., directing a test pilot for a television show, which happened to feature some friends of mine. Actually, I'd met him months earlier, served him drinks at the club, chatted briefly. Then, I had not taken note of how handsome and articulate he was. In those days, I was still with Jerry, and being involved with one man always precluded my looking at another, even for innocent, window-shopping pleasure.

Our paths crossed again, when I was assigned to interview Nick for *Texas Monthly*. That interview got canceled when the show was put on hold, but I invited him over anyway, to a dinner party. He walked into my house like a long-lost friend, took to Henry as immediately as Marty had, and dove headfirst into the ten simultaneous conversations going on among the other guests.

One by one they filed out. Nick stayed though, apparently in no rush to leave. At Henry's request, we spread a blanket on the floor, popped an inane video into the VCR, and in my son's words, acted "just like a family." Cartoon catastrophes and superhero mice held Henry's attention while Nick and I talked beside him.

As we swapped tales of our lives, that old crush-alarm went off. I tried to muffle it. I was very serious about getting my life organized, about not chasing after yet another unavailable man, another man who, no doubt, would have some elaborate set of rules and regulations for me to follow in order to earn minuscule portions of his attention, carefully rationed dollops of his affection.

Muffle my ass. Before he even walked out the door, I knew I was on my way once more, about to be lost in the fantasy of having one man pop into my life, love me forever, make me feel whole. We saw each other several times over the next few weeks, though neither of us made a move past friendly discourse. I still had not discovered whether he was seeing another woman. If that was the case, I swore, I would refuse—crush or not—to pursue him further.

Too shy to flat-out ask if he was single, I decided to cleverly test his availability. I called one night and asked him to join us for supper "next Tuesday," knowing damn well "next Tuesday" was Valentine's Day and a yes would mean that there was no other woman in the picture. He agreed. I wanted to faint, like a Beatles fan, front row, Shea Stadium, 1965.

We continued to hang out platonically. Some nights he stopped by the house to wrestle Henry and then, child tucked in and lullabyed to sleep, we just sat and talked for hours at my kitchen table. He was so straightforward, looked right into my eyes, paid attention to what I said, offered genuine insight in response to my verbal meanderings on topics like writing and fathers and parenting. Which is to say, he was normal, kind, and not as self-absorbed as so many of the other men I knew. What a shocking change of pace. I adored him.

Still, I could not figure out how to get him from Point A, the table, to Point B, the extra-firm queen-size mattress upstairs in my bedroom. Nick was a baby boomer, seven years older than me, and this made me less inclined to attempt a power play. Something told me that men of his generation preferred to lead. The bold girl I had been in Knoxville grew timid in this man's presence, did not dare make a move, just dropped far too many of what she hoped would be obvious hints.

Nick had one little habit that was annoying in the beginning, and quite telling—and painful—in the long run. He would call to say hi. I would hint that I wanted to see him, unsuccessfully act nonchalant as I ticked off my minute-by-minute itinerary for that evening. He would say he had other plans, that *maybe* he could meet me later, but really, he just could not make any promises.

His "maybe"s always translated to yesses in my ears, as if he had told me we were leaving for Paris in the morning, but not until he'd ravished me the night before. I was not one to pay much attention to my clothes and never one to wear makeup, but the thought of a run-in with him drove me to new girly heights. I'd try on ten different outfits, attempt to apply lipstick evenly (impossible), wear my nicest underwear, clean my house, stock the fridge with the kind of designer food and beer no real poor single mother would have "just lying around," cue up a romantic CD on the stereo, remove the rubber sheet I kept on my bed for Henry's late-night visits. All this just in case—please, Baby Jesus—I might somehow lure him to my lair.

One night he'd told me *maybe* he might join me at one of my weekly poetry slams at the Electric Lounge. And so I went through all the rituals of a pathetic girl, more hungry than ever before, desire bordering on obsession. My nervous energy served me well, gave me an edge over the competition as I spewed my funny-angry words at the appreciative crowd. I hope he's out there, I hope he's out there. . . .

He wasn't. I'd step down from the stage, scan the crowd. Nope. Nada. As the night wore on, my lipstick and patience wore off. I'd set out, determined not to get drunk that night, wanted to be clearheaded when he arrived. He didn't, and so I headed over and ordered my third pint. As the effects of that drink hit me, hard, I noticed him walking across the room.

He slid into the booth beside me, just as I was announced winner for the evening. He used my triumph as an excuse to hug me and I used his hug as an excuse to lean a little too far into him, to let my leg linger when it brushed his beneath the table.

"Do you have a curfew?" I giggled.

"No."

"Me neither. Henry's at a friend's. Want to get in trouble?"

The lines I threw at him were some of the silliest that had ever left my mouth. He ate them up, flirted back. We hit another bar in time for last call. I, cleverly, had claimed to be too drunk to drive myself anywhere, and so now, at 2 A.M., we sat peripherally face-to-face, seat-belted in (like responsible adults) in the two-by-two-foot interior of his subcompact car.

"Um, could I give you a kiss?" he asked. Well either that or push me out of the car now, I thought. No words, in any language, could do justice to what that kiss did to me. I think, beyond his skill (and I was happy that the man was skilled in matters mouth), something else sent me spinning. Here I was, being kissed by a man who was, for once, not a fuckup or a drunk or a recluse or a slacker. He was mature, employed, confident, and handsome. His attraction to me bolstered my self-esteem. I could win a man like this?

"WOW!" I said, when he took a break.

"Wow?" He laughed at my twelve-year-old's response.

"Yeah, WOW!" So I sounded stupid. It was the only fitting description that came to mind.

Back in my apartment, cued music playing in the background, we rolled around on my couch. Nick finally came up for air and to make two announcements. One, he wanted sex. Well, I would hope so. Two, I *had* to understand that, project being over, he was returning to L.A. at week's end. I had to *promise* to recognize this as love of the one-night variety. Could I handle that?

Could I? Why, sure I could! I assured him as much as I could, short of listing all my other one-night stands in résumé fashion. I mean, in a perfect world, *of course*, I would have preferred that he stay, move in immediately, marry me, and never leave my side. But one night was okay. One night would work.

One night would leave me with a romantic memory to gnaw on as I sat, years hence, a spinster on the nursing-home porch, rocking and reminiscing about all the men I'd let get away. Especially that normal one.

One night? Not a problem.

We kissed good-bye the next morning, post–scrambled Chomsky eggs, at the scene of the original crime—the parking lot where I'd left my truck. As I stuck the key in the ignition, I immediately began that mantra Christ invented on the cross: It is finished.

I would let him go. I could let him go. Proving he wanted me was enough. I could now march forth in the world— once I'd had a good nap—and be confident, knowing there were others like him. He would leave. I would be fine. He wasn't the destination, the perfect man, he was just a sign at the starting line, that I was worthy of a mature man, that at last I had found the right road, the road of ideal men.

But he didn't leave at the end of the week. Which turned out to be problem number one. And so I wasn't fine. Which turned out to be a much, much bigger problem number two.

As he would do over the course of the next six months, Nick called a few days later to say there had been a change of plans. He'd picked up a little freelance work, was sticking around; did I want to have lunch?

That first lunch—postponed several hours by long, luxurious afternoon sex and postcoital whispers as we listened to the rain pelt the roof in my bedroom—gave way to many more lunches. And dinners. And cocktail hours. Whatever. He squeezed me in when he could, and I squeezed him in gladly, anytime, canceling all other plans if necessary, all the times he said he might swing by, maybe, but never with the promise of a sure yes.

As week one gave way to week two, then month one to month two, certain things were emphasized on his part repeatedly, certain assurances offered in retort to mine. "I am *not* your boyfriend. You do understand that?" said Nick, time and again. "Oh, yes, loud and clear." I nodded, emphatically. "I am not ready for a relationship, I'm not even through with the divorce yet," he explained clearly. "Makes sense, given all you've been through," I stroked. "I am leaving soon. Really. And I will not be involved in a long-distance romance," intoned Nick. "That would be so wrong," I concurred.

I lied more to myself than to him. I tried so hard to mean what I said. I walked for miles and miles every day, coaching myself to figure out ways to deal with his inevitable, if indefinable, departure date. But truth, too painful to say out loud to all but a small handful of close friends, was that I was going a little wacky watching this guy's footwork. His advance and retreat moves were worthy of a champion fencer.

Petrified of missing one single phone call from him, I carried my cordless phone around the house like an emphysema victim pushing an oxygen tank. When I simply had to leave the house to, say, pick up my son at school, I would leave embarrassingly detailed descriptions of where I was going and when I could next be reached. Once, I answered the phone in the shower only to have a girlfriend, on the other end, tell me I was being a complete idiot and *never* to do that again.

When I did see him, more and more often I panicked, unable to be that fun-loving gal he had been attracted to at that first dinner party when, having no designs on him, I was just me, loud and silly. I grew increasingly serious in his presence, danced gingerly around topics, trying to say what I was thinking: *I am not okay that you are leaving me. I am in love with you.* I never got the words out.

After each date, he would disappear for days, usually refusing to spend the night, even when we'd had sex. Each time he left, a feeling of sick apprehension would fill me. The next call could be the last one. This was both more devastating and more exciting than unrequited love or a love that gave no hint when it would fade. I had my work clearly cut out for me, needed to find the magic formula to make him love me back, to want to stay or at least to continue things once he was gone.

No amount of wishing or effort worked, though. He did leave, eventually. But curiously, inadvertently, I left him first. I'd scheduled a late spring trip to New York to see Jonathan and track down more writing assignments. Had I known Nick would still be around, I probably would have scheduled the trip for after he'd left. To my pride and credit, when I learned he would still be in town during my vacation, I did not cancel or reschedule. Somewhere, that voice inside of me that wanted to grow up, be strong, forced me to follow through.

It was this voice that fought constantly with the rejected teenage girl in me. The strong me was challenged at every turn by the weak me as I walked the streets of Manhattan with my oldest, dearest friend and my son. At least I didn't have to make excuses to Jonathan, who had nursed me through so very many of these infatuations. I just pined and whined to my broken heart's content, and Jonathan indulged me.

I insisted we take detours to out-of-the-way places I'd heard Nick mention as his favorite places in the city. Jonny obliged. I had him snap pictures of me in front of this obscure Italian restaurant, that sculpture in Central Park. I was not on vacation. I was not seeking work. I was not successfully putting Nick out of my mind. Even a stranger could see I was on a pilgrimage to capture celluloid proof of my love. I never stopped to consider that this intense effort on my part might be perceived as scary or obsessive. And Jonathan knew better than to try to steer me away from this path.

I was thankful that Henry provided a marvelous reality check during this excursion. It was the first time I had brought him to Manhattan; usually I dropped him off in Jersey with my sisters and took the trip alone. Without him there, I would no doubt have gotten loaded morning, noon, and night. As it stood, I had an eager four-year-old who could not believe places like FAO Schwarz existed outside of dreams and movies. There was no way, despite my maudlin romantic woe, that I could not stop and laugh as I watched my child observe the crazies in the Village, re-peat—in his own way—some story I told him to explain a religious painting in the Metropolitan, marvel at the polar bears in Central Park.

For all the thought I gave to Nick on that trip, Henry forced me to examine other things. My whole life, I had been terrified of traveling alone, thanks to Daddy's admonitions that this would result in my rape and murder within moments of my setting foot in a strange city. For years, I relied on friends, usually Elaine, to travel with me, to read the maps, show me the way, make all the decisions. When I was alone with Henry, this was not an option. Forced to steer the ship, to make the choices, I had to acknowledge I wasn't an idiot after all, as I got us from place to place, even on the dreaded subway system.

We returned to Austin, and the actual final stage of the relationship that wasn't a relationship. Before I'd left, I'd handed Nick an agonizing, endless letter detailing my pain, full of metaphors of the sort that likened me to a starving diabetic locked in a room with him, a five-pound bag of M&M's. The letter, he admitted, had frightened him. He still came around, rarely, but the night we'd shared in my bed, ending five hours before my plane had taken off, turned out to have been our last.

I thought I had ended this rather maturely, soberly, sanely. But the bad old days weren't gone yet.

19

WITH major effort, I demand that my brain locate the necessary neurons and have them send a message to my soldered eyelids: OPEN. Eyelids respond, tentatively at first, but as slits turn to cracks, cracks to wider cracks, pain shoots through my body. Oh god. Major, major backslide here.

Without moving—I do not want to disturb my own self any further or Barry sleeping beside me—I attempt to pinpoint the precise location of the hatchet cleaved into the back of my skull. If only I can extract it, surely the pain will at least partially desist, if not cease altogether.

Barry stirs. Shit. I must've made a noise. "You have to tell me," I croak, alarmed. "What happened?"

Barry, my best-sport-ever boyfriend, smiles kindly and slyly offers that nothing awful has occurred. Well, okay, I did demand that the uniformed elevator operator reveal his rank. But other than that . . .

Elevator operator? It begins to come back to me. Tiny pieces through the shattered reflection of my too-damned-accurate memory, the memory that will not quit no matter how much booze I splash upon it.

I was in New York again. It was mid-February 1996. I was in a small, unfamiliar apartment on Central Park West. Henry was across town, safe with Jonathan. Ten hours ago I was admiring a full bottle of very expensive vodka in Jonny's kitchen. Now I was lying beside my latest beau, realizing the hard way that one need not drink half a liter of said vodka—on an empty stomach, no less—to merely loosen up.

I think I nearly killed myself. Looking gratefully at Barry, I begin to remember more. How he made me shower, checked on me frequently, force-fed me Chinese food—much of which, not content with my own, I stole from his plate, ate with my bare hands. I remember hearing him in the hallway, trying to find a common language with which to haggle prices with the delivery man. I remember mounting him, momentarily, falling off when said delivery man knocked. There is no chronology. Just all these flashes. And with each flash a pain, like an electrical probe wired directly to my brain, rips straight up my spine.

Barry pats me, reaches over the side of the bed, retrieves another bottle of water. This rings a Pavlovian bell. My non-drinking man, fearing the worst, woke me every hour through the night, poured gallons of rehydration down my throat, willed me not to slip into an alcoholic coma.

What had I been thinking? Theories began to formulate as I stood in the blinding snow, trying to hail one of the few cabs running in those horrid conditions, all of them running the wrong way, away from Jonathan's, away from Henry. I got drunk, I reasoned—so, so dangerously drunk—to avoid confronting Barry, to skip out on telling him I just could not go on anymore.

No, wait, I'd already done that, two nights earlier. And he was so calm and kind about the whole thing, so let's-meet-for-dinner-anyway, I'd decided maybe I should stick with him.

Okay then, I got drunk because I always get drunk in New York. I always get caught up in the energy and excitement and thrill of it all and I forget to eat and then I decide to drink. Besides, I love drinking with Jonathan. Always have. Okay, that's it.

It takes me several hours to come up with the reason I finally count as accurate, though I hate to acknowledge it. Hate to even contemplate it.

I am in New York again, with yet another man—nine months since my pretend-to-escape-Nick trip—due to a wild assortment of random factors. It was on the last trip here that I made the acquaintance of the editor friend of an editor friend. Without warning—she simply remembered my big mouth and the writing samples I'd mailed her—she called me in the late fall and offered me a job as a women's issues columnist for a major Internet provider.

Barry, too, had come to me via the Web. He was the L.A.-based writer friend of an L.A.-based writer friend of Marty's—oh, how electronic communication lent itself to such introductions. We had flirted for weeks online and then on the phone, meeting finally, face-to-face, at a computer conference in Vegas, a trip I took courtesy of my new employer. There, in the Hard Rock Hotel, we had fallen deeply in lust, and I had spent more time exploring the mattress than my new job description.

Barry wasn't the first man I dated to help me forget Nick. Actually, that honor went to Andy, without whom I could never have carried on the way I did with Barry, which is to say in a fun, relaxed, commitments-are-not-us sort of way. Andy, nearly twenty years my senior, was handsome, hysterically neurotic, a brilliant writer, and far more wise to the ways of the dating world than I. He pursued me somewhat steadily but without obsession, made me laugh constantly, took ironic pleasure in toting this Jersey waitress out to his country club in his brand-spanking-new convertible Saab.

Andy loved and respected me too much, too fast, for me to ever consider fixating on him. Where was the challenge in a nice, nonrejecting man? Not to mention that, though Nick was long gone, I still could not shake him from my mind. Andy was wonderful, yes, but his biggest flaw was that he was not Nick.

I dated Andy for roughly fifteen minutes, took turns with him breaking the romance off humorously, with me finally declaring age difference the obstacle I could not overcome. He shrugged the shrug of a seasoned playboy who knew all about the big ocean out there. I believe we smiled as we parted, both of us satisfied to move on to an intimate friendship that remains to this day.

But in that brief, brief period during which he wined and dined and fucked me without all the usual heavy analytical bullshit, Andy got a message across. I did not have to contemplate life ever after with each man who came up the pike. I could just date, be a more refined, less drunk version of the noncommittal woman I had been in Tennessee.

Which made it easier to accept Barry's generosity, both in spirit and cash. He had sold a half-million-dollar screenplay just prior to meeting me, so money was a nonissue for him.

If we wanted to see each other and I had no money—always the case—Barry made arrangements. He did so, as Andy had, without fuss. Trained by Andy to sit back, shut up, and not protest a bill I could not afford to pay, initially I was able to accept Barry's generosity.

But Andy's message, and Barry's follow-up, never totally took hold. Four months into our relationship, I felt pangs of deceit as I flew to meet Barry for a weekend in San Francisco. Did I feel like a whore? No. But I did still cling tightly to the myth of one perfect man. Barry and Andy both came close in so many ways. But neither evoked that indescribably in-love sensation I so craved. To carry on with either, to let them continue to spoil me when I did not feel one hundred percent committed, meant in my mind that I was being terribly dishonest. I wanted the real deal, or I wanted nothing.

I looked forward to the latest Manhattan jaunt, and Barry hookup, with major trepidation. The real cause for the trip was, again, business. My company had arranged a series of readings and parties to promote my column. It was a dream beyond dream come true. Reading my poetry in New York was something I both always hoped for and had not dared hope for. That Barry would be in town at the same time was merely a coincidence; nonetheless, we couldn't be that close and not meet.

The main reading went smashingly. I was Miss America there up at the podium of the tiny packed coffeehouse. I was delighted that Henry and Jonathan were with me but that Barry had other obligations. The more I thought about him, about us, the more I felt I had to end it soon, because "it" was not going anywhere.

And so I found myself, a few nights later, drinking heavily

before he arrived to pick me up at Jonathan's place and cart me off, to what would be our last liaison, in the borrowed apartment of a friend. Only the following morning, as I stood in Penn Station with Henry waiting to catch the train south to Philly, did I realize that Barry was not the main source of my discontent, was not by a long shot the man I had really hoped to escape as I drank myself two times three sheets to the wind the night before.

The Amtrak train was delayed for hours on account of the snow, and the time dragged like a corpse behind a horse that had been running five days straight. I stood there, head pounding, feeling like a total shit, a complete failure as mother, lover, daughter, human.

Henry asked for a doughnut and I didn't even try to talk him out of it. Grease and sugar actually sounded like the only smart plan at that point, so I bought us each two. I clung to him there, as much as he would let me, and though this sometimes annoyed him—apparently I'd given lessons in independence a little too well, too soon—he was a good sport on this day.

I needed so much to be loved and forgiven for my stupidity the night before. And my little man always did those things for me, which eased and reheated my pain simultaneously. How unfair of me to drag him through this drama of my life. How comforting, though, to have him, and all that unconditional love, bolstering me, driving me time and again to pick myself up from the floor of distress and forge ahead, his thriving a sign that at least I was doing something consistently right.

I took his sticky hand in mine and I began to discuss my apprehension with him, the growing knowledge of why I'd gotten so smashed on this trip, after such a long stretch of managing to drink moderately for so long. We may have appeared strange to others, the way we had such serious adult-to-five-year-old discussions. But for us it was not unusual at all. We were a pair, we had no father/husband guy or other siblings to divide us, and so we turned to one another when we needed an ear.

"Now honey," I said, looking at him with my bloodshot eyes. "You know we are going to see my mommy and daddy. And you know I don't get along well with my daddy—"

"I know that, Mom," he said, a bit impatiently. "But why?" Then, before I could answer, he answered himself. "Oh, I know! Because he ripped up your coloring book when you were little like me, right?"

The kid had a memory better than mine. Long ago I had told him that story about the time I was four and my father, frustrated that I would not heed the bedtime call until I finished what, to me, was an urgent task, had torn my coloring book from my hands and shredded it. I told him that story foolishly and without forethought, trying in some twisted way to let Henry know how much better I was than Daddy. It was too late to undo the telling, though; Henry had taken the story for his own, had never forgotten it.

"Yes, honey, he did that. But listen, when we're there, promise you won't talk about it, okay?" All I needed was for my son to let on to my father that he was aware of our hostilities, to rock the boat that was already clearly sinking, was perhaps halfway to ocean's bottom by now.

It was this stress, this having to face Daddy, that had driven me to drink, I decided. Because, while seeing Daddy always made me sick with fear and worry, this time was worse. This time, I would be seeing him for the first time since I sent The Letter.

As it happened, Nick's departure triggered a clinical depression slow in buildup, but lightning fast in its ultimate destruction. Fully two months after he left, the impact crashed upon me, and I found it nearly impossible to get out of bed, a task I accomplished at all only thanks to my child, who needed me far too much for me to fully cave in to the anguish that ate me.

With the help of Grace, Elaine, Marty, and Alan, Grace's new husband, I began to examine the depression more closely. As I walked, weeping, sometimes eight miles a day, feeling sorry for all those happy joggers who had to witness my tear-stained face, feeling sorrier still for myself, I had a revelation. Surely others must have realized it years before. I had not been able to face it head-on until this point.

It was not really Nick's rejection—for no apparent good reason—that had such a paralyzing effect on me. It was that Nick's actions evoked for me those of my father. Neither had any legitimate cause I could see to treat me as he did, to leave me like that. My father, especially, being a parent, had—I thought—an obligation to love me. But he didn't.

Watching my own son thrive over the years brought me comfort, but it brought me painful realizations as well. In Henry, I constantly saw a brilliance, details both tiny and large that filled me with love and, most important, brought me flashes of the child *I* had been. And so I came to realize I had been a lovable child. Okay, then, how come my father had not adored me as I did my son?

This revelation and its related depression coincidentally and tragically came to me during the worst financial period of my career since I'd jumped into writing full time. My latest article had been rejected, and I had none on deck. Which meant I had no income to speak of, and none on the horizon. Broke, I panicked. I called my sister, Bridget, for help, asked her to co-sign a loan. Generous in times past with gifts, hand-me-downs for Henry, and once a check for groceries, this time she said she would have to consult her husband. Angered at what I viewed as weakness on her part, I told her to forget it. She suggested I pray.

Jonathan stepped in and helped me procure that survival loan. But the feeling of rejection I felt at my family's hands intensified. I tried to convey this sadness to my mother, who simultaneously told me to get over my self-pity and sent yet another of my father's checks, this time for twice the usual amount.

In a rage, humiliated that he could send money but no love, I shredded that check, sat down, and fired off an angry missive to my mother, accusing her of loving him more than me. Not satisfied with that—feeling I was missing my mark—I also stuffed into the envelope a much shorter letter to my father, demanding an apology for how he had treated me over the years, threatening to stop bringing my son to see a man who showed nothing but disrespect for me.

My mother responded angrily, telling me how selfish I was, and how crazy, too; clearly I should see that she loved us both equally but differently. My father's response was nonexistent. I wondered if he even had read the note intended for him. But my mother, in a heated exchange, assured me that he had.

And so, here I stood, about to see them all—my siblings, who were informed of this altercation, were more than a little vocal in their disapproval of me—and I was terrified. How had I come to be the wayward daughter? Why had they labeled me the wacko just because I refused to settle down in the manner they saw fit? And could not one of them acknowledge that I wasn't crazy—that Daddy had treated me like shit?

Actually, one sister had conceded—just once and years before—that Daddy was particularly harsh on me. I mentioned this, without naming which sister, in the letter to my mother. Had said I had a witness to my abuse. This only made matters worse, netted me an angry call from this particular sister when she found out, how-daring me that I had referred to her, even anonymously, after all she'd done to build a good relationship with them over the years.

These memories swirling in my still aching head, I walked into my parents' house, feeling defeated before my feet even crossed the threshold. Not even pretending to be anything other than the hungover mess I was, I announced I was going immediately to bed. I stopped on the way to check in with Henry, who had already tracked down Pop-pop, and was eagerly heaping him with affection, which my father returned in equal measure. No matter the bad blood between us, Daddy always loved Henry, always showed this love openly.

"Hi, Dad," I offered, waiting for him to turn, perhaps spit, tell me I was an asshole because of my letter. Instead, he said nothing. And, as I prepared to leave late the next day, he said nothing again, when I looked into his eyes and said good-bye. Instead, he stared through me. Clear through me. I had spoken my mind, and that was the ultimate cardinal sin. There was only ever room for one right opinion in my father's house, and mine was not that opinion. I was dead to him. Invisible. As he had so many times before, he spoke loudest when he did not speak at all.

In the Thirtieth Street Station, I sat, chain-smoked, felt for a minute or two that I might crack, fall upon the floor, walk up to a stranger and beg her to take my child, to raise him as her own. I beat back these feelings, this hideous agony I felt at my father's refusal to love me. I got on that train, and I held my baby tight.

And then, on the way back north, something akin to a miracle occurred. I had spent the week before observing what a city of layers Manhattan is, particularly in the winter. Layers of vertical floors ensconced in layers of horizontally placed buildings, layers of clothes to fight off layers of snow. Layers of thoughts and layers of fears among layers and layers and layers of people.

But the closer we got to the city, the more these layers peeled away. Instead of feeling weaker and more scared, as I had expected, I felt suddenly lighter, relieved of some burden. I could not wait to get back to Jonathan, to race into his comforting arms.

It occurred to me then, as we pulled back into Penn Station, that mine was a Kryptonite Daddy, a piece of my home planet who paralyzed me and ripped my strength away whenever I got too close. I had run from him, his ideas of me as stupid, incapable, bound to fail, when I ran to the planet Tampa. I had run from him to Tennessee and Missouri and Texas. I would run no more.

When I was back in Austin, a few days later, my mother called as she always did, to make sure my plane hadn't crashed. "You sound much better than when you were here," she said.

I responded, honestly, that that was because I was away

from Daddy. "He wouldn't even look at me, Mom; did you notice that?"

My mother, in total denial, went on. "Well, you did have your period, didn't you? And wasn't your hip bothering you?"

I persisted. "Mom, I tried to communicate with him. . . ."

Finally, she acknowledged the point I was trying to make, but did not give me what I was asking for. "Well, you were the one who wrote that letter. You told him you weren't going to talk to him again."

That was it. He had won again. If my mother put similar pressure on him to work things out with me, I never found out about it. Things grew more strained between us. I had little left to say. Not wanting to perpetuate the estrangement I felt, I taught my son to speed-dial his grandparents, to visit them by phone whenever he desired.

Me? I just withdrew completely.

Hell

20

———————

"ARE you sure?"

"Yes, Marty, I'm sure. Positive."

I was sitting on the low, broad bottom shelf of my walk-in closet, the door to both the closet and my bedroom shut tight. I did not want Joe to hear my side of this phone call, knowing he might misconstrue.

Marty had grilled me often over the years, usually leaning more toward brotherly teasing than serious interrogation. Now, though, he was beyond somber. The only other time I remembered such a tone in his voice was back when James and I were in his office, signing papers to terminate James's parental rights (a decision made not to punish him—he was still welcome to be part of Henry's life—but to insure that in case of my untimely demise, guardianship plans laid out in my will would be uncontestable).

As he had then, Marty now approached me wearing his entire collection of hats. He spoke to me as my lawyer and my friend and my son's surrogate father. He had nursed me through contract decisions and broken hearts, career crashes and parenting dilemmas. He knew he could never stop me by telling me what an idiot he thought I was being just then, knew that would just drive me to defy him as I often defied authoritarian imperatives. But given the implications of what I was about to do, he wanted to be sure he had done everything in his power to calmly dissuade me.

"Do you love him?"

"Marty, yes. Yes, yes, yes."

"You're not just doing this because you think you have to? Because you think it's too late to say no?"

"Marty, I'm sure."

"Do you understand, legally, what you're getting into?"

"That's why I have you." I could have giggled, but I didn't. I followed Marty's lead, caught on pretty fast that he wasn't trying to get me to convince him—as I initially thought—but rather he was trying to get me to contemplate for myself possible unforeseen land mines.

"Have you stopped to consider that he might have some potential quirks and habits that might embarrass the shit out of you?"

"I haven't noticed any."

Here, Marty gave me a little leeway. "Well, I haven't had enough time to get to know the guy, but so far, from what I've seen, I have to say I do like the way he seems to treat you."

"Thanks, Mart. I do, too."

"Okay; now what about Henry?"

Marty's last question was a good one, both ethically and as a way for me to segue into a lighter mood. I told him, proudly, about our little man's reaction to my decision to get married. The day before, I took Henry away from the crowded brunch I threw to introduce my closest friends to the man I'd met six weeks before online, two days prior in person, and whom I planned to wed immediately, without ever having dated him.

"Henry, I'm thinking about marrying Joe on Monday," I started.

"When's Monday?"

"Tomorrow."

"Oh."

"So, honey, do you think that would be okay with you? Do you like him?"

Henry, now five, looked straight at me. "Mom, he's a good wrestler. And if getting married will make you happy, it will make me happy."

Not stopping to consider that my son might be parroting a line from some movie he'd seen where the single mom finds happiness ever after, her children finding nothing but sheer joy in a new stepfather, I squeezed my baby tight. I like to think that, if he had responded negatively, I would have gone along with that choice, too. But I know, as much as I let him help with so many decisions, that I would've convinced him to go along had he raised any objections. My mind was made up.

Who can ever say, even now, what wire shorted in my brain when I met Joe Smith and married him blindly, fewer than seventy-two hours after first laying eyes on him? It is one case in my life where hindsight is not twenty-twenty, but closer to twenty-two thousand. My friends, my therapist—none of us can figure it out. Was it the way Daddy cut me off so clearly, for the last time, when he stared right past me? Was I in a hurry to prove once and for all a man loved me? I suppose that's possible, given that I got involved with Joe immediately upon returning from that last trip home.

Or could it have been Joe's marketing skills? Because there is no denying, even now, that he is a brilliant man, a master of publicity, particularly for himself. The guy was so smooth he could easily have sold StairMasters to quadriplegics. Unfortunately, I came to believe, he was also the kind of guy who would have done so, if such opportunity ever presented itself.

But I get ahead of myself here. As I stood upon the highest scenic spot in Austin that warm and sunny spring Monday afternoon, looking over Lake Travis, my mini-dress grazing the tops of my thighs, passing joggers beaming at me and my tiny wedding party, I made myself believe the dream had come true at last. For all I'd learned in my Women's Studies classes, for all my proclaimed independence and feminism, there I was, Cinderella at the ball, at last having wedged my foot into the fragile slipper of wedded bliss.

Henry stood beside me, stopping us midceremony to ask why I was squeezing his hand so tight. Joe stood before me, smiling down from his towering six-foot, three-inch height. Marty, in a show of love for me, if not support of my decision, arrived at the last moment. Benny, another lawyer friend, played witness. And Harold, also a lawyer friend and Universal Life Minister, listened to us read the vows we had written, said the magic words, signed the magic papers, and there I was: firmly ensconced in the hell of the worst marriage ever made.

I met Joe quite by accident. A colleague of his, a woman I once profiled in my online column, turned him on to my writing. Consequently, he e-mailed a request to subscribe. I answered—as I answered everyone—thanking him, confirming his request. Because his note came in with a crush of mail that arrived during my Manhattan trip, in my confusion I sent him a second note.

His next response—all flattery and flirtation—coupled with a note from our mutual colleague stating he'd told her, based on my writing, that he wanted to marry me, went to my head. Though marriage was something I always claimed to have proudly avoided, Joe's pitch drew me in, touched the part of me that longed to be wanted fully by a man.

Somehow, our brief, early notes led to six hundred pages of correspondence between us—sometimes in the form of thirty or more e-mails a day—over the next six weeks. No matter how fast I typed—which was very—or how quickly I hit the Respond button, Joe was faster. The speed and overwhelming quantity of attention hooked me. I hated to log off at night, woke up extra early in the morning to find a note he invariably had waiting for me—having gotten up earlier than me though he lived on the West Coast.

Naive as ever in matters of men, I did not consider that each column I wrote, each personal e-mail I sent him, gave the boy genius more information with which to seduce me. Not until way, way too late did I learn that there is an entire breed of men who listen to the wishes of women they want to attract, and slyly echo back assurances that they possess whatever qualities are named as most desirable.

I thought, given the vast array of all those I'd dated, that I already had encountered every possible type, from the married to the addicted. Not once, in all my years and errors, had I been involved with someone who could look me sincerely in the eye and tell story after story that later seemed preposterous. Therefore, I reasoned, liars did not exist, or at least I was smart enough to avoid them.

Without my noticing, Joe mirrored thoughts I shared in e-mails, responding in turn with tales of his amazingly, almost bizarrely, similar background. He latched on to the facts about my broken relationship with James, my adoration of my son, my struggles with drinking, my fear of rejection, my stormy Catholic past. He then turned around and eagerly detailed his successful recovery from alcoholism, his own intense Mormon upbringing, rejection that had crushed him in his twenties, his desire to one day (soon) have a family.

I was, time and again, impressed. By his accurate descriptions of overcoming the hell of a drinking problem (not only that, but unbelievably, like me, he too said he had mastered the art of moderation), by the rapt and constant attention he paid me, by his knowledge of nearly every book I'd ever read, by his proclaimed love of practically every one of my own proclaimed loves in life. Could such a man really exist?

Yellow lights, red lights, even flashing blue lights and sirens that appeared throughout our courtship could not stop me. I saw only what I wanted. So he was in touch with a woman who, he admitted, believed him to be her boyfriend. He assured me that he'd assured her that they were just friends. So he had panic attacks which he had to control with Xanax. So? Nobody's perfect.

Delighted at what I saw as playful and spontaneous—and that Marty thought bizarre—I found Joe's ongoing references to marriage and our happy life together endearing and exhilarating. Through the smoke and mirrors of modems and monitors, he—thousands of miles away in San Francisco—created just the sort of man I wanted. And he named the man Joe Smith.

As the weeks wore on and the manic pace of communications escalated—now we talked on the phone often, too—I thought how absolutely nutty and romantic a fast marriage would be. Better still, April Fool's Day was just around the corner. And as the woman who had said so often, in private and in my public forum, that marriage was for idiots, I decided it would be most fitting for me to marry on this date. Most fitting indeed.

At that wedding's eve brunch, my friends had varying responses. Though she spoke little, Elaine's face revealed disappointment that was palpable. Grace, ever validating, was more supportive. When Joe grabbed me, swept me up in his big arms, and held me tight, she smiled. "That," she proclaimed, "was the most nourishing hug I've ever seen anyone give her."

I wanted votes of confidence from all. When I did not receive them, I tempered my disdain with the knowledge that I would prove to every one of them—supportive or not— that I knew what I was doing, and what I was doing was right. I would invite them over for our first and second and tenth and twentieth anniversaries. There was nothing wrong with my plan. They just worried too much.

The crowd dispersed, Henry went off with Grace and JohnHenry, and my intended and I lay down for a nap. I awoke alone, went downstairs, found him and a drained bottle of wine. A bell went off. I silenced it. I asked about it in the most lighthearted tone I could muster. He joked back. No, really, he was a moderate drinker. He just got thirsty. He just got nervous. He just . . .

The morning of the wedding, he woke me up early, asked me to promise not to read any correspondence from Tricia, the woman he kept denying was his girlfriend, the woman who kept insisting she was. He'd spent weeks painting a picture of her as an insecure possessive woman from whom he had tried again and again to shake himself free. He assured me that, on my earlier insistence, he had clearly explained our marriage plans to her. But if so, then why, hours before we married, did he insist on a private phone call to her, a phone call I could hear though the door was shut, his voice rising and falling?

He brushed off this call when I asked about it, again chalking up the obvious drama of the conversation to what he declared was her emotional temperament. An e-mail I received from her the morning of the wedding seemed to confirm this. In venom-laced words, she told me what a fool I was, that this man I was marrying was an asshole, with a whole host of qualities you'd never want in a husband.

Clearly, Joe reasoned when I quizzed him, these claims were outrageous, the workings of a mind sick with envy. Clearly, I tried to tell myself, fighting the twist in my stomach, he was right. I knew better than to believe her even without his assistance. After all, I had spent *six whole weeks* swapping e-mail with him.

And further, as he pointed out, he had business colleagues and ex-girlfriends who vouched for his integrity. Had not the people I asked, just to be sure, given him glowing reviews? Well, yes, they had. Besides, if he was really so awful, why was this Tricia character so interested in him still, and why was she interested in helping me, whom she clearly despised? I listened to my man. This chick was nuts.

Although I granted Joe the courtesy of a private phone call with his closest female companion—no matter how horrible she seemed—he responded differently when he learned I had been speaking to Marty as I hid in my closet. Extremely threatened by Marty's earlier crack that there must be something wrong with a man who proposed marriage that fast, Joe could barely hide his anger that on our wedding day I would stop to talk to such a man, never mind that Marty was one of my best friends.

Joe took only Monday off from work, despite the grand occasion, and needed to be back at his job early Tuesday, which meant that we did not spend our wedding night together. Some might think that a sure sign of . . . something amiss. I just tossed it in the mix as one more wacky factor of nonconventionality. I dropped him off at the airport late that night and headed over to Grace's.

She and the boys were already asleep, so I tiptoed through the house and located Henry deep in dreamland on the futon. I quietly made my way to the bathroom, slipped on a huge shirt my 260-pound husband left me, inhaled deeply, trying already to remember what he smelled like. What he looked like.

Though I did not spend the night with my husband, I did spend it sleeping beside the most perfect little man in my world. I crawled in beside my child, wrapped myself around him. I inhaled deeply again, this time Henry's sweet sweaty hair. I looked at his beautiful, peaceful face and felt overwhelmed with joy at all my blessings, at the sudden turnaround in events after so many months of sadness, so many years of conflict with my father.

Henry woke up first, shook me, his face registering surprise as if Santa had randomly dropped in on the wrong holiday. "Mom!" he shouted. "How did you get here?" Still dazed from the events of the day before, I just smiled at him, squeezed him until he squirmed away. Grace came in from the kitchen with two mugs of coffee and lay down beside me.

We stretched out side by side, our sons busy playing in the other room, and went over the details again. How lucky I was, we declared, to have found such an adoring man, a man with a job, a man with goals, a man who loved me so much.

At last, I got up, collected myself, my things, my son. We got in the truck and headed off to pick up where we had left off. How convenient to have a faraway husband. I could continue the life of single parenting I loved, until he found a job in Austin and moved here. And, better, using the excuse of marriage I could now finally—once and for all—quit constantly seeking a man. Having one, a permanent one, meant I could focus on more important things.

Henry and I got to talking as we bounced along in the truck on the way to his Montessori school. "I want to make sure you know something, honey," I said. "I married Joe because I have faith in him, in us. Do you know what faith is?"

"Sure, Mom," he piped up. "Faith is when you believe you can make something work. And if it doesn't work, then you can get Marty to fix it."

I tried to suppress a laugh. "That's right, Hen. Sort of. Only Marty won't need to fix this. Because I have faith that this one is going to work."

21

THREE weeks postnups, Henry and I took a trip to San Francisco to get to know Joe better. This task was not without challenge, given that my new husband turned out to be a workaholic, gone twelve or fourteen hours at a stretch. Still, Henry and I had no trouble entertaining ourselves.

We took boat tours of the bay, played Frisbee in Golden Gate Park. We amused ourselves on all the various modes of public transportation and tromped on foot up and down the hills of the city. We stopped to admire the endless, gorgeous, intricately detailed architecture—all those beautiful pastel houses lined up like freshly iced cakes in the window of an exclusive patisserie.

There was no shortage of museums and festivals and parades to keep us busy. Also, I had a dozen or more friends in the Bay Area, all of whom took turns and pleasure in playing Host for a Day.

Nights, Joe joined us for supper. Afterward, he'd play a board game with Henry, or the three of us would wander through the nearby Haight-Ashbury neighborhood. Once Henry fell asleep, Joe and I would lie in bed and talk, have sex, delight in our wacky decision to marry hastily. Weekends, we'd take the bus out to the Pacific, walk along it for miles, take Henry to see the giant camera obscura, or look through binoculars at Seal Rock. Look at us! Look at how happy we were!

I made one huge error on that trip, though. Before we married, I emphasized that I had no plans to leave Austin. Henry and I had spent five years building a chosen family there, and it was our home. Joe, in love with his new, high-paying job in California, had wept at this proclamation. I held firm. Said I understood his conflict, would wait six months if I had to for him to find a job he loved equally in Texas. But if he couldn't abide by my choice, to come and live with me where I was happy, I couldn't marry him.

I did not feel particularly bad or selfish in my unwavering attitude. Joe had only lived in San Francisco a short time, had only a tiny handful of friends there, most of them of the co-worker variety. In fact, more than once he mentioned that he had considered a major move to another state to be closer to his last serious girlfriend. Then surely, I reasoned, he should be willing to move for his wife. Also, the computer industry—Joe's marketing specialty—was growing exponentially in Austin. It would be far easier to replace his job than my circle of intimate friends.

But that first ten-day trip to San Francisco melted me a bit. I brought hardly any work along. The weather was absolutely perfect. And being on a vacation of sorts, I spoiled myself, eating out often, buying little treats for all of us in North Beach and Chinatown. Succumbing to the affliction that often strikes travelers when they cast off real-life duties for carefree relaxation, I started to muse that perhaps I could live in San Francisco, if only temporarily.

I voiced this fantasy aloud, and Joe lit up like an octogenarian's birthday cake. "You can change your mind if you want," he said, quite unconvincingly, as he raced out the door to buy a guide to area schools. Thus part two of the Joe pressure system began to build up into a devastating storm, waiting just around the corner, me totally unsuspecting, fooled by the comparative calm that preceded his thundering outbursts. I had the flash of a feeling then that perhaps this was his plan all along—to get me away from my friends and work on me to change my mind about which city to live in. But wait—he hadn't said a word about me moving. Had he?

Back in Austin, surrounded by the people I knew far better than my husband, the ones I loved truly because it was a love built slowly, over time, I had second thoughts. Feeling deeply sentimental, and again overwhelmingly attached to Austin, I called Joe and reneged on my offer. He exploded, demanding to know how I could have raised his hopes like that. His reaction was so unexpected that it startled me. I apologized profusely, said I knew it was awful of me to back down, but couldn't he see that I had been unduly influenced by the fact that I had been on vacation?

He could not. Frightened, feeling bad that I might be a liar as he said, rather than merely confused, I grew depressed. Pouring gasoline on that fire, I began to drink, an activity that had nearly screeched to a halt for me as I tried to show support for my recovering husband. For a week I drank heavily, more than once in the afternoon, chewing on a mouthful of mints as I walked to pick up Henry from school.

Drinking proved to be major marital crisis number two, though I didn't think it was my drinking that was the problem. I got a grip on my little spell of overindulgence quickly, thanks to a phone call from an editor willing to offer me the biggest assignment of my career to date. There was a catch: He wanted a pitch, a perfect pitch, inside of two weeks. Otherwise the deal was off. Excitedly, I called Joe to share the good news, glad for his reciprocal enthusiasm and purported support.

I set myself soberly and intently to the task. I would not screw up this opportunity, would not allow this writing gig to be killed, as too many earlier ones had been. I still had bread-and-butter work to do by day, and I wrote better in the evenings anyway, so much of this undertaking occurred once I'd tucked Henry in and sung him to sleep.

Each night, just as I got really rolling, the phone would ring—Joe. I would chat briefly, then beg off, swearing love and allegiance but pointing out this project was too big an opportunity and too time-consuming for me to linger for long talking. Considering that he worked fourteen-hour days, was willing to sleep alone on our wedding night to insure that he could be at work the next day, I assumed he would understand. And he would *say* that he understood. But ten minutes after hanging up, he'd call again. He just had to tell me one more thing. Just thirty more seconds, he would beg, and launch into a twenty-minute monologue.

Some nights, as I tried to concentrate, the phone rang ten or fifteen times—every single call his. I would turn off the ringer, then feel guilty, check my voice mail, and listen to messages that got increasingly longer and more absurd. The more I listened to him—live or recorded—the more I began to suspect that he wasn't making sense because he was drinking.

When I confronted him, he defended himself. He just had a couple of drinks because he was so hurt that I'd lied to him about moving. How could I lie to him? Then he would begin to weep, playing upon my guilty streak, that Achilles' heel of mine he was well aware of. I struggled to calm him. I struggled to get him to hang up and not call back. And I tried to fight the realization that this man was testing me, trying to get me to set everything aside for him, to prove he ranked first, above my writing, my son, myself.

After a number of these episodes, I could no longer ignore my misgivings about his drinking, despite his claims that he had mastered drinking responsibly. Sometimes, I suspected, he drank during the day, or hours before he called, waiting until he could feign sobriety to speak to me. But regardless of what or when or how much he was drinking, he had two things on his side. First, he was thousands of miles away, so I could not definitively prove he was drunk. Second, he was married to a woman who was, as they say, the queen of denial.

Okay, so maybe he wasn't as recovered as he said. Surely, he wasn't as fucked up as James. I mean, he held down a very prestigious job. Also, he was my husband, not just some guy I was dating. I owed it to him, whispered my inner traditionalist, to stick with him, to believe this was just another small slipup. Though our vows had not included anything about "in sickness and in health," I'd seen too many TV and movie marriages to think I could up and ditch a husband after just one month on account of his drinking.

So I waited ten.

I assure those who said, of my marriage, "Well that sure didn't last long," that it did. It lasted long enough to more than double the gray hairs I had sprouted pre-Joe, the ones he gushed over for some reason as being incredibly attractive to him. In fact, my gray hair was one of the few areas that escaped criticism. Joe wasted precious little time using our visits to detail how I could improve myself, make "better" the me he had declared pure perfection in his courting e-mails.

"Did you ever think about getting rid of that hair on your upper lip?" he asked two hours after we said, "I do." This question was followed by others. Did I know I was the only nonpetite woman he was ever involved with? Had I thought about getting into better shape? I pointed out that at five feet, five inches, 123 pounds, not only was I in shape, but I weighed less than half as much as he did. But we weren't talking about him. Hadn't I noticed my stomach wasn't very firm? And maybe I might like to trade those Levi's and running clothes in for some nice Ann Taylor fashions? And look at these Cole-Haan shoes—are they a sight better than those Birkenstocks, or what?

His requests, thinly veiled demands to which I sometimes gave in but most often did not, grew more staunch. My writing was a favorite target. Yes, he had gushed over it before marriage, and he still complimented it, but . . . Well, you see, he had been an editor for years, and if I would just work with him, he could really help me polish my style.

Sometimes I took him up on his offers to edit; sometimes

I didn't. The rare times I mentioned him in my column, I did feel obligated to let him have a peek, the same courtesy I extended to any friend I described intimately. I gave him an opportunity to proof my portrayal of him, debate any points he disagreed with. Not satisfied to stop there, he developed an interest in rewriting my work.

In one essay, I wrote about the double-edged sword in our society that still exists regarding men and their past lovers, and women and the same. I used myself and my husband as examples. He had assured me, premarriage, that he was well aware of all my past lovers (how could he not be; I wrote about my exploits for a living), and that, further, they meant nothing to him. Also, he bragged about his exes all the time.

Once we were married, though, a different side showed. Actually, it bothered him, much more than a little, that I had freely slept with dozens of men. Didn't I feel bad about that? And did I have to talk about my old lovers? Couldn't I write about other topics?

When he saw the piece I had written as a result of these ongoing debates about what he viewed as my slutty past, he went ballistic. We argued through the entire night, and I sat and wrote and rewrote the piece until at one point it came off sounding as though, if I could have just one thing in the world, it would be to regain my virginity to make my man happy. I felt sick reading this false sentiment. He watched over me like a stern taskmaster, and each time he proofed, he would add in his own paragraphs.

Another time, when I was in San Francisco and without my computer, I wrote a piece longhand and asked him to type it at work and e-mail it to an editor. He asked if he could "tidy it up." I thought he meant spelling and punctuation, and so agreed.

When the piece came back from my editor with suggested revisions, I was astonished to find that Mr. Overhelpful had taken the opportunity of my absence to change my description of him in the piece (which was nothing but flattering to begin with), padding it with a series of descriptive clauses singing his fabulous praises. Instead of the light-hearted essay I intended, "my" words read like an overembellished résumé for my husband.

I alternately gritted my teeth and lashed out at him when he pulled stunts like this, when he made requests that I drastically alter myself physically or ideologically. Was he nuts? No, not at all, he reassured me. He just knew what was best for me.

He didn't stop, in his Pygmalion efforts, with my clothes and my words. While I'm sure he would have liked me to change my last name to his, he did not protest when I kept mine. However, about my first name . . . wasn't Spike a little harsh for a woman in her thirties? Never mind that I'd spent more than a decade soliciting work and cultivating an audience with my nom de plume. He thought I needed something less butch, more professional.

But it was the will incident that really made me recoil. From time to time I went to my friend and probate lawyer, Benny, to have him alter my final testament. Outside of a twenty-thousand-dollar debt, I had no financial picture of particular note. My possessions were few, and 90 percent were of the thrift store variety. My only purpose in continuing to update this legal document was to make certain that Henry's named legal guardians—in case of my death—

were appropriate. Sometimes friendships changed, people moved, and I, in turn, changed my requests regarding my son's welfare to reflect such shifts.

I reworked my will once during my marriage. I was not stupid enough to name Joe a guardian—even I had my limits to wackiness, and besides Marty would sooner have killed me than allow such idiocy—but I was stupid enough to apprise my husband of the alteration. He was still in California when I made the changes, and I sent him an e-mail, jokingly asking him what he wanted me to leave to him, expecting a funny response. You know, like "Leave me the underwear drawer, my darling."

No. The lightning-fast return e-mail informed me in no uncertain terms that my betrothed expected me to sign over my publishing rights to him should I die first. My publishing rights? Huh? They were worth nothing. No one reprinted my stuff. I was not famous. I had written no books and hence there were no royalties, real or potential.

But his request got me thinking. If such a shrewd businessman saw future value in my publishing rights, shouldn't I, too, give weight to this "possession"? I informed my husband that, while I was currently worth less than nothing, I would feel more comfortable leaving any such pending profits to my son. After all, Henry was five and had no job. Joe was thirty-four and made nearly six figures.

As he had when I decided not to move, again he exploded. How dare I? The idea had been his, and so he deserved the rights, and that was all there was to it. This angry retort made my skin crawl. Who was this man I had married?

I didn't want to focus on the nagging voice in my head

but could not turn away from it. Could it be possible that Joe had latched on to me because he saw me as a potential gold mine, someone he could profit from, someone he could one day falsely claim to have single-handedly molded into a money-making star? Was he a starfucker in reality? Was that why, at parties, he glommed on most quickly to my more well-known friends rather than my "mere"-waiter buddies? I stopped myself. I couldn't think like that. I was being paranoid.

I compromised. I cut the rights, still worth absolutely nothing, right down the middle, dividing them between husband and child. My logic was this: If I did die young, Joe seemed like the only one eager enough to push my collected writings and profit from them. Okay, if he wanted to hypothetically make money over my dead body, he could hypothetically work for it.

There were other conflicts. He'd never mentioned, prior to marriage, that he was a Republican. This, in and of itself, counted as grounds for divorce in my book. But by the time I found out, I was getting so accustomed to his "confessions" that again I overlooked what typically would have sent me running from a man I was merely dating. Somewhere, though, my mind was registering all these revelations that were slowly materializing. And I grew increasingly pissed off, more and more wary of the things he told me, suspecting he would soon enough do a three-sixty, and then try to convince me I had imagined his original statement.

I hid nothing from my husband premarriage. Hell, I had hid nothing from my audience. I was balls-out honest at all times. When Joe particularly irked me, I would remind him that he had to have known what he was getting into when he married me. "Well," he would counter, using debating skills he had learned as a philosophy major and onetime Mormon missionary, "you hid your temper from me."

Now that was sticky. He did have a point. More and more often I screamed at him, lost my temper, felt hatred boil up inside me. But I finally discerned for myself, and pointed out to my husband, who argued me down nonetheless, that this was the only relationship in which I had ever grown so ugly. It was true. There had been no real, ongoing fighting and shouting with James or Jerry or Nick or Barry or Andy.

But I could not keep from lashing out at Joe. The verbal swipes came from the place in me that felt trapped, and worse, that felt I had been tricked into marrying him. Now, legally bound, and worse, oddly obligated by this sense of tradition I could not deny existed within me, I was angry, pissed to feel I owed this guy something just because he was my husband.

More than once, many more times than once, over the course of the long-distance phase of our marriage, I begged him for a divorce. He had promised—we had promised each other—that if our marriage didn't work we would ditch it. But every time I tried to hold him to this vow, he slammed me, verbally, against the wall.

There was always always always another excuse at the ready. "You can't divorce me before we even live together" was a real favorite. When I told him that I was sick of his excuses, he would cry. He would wake me up all through the night if he had to, knowing, I suppose, that such methods would break me. At four in the morning, sick from a lack of sleep, I would say anything—"Okay, okay, I forgive you"—just for the chance to rest.

Like Ingrid Bergman in *Gaslight*, I was weakened by my husband's persistent tactics. But this marriage, so suffocating to me, made *Gaslight* seem like an animated Disney feature. This marriage, should it ever be fodder for screen, would more aptly be titled *Gas Chamber*.

22

FOR all the bullshit and fighting, unbelievably there were times—quite a few times, in fact—when I convinced myself I was, indeed, in love with my husband. Or, more accurately, I allowed myself to be convinced by him. He had a bag, bigger than Santa's, full of excuses to wiggle out of every tight spot. He had just as many ploys to jog my memory, to make me feel bad anytime I threatened to break my promise to love him, to give him a chance to prove himself.

But beyond his excuses, and the ones I made up myself to maintain my sanity, there was something else, something much bigger that kept me going back for more. In July, Henry and I flew to Utah with Joe to meet his very large extended Mormon family for the first time. Though they had been shocked—and his mother admittedly hurt—by our out-of-the-blue wedding, they wasted no time chastising. Eagerly, they welcomed Henry and me into the fold.

They threw a wedding reception for us, and aunt after uncle after cousin after cousin after cousin warmly greeted us, hugged us, told us sincerely how happy they were to have us as part of their family. Mormons are deadly serious about marriage, their belief being that once united, spouses remain so for time and eternity. Some of my friends teased that I had married into a cult. If they were a cult, though, they never tried to recruit me. They were nothing but completely sincere and kind.

Henry and I were bowled over by this kindness. At last, a supportive family to fit in to. Well, okay, I didn't exactly fit with my tattoos (which desecrated the holy temple of my body) and my liberal beliefs. But no one criticized me for these things. At most, there was some gentle teasing, some pleasantly heated dinner debates over politics.

Of all of my new relatives, I was drawn most of all to my mother-in-law, Marie, and her sister Darla. They were both genuine, brilliant, compassionate, and strong. Both adored Joe and, by extension, adored me for being his wife, since, at least in the fairy-tale version, I must have shared their adoration for him. Along with other family members, they pulled me aside time and again to marvel at how healthy Joe looked—they hadn't seen him this healthy and sober in years.

But Marie was not blind, and she was anything but stupid. No matter how much she loved her son, she knew that although he was sober in Utah, Joe still struggled with his drinking. We had discussed his problems at length over the phone, as I grasped for strategies to help him, to deal with my own anger. Her own husband also drank too much. Marie and I bonded over this common denominator: husbands with the same name, the same susceptibility to alcohol.

While she and Darla were frank with me in discussing

problems that had come up over the course of my brief marriage, I realize now that the entire family carefully neglected to dwell much on Joe's history. Only much later did it occur to me that there might be an unspoken dark side to the ongoing exclamations that Joe had not looked or acted so healthy in years. There was a parenthetical, unspoken *because*. And the *because* was this: Joe's drinking could cause a lot of trouble.

I don't think they remained quiet about these things to be deceitful, though. I think that, when they saw us together, they really thought that finally, as his mother put it, Joe had turned fool's corner. Sometimes, I think Joe also believed this: that I was some sort of talisman, a reason to straighten up. That once he had a loving wife, his problems would miraculously disappear.

In a vacuum replete with no work stress and seemingly more offers for child care than I'd had over the past five years combined, Joe and I did thrive lovingly in Utah. "See? It *is* okay. We just need to be together to get along," he would say, admonishing me as he held my hand and we strolled for hours on long walks through Bountiful, Utah, surrounded by breathtaking mountain views wherever we turned.

At these times, I really felt I loved this man. Here he was, on his best behavior, living up to the portrait he'd created in all those e-mails. He lavished me with attention, took his time during sex, used his expertise—though raised in New England, he had lived in Utah through college—to show me gorgeous natural wonders and out-of-the-way places that delighted me.

And all the while, that chorus of his family sang out in

the background. How pretty I was. How wonderful my son was. What a great cook I was. What a wonderful couple Joe and I were. How blessed they were to have us in their family. And how blessed I felt, when I was among them, to be a part of all this love.

See? I told myself. Joe *was* right. We were made for each other. We were just suffering the stress of long distance. Once we were under the same roof, things could be this wonderful all the time. Which begged these questions: When would he find work in Austin, and what was taking so long?

It took him until October to land a job in Austin that would start in November, giving him ample time to resign and get his tiny apartment packed up and shipped out. I was relieved; the novelty of a long-distance husband had long worn off. Finally, eight months into our marriage, we would be living together. Finally, we could prove to each other and the world that our problems were only due to our awkward living conditions. To celebrate, I flew west for a long weekend without Henry, my first such solo trip to be with Joe.

Friday night we slept close together, and I was comforted by my husband's huge body, keeping me warm against the chilly autumn air. I told myself I had been too harsh on him in my anger all these months. It had been me, my stress, that was the real problem. He was sober now, for real and forever, he promised.

As far as I could tell, this was finally true. He no longer drank around me, not even in his proclaimed moderation. Again, hope sprang in my heart, replacing the bile in my stomach that had churned miserably all those times he'd "slipped."

Saturday, we spent the day my favorite way. We hopped on the N-Judah, took it out through Sunset Valley, and hopped off a couple of blocks before the ocean. There, a few trips back, I had discovered an Indian restaurant, sandwiched in an ugly strip mall between a laundromat and a 7-Eleven. It was dingy inside and always empty, but the food was nonetheless exquisite. We stuffed ourselves and then walked for miles and miles along the Pacific, up to the Cliff House, overlooking the remains of an old, burned-down bathhouse.

Back in Joe's apartment, I felt content, eager to use this calm, loving time as a new starting block for our marriage. I looked out the window of his third-story walk-up, took in the magnificent view, turned around to smile at my husband, and as I did, I noticed him extract a small, jeweled box from his shirt pocket and place it on his desk.

"What's that?" I asked, trying to sound innocent though a nervous feeling stung me.

"Nothing." The panic in his voice was a dead giveaway. Guilty. Before I even looked, I knew.

Now Joe had told me before we married that he took a prescription drug, Xanax, to control his panic attacks; he had even convinced me to pop one or two: "They're great. You'll love them." Being completely unversed in matters pharmaceutical, I assumed the drug was some sort of antidepressant. Plenty of my friends took such drugs, and none of them had any resulting problems.

But as I learned, Xanax was a more powerful drug, often prescribed for short-term use. Joe had been taking it for much longer than seemed wise. I'd watched him from our wedding weekend through the early summer and noticed that he seemed to pop the pills like Pez. I'd quizzed him on this consumption, only to be reassured that he "needed" his Xanax, that it was crucial to his survival, that panic attacks are paralyzing.

Given that his claims of moderate drinking had been so facetious, nervously I began to research Xanax. Marty, who had taken it, condemned it when I asked his opinion. I called doctor friends, a former drug counselor, surfed the Net for more information. Everything that turned up was bad news, and seemed to explain some of Joe's behavior— the times he fell asleep without warning in the middle of a conversation, his night sweats, his insomnia. Perhaps not all of these were due to the drug, but all were clearly listed as possible side effects.

Presenting him with this information, I told him that while I believed his claim of panic attacks, I did not support his use of Xanax. The fact that a doctor continued to pre-scribe it held no water for me. I told him he could keep that excuse. But he asked defensively how I expected him to cope with his debilitating condition.

I offered a number of possibilities, from talk therapy to homeopathic tinctures. I suggested several other less po-tent, less addictive prescription drugs. Like a tired, hungry child throwing a tantrum, he discounted every alternative I offered. He wanted his Xanax.

And so we fought, yet again. And I gave him an ultima-tum. I told him over and over that I had no intention of liv-ing with him if he was going to be dependent on Xanax. I had put up with his drinking. I would not put up with his gobbling down a potent drug with so many potentially ad-verse side effects.

The high drama that ensued after this particular argument was worthy of a daytime Emmy. My husband cried, yelled, begged. I stood firm, giving more fuel to his argument that I was an angry, unwavering bitch. I didn't care. I was so sick of his behavior. My God, how much did he expect me to tolerate?

And so, on that very dramatic June day, with my son observing from the other room in sheer terror, we had argued vehemently until Joe, in a gesture as stupid as it was melodramatic, flushed his Xanax, a drug you are absolutely not supposed to quit cold turkey, down the toilet.

All that had happened months ago. Joe had hated flushing his Xanax, but he had done it anyway, swore never to touch it again. I, to offer solidarity, completely quit drinking after that incident. We'd moved past it. We'd gone to Utah for that first boost, and now a sober, drug-free Joe was moving to live with us, to finally get going on a long, healthy, substance-free life together.

I demanded to see what was in the box as he reached to grab it, withhold it from me. Finally, he opened it, holding it out for me to see a Xanax pill nestled inside. As he lifted the lid, the excuses poured from him. My husband looked me in the eye and explained that he really had given up the drug back in June, during that dramatic fight over my concern that he might be addicted. He said he'd gotten one last prescription to help deal with the panic he felt as the time to move to my town approached, taking him away from the job he loved.

Maybe someone else would have been sympathetic, but I was not. For me, there was more to it than the question: Did he really need this drug to deal with a genuine condition? Perhaps he did. Surely he seemed to think so. What upset me was that he'd made a promise to quit and then he had broken this promise. Not the first time. Also, though clearly a doctor was agreeing to prescribe the medication, I wondered whether Joe was ingesting more than the designated dosage. I wasn't merely looking for some point to bully him on. I was sincerely concerned for his health, for the dangers I'd learned abuse of Xanax could bring. I wanted to know exactly how much he was taking.

I demanded to see the vial. Reluctantly, and only after much foot-stomping on my part, he extracted the little brown bottle from a shelf high above my view. The label indicated the prescription had been made a week before for a month's supply of ninety tablets. There were twenty. I glared at him.

Another excuse. Joe explained that he'd been so torn over breaking his promise to me that he'd flushed most of the pills. I refused to believe him and stormed out of the apartment. Ironically, I went to buy cigarettes. Though I accused him of addiction, I had to admit I still had my own demons. Then again, I'd told him from the get-go that I was hooked on nicotine, wished I wasn't, but had no immediate plans to quit.

His initial response had been to inform me he found smoking sexy. Only after he "owned" me, via our marriage certificate, did he change his stance, berating me that smoking was "unclassy." In fact, I think it was his only solid comeback to my suggestions that he had much more serious substance problems.

I stood on the sidewalk, deciding which way to turn to find a store. Fear and sadness gripped me. It didn't matter, really, if he needed his pills, if he was addicted or not. The bottom line was that we did not see eye-to-eye on our respective habits, a symptom—to me—of much bigger problems.

I think I knew then that we were doomed, caught in patterns we would never break. He would do something that I disapproved of. I would get angry. He would cry to soften me. I would do anything to quiet him. It seemed like a never-ending game of cop-meets-pope. I'd "catch" him doing something I told him I didn't like, he'd beg me to forgive him. I would grow frustrated at how much time it felt like we wasted arguing these points into the ground—was he an addict or wasn't he? should we be married or shouldn't we?

When I pointed this pattern out to him, he accused me of not working hard enough. Marriage, he informed me, was about hard work. It was my fault that things were so rocky—I wasn't applying myself. Okay, I would cry back, but when do we get to have FUN? Does it have to be hard work all the time?

Looking for the cigarettes, I headed west a few blocks and my mind switched gears. For a thankful moment, I pushed my hideous husband from my mind and thought of Marty. As Jonathan had been in my twenties, Marty was now the one who came to mind whenever I panicked, got scared, needed a calm voice to reassure me.

I thought about my options. I had twenty dollars in my pocket. I went over a mental list of things I'd left in the apartment—my wallet was there. But I could replace the things in it. In fact, if I stopped and made myself think as Marty would, I realized nothing was irreplaceable. Okay. I could convince a cab driver to take the twenty and drop me off at the airport. I could call Marty, and he would charge me a new ticket. I could be home in a few hours. Just as Henry said, Marty would fix things, would make this nightmare go away.

Instead, feeling guilty, I went back to the apartment. I refused to sleep with Joe, so he refused to sleep, period. He woke me up all through the night, crying loudly, begging profusely. Time and again I shoved him away. Time and again he came back to me until finally, to get some sleep, I let him lie beside me, though I hated doing so.

On Sunday, we must've walked ten or more miles through the city. After about five angry, silent miles into this walk, I decided to speak to him, to lecture him, to tell him how messed up I thought he was, to ask him—after we had finally come so close to moving in together—how he could do something like this. As if clicking some internal remote control, he switched channels. I think he knew that once he softened me up enough to speak, the ball was back in his court, and he could get me to do anything.

Suddenly he became the calm, rational, sales-pitchy marketing guy/former missionary. He listened to me with the most sincere look in his eyes. He reached for my hand. He apologized again and again. I had to believe him. This was just a small slipup; really, it was. And it was the last small slipup. Never, ever, ever again would he take a drink or a pill. In fact, he had written this in a card, pressing hard into the paper, promising he would understand that if he ever broke this vow, he would not try to stop me from divorcing him. If he ever did break this promise, I never found out about it. Even after I left him, he wrote and insisted that since he moved to Austin he had not touched a drop or taken a pill.

We ate Japanese for dinner and made long, slow love, the electric kind of sex that occurs after fights and especially between people who are totally, utterly, dangerously wrong for each other.

I flew home the next day, reluctantly and embarrassingly recounting the weekend for a few of my closest friends. They wanted so much for things to work out in my life. They knew, despite the growing odds against it, that something inside me still wanted my marriage to work out, still thought I could turn pig shit to crème brulée.

Let him come. Let him move here. Don't give up now, they said. He did quit his job for you; he is willing to move. . . . They really didn't need to say these things. Hell, maybe they didn't. Maybe I just imagined the words I wanted to hear coming from their mouths. Whether they had urged me or not, though, really made little difference. I'm sure I would've rationalized such stupidity on my own. I mean, look what else I'd already managed to accomplish by thinking for myself, right?

23

I STEPPED out of the bathroom and into the kitchen and, as three six-year-olds swarmed around my feet, I held up the stick. Grace and Joe leaned forward to look at it. I think they thought I was playing a coy guessing game. Actually, I was too numb to speak.

"What does it mean?" Joe asked.

I went back to the bathroom, still speechless, and returned with the box, holding it up so he could compare the instructions with the results.

He leaped up. "Oh, this is *great!* This is so *great!* I'm so *excited.*"

I felt sick. Actually, I'd felt sick for a week or so, which is why I asked him to pick up the test on his way home from work. While he jumped around, fitting in perfectly with the children, I slumped down on a chair next to Grace. She, far more attuned to my true feelings than my husband, reached over and rubbed my shoulders. "I'm just . . . I don't know . . . shocked," I whispered.

She nodded. Not all of my friends were intimately familiar with the workings of my marriage. But Grace and her husband, Alan, were my chosen confidants. They knew about the fighting that never did stop, even when Joe moved in. They knew about his drinking "slip" a few weeks earlier that had caused an explosion so big I had taken Henry to spend the night at Elaine's.

The rest of the world knew only what they saw, only what I let on. And what I let on anymore was less and less. As I had informed him of so many aspects of my life prenuptially, I told Joe that I had a tribe, a special chosen group of friends, my real family, with whom I shared everything. Intent on proving that he understood, he wrote into his wedding vows a section about honoring them.

But like so many other things, his reverence for my circle diminished greatly once he applied that wedding noose to my finger. Once or twice I'd told him that I'd discussed a problem of ours with my friends. He erupted angrily each time.

Like my father, he let me know we were to keep our business behind closed doors. When I disagreed, and insisted I would say what I wanted to whom I wanted, his contrary response took a toll. After this privacy lecture, I would begin to reveal a secret to friends, to get feedback, only to edit my words as they left my mouth. It just was not worth the fallout of his reprimands should I slip, should I mention seeking advice from my friends.

Most unsettling was Joe's seeming allergic reaction to Marty. Though Marty went out of his way to welcome Joe, Joe still harbored a grudge over Marty's loving, concerned phone call the morning of our wedding. The more I grew to know my husband, the more I realized he felt threatened by everything and everyone in my life. He once asked me whom I loved more, him or Henry. I told him that, obviously, my son came first in my life.

When this set him off—and he really did get mad—I turned it around and asked him whom he loved more, me or his mother. He could've answered the Queen of Sheba; I wouldn't have cared. I had no trouble with the concept that there are different types and intensities of love for different people. Caught in his own childish game, he declined comment, though I knew, without feeling threatened, that his mother had always been and would always be the most important person in his world.

Joe's obvious jealousy of Henry alarmed me. Certainly, some settling-in time was to be expected as we adjusted. But his admitted jealousy made my stomach tense the rare times I left the two of them alone for more than an hour. I didn't think that Joe would hurt Henry physically. But not living up to the parenting potential he'd sworn he'd had (he preferred to come home from work, get in bed, and read rather than do anything with Henry) caused me to worry that he might not pay enough attention to my active child.

Proving me right at least once in my presence, Joe took Henry out to play Frisbee on the lawn one day. I went upstairs to write. I came downstairs a few minutes later and found Joe in the kitchen. "Where's Henry?"

"He's outside. He got mad at me."

I raced out to the lawn and found my crying then five-year-old hunched over and unsupervised, close to the curb. Apparently, they had argued about how the game was going and Joe had gone inside. I avoided leaving them alone together after that, except to let Joe drive Henry to school in the mornings—we only had one car, mine, and Joe needed it for work.

In public, at parties and dinners and informal gatherings, my husband went overboard in the affection department, hugging me, kissing me, pulling me into his lap. True, I had longed so much for others—Jerry, Nick—to dote on me this way, to show the world we were together, but this was different. Joe was so clingy that it made me wonder whether he was showing off for others, as if I were some possession. I found his behavior annoying, and he resented me for refusing to make out with him when we were on buses, while I was driving, or when we were out with friends.

Nonetheless, I confess I often went along with at least some of his p.d.a. antics. Once in a great while, during a rare occasion when we were getting along well, for instance, I even enjoyed it. Compared to the hellishness of what typically went on, these gestures were a welcome tonic. My reciprocal affection in public, though, left my less privy friends thinking we were a happy couple.

Grace knew better. I never stopped telling her the odd and controlling things Joe did. She saw the tears in my eyes as I sat there, trying to cope with the idea that I was pregnant. She, too, looked sad at the news.

When, finally, the dancing idiot stopped hopping around long enough to notice the pained look on my face, he came over to me. "Are you okay?"

Grace spoke for me. "Being pregnant comes with a whole mix of feelings. It can be a really tough thing."

Later, when she left, I elaborated for Joe. He was in bed already, reading, when I tucked in Henry and finally, dreadfully, went to our room.

"How do you feel?" he asked.

I climbed into bed and began crying. I couldn't look at him. "I'm scared," I answered. "I know I should be excited, but I feel this incredible sense of loss."

I later turned this answer into a long story of how I was scared that, based on Henry's birth, I would die delivering this child, would leave my darling son alone in the world without a mother. I was not ready yet to examine the full scope of this fear, the other side of it, the part involving Joe.

But I couldn't deny for long the real source of my terror. If something awful happened to me, Joe would be left to care for this baby, might somehow get custody of Henry, too. The feelings such thoughts evoked made me want to double over in pain. But they were unavoidable, intuitions planted as deeply in my mind as that zygote in my belly.

As for the sense of loss I voiced feeling, that was another thing I could not detail too deeply for my husband for fear of setting him off yet again. So I sat down the next day and wrote a long letter to my son—to myself, actually—an apology for this foolish misstep of mine that now meant a total end to the happy world of two we had been for so long. Now, with another baby coming, we would be four, could not ever go back to two again.

Even if I did divorce Joe, Henry and I would never be the same. I felt that this potential child, through no fault of its own, was more like an intruder than anything else. Its presence would mean Joe's presence in our lives forevermore. And that was the biggest kicker, the revelation that hurt the most. Self-loathing filled me: I had to go way, way too far, to get pregnant, before I could fully acknowledge my marriage as the hideous mistake it was. I wanted my life with Henry back. I did not want this other child to come and change all that. I wanted Joe gone.

I would be remiss if I did not mention that there was a time, as recently as the month before, when I had cavalierly put myself in a position of purposefully not preventing the high odds of pregnancy. We were in Utah for our second trip as a family, this time for Christmas. Again, we were surrounded by literally hundreds of relatives who poured out genuine love for us. I loved trips to Bountiful so much—the calming effect they had on my marriage and my mind—that I got carried away, as I seemed to do in those surroundings, in fantasy upon fantasy.

We stayed with Aunt Darla, who asked, lovingly and jokingly and nudgingly, when I planned to have a baby. She even offered to draw a candlelit bath for Joe and me to "help you along." Joe and I would again take hours-long walks, now in the pure falling snow, and again I would think how wonderful he was.

It was as if the altitude, the thinner air in Utah, cast an odd spell on me, deprived my brain of the oxygen I needed to remember that the week before we had been screaming at each other. Things felt so damn right there I sometimes thought I could move, leave all of my friends behind, become a small-town wife, content myself in raising ten children.

On Christmas Eve day, with Henry preoccupied upstairs with an assortment of cousins, I crept down to our room in the basement. Joe, who interacted far less with his family than I, was reading, as usual. I climbed on top of him. "I love your family so much. Do you know that? I love you, too. God, this has been so hard. But we are going to make it work."

Across the room, in my suitcase, was a collection of condoms. Joe, initially irritated at being distracted from his book, caved in and let me rub against him. I knew I might well be ovulating. I thought about the condoms. Fuck the condoms. Another baby would be wonderful. Hell, before Joe had come along I had toyed with the idea of having a second baby on my own. And if the marriage didn't work out, so what? I could raise the child without a man. I'd proven that already.

Not that Joe would've consented to use a condom. He hated birth control. His excuses varied. In the beginning, he explained that he just could not deal with having me use a diaphragm that had been tainted by other men. Though I found his argument totally ridiculous and utterly sexist, as a wedding gift of sorts I'd gone out and gotten a new one. But then, suddenly, that didn't work for him either. He looked at it, and then announced that the idea of it just didn't feel "right."

Not a big condom fan to begin with, and once again casting aside my feminist wisdom to give in to a man, I often used Joe's attitude as an excuse not to deal with a messy diaphragm. Ovulation occurred mostly when we were thousands of miles apart anyway. On the off chance that I did get pregnant, I told myself, at least I would be with a man who wanted kids. In fact, Joe started pushing me to get pregnant in the first month of marriage.

When that spontaneous risk didn't take in December, when we returned to Austin and our fighting ways, I rethought my holiday stance. I told him that no, we would not be trying again, intently or spontaneously, in January. As I had before, I went back to my request that we wait until we could go an entire month without a wild blowout over some petty something.

Well, well, well, didn't I just jinx myself with those words? Knocked up, no doubt, on the very night I said I wanted to wait—another statistic of the ain't-got-no-rhythm method—to my great chagrin and to the giddy delight of Mr. Control, I paced the house daily, fretting. I was sick as a dog and more scared, still. Every day the thought came to me, obviously way too late, that I did not want to have a child with him. Every day, I listened to him insist that this fear I had was nothing but a bad case of overactive hormones.

It didn't matter, really, what either of us thought. We both knew abortion was out of the question. And he was far too delighted now at the thought of fatherhood to even consider termination, even if I could find a way to bring myself to do what clearly would be the best thing for all involved.

The thought of sleeping beside him repelled me. I curled up in a tight fetal ball nightly, wishing I could sleep on the couch without his raising a fuss. But actually, regardless of where I laid my head, this was no longer home. Faster and faster it was becoming the asylum, a place of insanity and surrealism and insomnia. As he had throughout the marriage, but particularly since he moved to Austin, my husband woke me up almost nightly. He could never sleep. Things worried him. And these things could never, no matter how much I begged, wait until morning for resolution.

One night, before the pregnancy, I turned to him as he nudged me awake, not even trying to hide my irritation. How many times did I need to explain to him that without eight hours of solid sleep I was cranky and unreasonable? "What?!" I asked, beyond impatient.

Already, he had started crying. "I have to tell you something. It's important. It's that—"

"Just *say* it, will you? God, Joe, I am so fucking tired."

"Well, um, remember how you told me sometimes you felt like I tricked you into marrying me . . . um . . . well, okay I didn't tell you everything. But . . ."

I shot him a look that could've removed all the tattoos from a Hell's Angel in five seconds flat. If he thought I was putting my pope hat on and forgiving him for this one, he was sorely mistaken.

"But you have to admit, I am still a good guy, aren't I? I bring you your coffee in the morning, don't I?"

Well, gee, yeah Joe. And I'm sure old Adolf probably did a good deed or two in his day, too. As for the coffee comment—I cursed the day I ever told him I enjoyed that ritual, even though I had for the first week or two. Because before long, each night as he came home and fell apart like a street-vendor Rolex, he would snap at me for snapping at him for not letting me get my work done. I, in turn, would ask—nay, beg—if he could please, please, hang on to his crisis for a little while. He would answer that he deserved my attention right that second. After all, he brought me coffee in the morning, didn't he?

This conversation had taken place a while back, but each time after that, when he woke me at 4 A.M.—nearly every night—I had a Pavlovian flashback to this sickening moment. And I had this self-loathing about the fact that, rather than do what I was perfectly entitled to do under such circumstances, I continued to stay.

Okay, obviously, given my condition, I continued to fuck the guy, no matter how mad he made me. And how did I justify that? Hey, he was my husband. I had morals. I couldn't cheat on him. And if nothing else, I wanted my physical needs met.

Now, even that one little perk—physical relief—was gone. The thought of sex with him nauseated me as much as the pregnancy. One morning, instead of going on to work after dropping Henry off at school, he came back home. He wanted to talk about our relationship. I cried. I hated that we had no intimacy left whatsoever. I couldn't stand the thought of being married to—and thanks to this pregnancy, stuck with—a man who did not appeal to me in any way.

For once, Joe did not launch into a poor-him soliloquy, one of his trademark, punctuation-free twenty-minute sentences in which he always managed somehow to segue into what a good guy he was. Instead, slowly, he undressed me. Slowly, he fucked me. I recoiled at first, closed my eyes, tried to get into it. And finally, oh thank you, Baby Jesus, I had an orgasm.

How had I come to this? Pregnant with the child of this man? Hardly able to have sex anymore after being voted most likely to fuck five guys in a week (and like it) back in Tennessee? Depressed at the thought of a second child when I so clearly adored the first, so clearly enjoyed motherhood?

That short, not unpleasant (once I shut my mind down) sex session was a fluke, though. The final straw, such a tiny one, came right on the heels of my last orgasm with that man.

Elaine took Henry one night so Joe and I could go to a

concert. On the drive there, we got into yet another argument. Like grains of sand. Like grains of sand. I, driving and hating driving, got distracted by his pettiness, his angry response to a story he didn't even let me finish before he started tearing me apart. In my anger, I missed a turn, cursing loudly at both his ridiculous accusations and my hideous sense of direction.

Joe, in turn, leaned toward me, got within an inch of my ear, and steeling himself with all 260 pounds of his fatness, screamed, "Goddammit Jesus fucking Christ; there—how do you like it when I yell at *you?!!*"

Stunned, absolutely paralyzed with fear, convinced that my eardrum had been shattered, I stopped. And did nothing. For a moment, we sat in the complete silence of suspended animation. By now we were in the concert hall's parking lot. Without turning to him, I broke the silence. "I am going home. If you want to drive yourself back to the show, that's fine. But I am not going."

On the rage- and tear-filled drive home, I lashed out at him. "Hey Joe, I have an idea, why don't you just go ahead and punch me? You know you want to."

It was the wrong thing to say, something I pulled from the bottom of my dirtiest bag of tricks. Joe had told me of arguments in past relationships that had escalated to a physical level. He had restrained me a few times, once squeezing my wrists so hard I thought he might break them. He'd restrained Henry, too. But he never, ever hit us.

Now, though, I wondered—might he smack me? Was he capable of such an act? I was so frightened by his unbridled screaming that I thought severe physical violence a real possibility. My fear was heightened by the fact that I was

234

trapped with him in a car, on a dark back road, both of us angry beyond reason. Anything could happen.

In fact, somewhere inside of me, I think I wished he had punched me. Maybe, too, I secretly wished I hadn't ducked all those years ago when Daddy took a swing at me. Because a gut sense that I was not in a good situation was never enough for me to leave that situation. I wanted solid proof—a black eye, a broken tooth—to prove to myself and the world that these men who are supposed to love a woman (father, husband) visibly did precisely the opposite. Anything less, at least at that moment, just did not seem enough to leave, to quit trying. So desperate was I, then, to believe I was loved, that any attack short of physical was not enough to convince me to move to safer ground, to make me believe a relationship wasn't worth fighting for.

Back home, I raced in the house. Packed a bag. Joe began to cry. Oh, God, not that again. I dialed Elaine, told her I was coming. Then, quickly, I hung up the phone and punched in Marty's number, hanging up after the first ring. I figured my clever husband might try to find me by hitting redial. If he did, I wanted him to have to speak to my friend, my safety net, my lawyer.

24

I COLLAPSED in the chair across from Marty, defeated, exhausted, hungry, and crying. He got up, walked around his huge mahogany desk, came to me, held me, a sure sign that this was a truly dire situation. Typically we touched twice a year, tops, usually on birthdays. I didn't have to tell him the nature of this call—he could see it in my frightened eyes—only the specifics.

I buried my face in my hands, shook uncontrollably. "I need a divorce." Then, after a pause, "And an abortion."

I cried harder, and Marty retrieved a box of Kleenex from across the room. "It's okay. It's okay. Try to calm down. You have to tell me what happened." For all the teasing we did, for all the levity that defined the greatest part of our friendship, whenever I needed a serious shoulder to cry on or some real advice, Martin Berger did not waste a second switching from goofy big brother to reverent listener, noble protector.

Stuttering, choking on my words, I managed to get out the story of what had happened at my apartment the night before and just that morning, moments before I jumped into the car and drove blindly to his office.

After a night at Elaine's, I decided to take Henry back to our place, to try one more stupid, fruitless time to resolve things with my husband. Like it or not, I was pregnant, I was going to have the baby, and I was going to have to deal with this man, so I figured I had better find a way to now.

Once Henry was asleep, we began to talk, but negotiations broke down quickly, voices rising higher and higher to a fevered pitch. I looked my husband, this stranger, in the eyes, and words spilled out from a place inside me I did not know existed. "Maybe I should get an abortion, Joe." I was at least as shocked as he was at this suggestion. Surely I was not serious.

Joe's panicked eyes flickered from semireasonable to something frightening. "How would you like it if somebody killed Henry?!" he hissed.

He could have stabbed me in the heart and hurt me less than he did with these words. I knew he was jealous of my son. I told him not to threaten my child. He insisted he wasn't threatening anybody. He was just "making a point." But I wondered: How could he think I would take lightly a sentence that included both the words "Henry" and "kill"?

Seeing his anger, and feeling terror well up inside, I'd tried to calm him down. "Joe, it was just an idea. Look, you know how I feel about abortion. But I was just thinking— we have so many problems. We know we can get pregnant. Don't you agree we don't need any more pressure right now? Or maybe we could get separate places, go for counseling, work this out. And if we do, then we can have a baby."

Not wanting to deceive him—he had taught me how awful that felt time and again—I went on to add some honest clarification. I told him that, frankly, I didn't feel like we could work it out. But if we wanted, really, to have this baby, we needed to learn how not to hurt each other, before our child was born.

He could have talked all night. And he tried. But finally, I begged off. His remark about Henry freaked me out so much that I went to my son's room, locked the door behind me—though Joe could've knocked it down with one finger—and tried to get some rest on the hard bottom bunk.

The last thing I asked my husband before I shut the door was to please, please, *please* let me get eight hours of sleep. I couldn't stress the importance enough. Sleep was the only thing that offered a tiny bit of respite from the morning sickness that exhausted me well into the afternoons every day now.

Six hours later, at 5 A.M., he began banging on the door. "I need to use the car!!" I opened the door, wanting to spit on this selfish man. That crazed look was still in his eyes. "I neeeeed the carrrr!" Henry stirred. I cursed at Joe and told him to shut up and leave me alone. Then I closed the door in his face.

Not that I could sleep, in my agitation and my rage, but I closed my eyes for a minute. And then I heard him crying.

"Jesus Christ! Will you shut *up* already?" I begged him as I ran downstairs to confront him. I stormed over to the kitchen and made him a mug of tea, handed it to him angrily when it was ready, retreated back to my son's room. An hour later, trying impossibly to feign calmness, I brought Henry down for a quick breakfast. Joe watched us, and I could see he was about to launch into another long, desperate speech. I cut him off before he started, told him I would deal with him after Henry was at school. But Joe never could stop himself. He continued to argue in front of Henry.

When we first married, I had given thought to how we would handle disputes. Would I, as my parents had done, keep all marital arguments from my offspring and give the impression that we never fought? I thought that was a bad idea, that part of the reason I often had a hard time resolving spats was that I had never observed my parents do so.

And so, at first, I concluded it would be fine for Henry to hear us argue, so long as he also heard us work things out. But we weren't working things out and my son had such a horrible reaction to our fighting that I could no longer subject him to my husband's debating technique, to my own angry outbursts in response. It wasn't that Henry cried. He didn't. Much worse, he grew visibly frightened, tried to work out our problems by changing his behavior, by suddenly going from fun-loving to somber and far, far too polite.

He didn't deserve that. And while he told me later that he sometimes sat on the stairs or outside our bedroom and listened to us bicker, I did what I could to protect him from this bitterness.

I refused to let Joe engage me this morning, carried on with giving Henry his breakfast. I dropped him off at school and then returned home. Joe, who really should have left for work by then, was sitting on the bed in his underwear, weeping, shaking, moaning. "I'm not going to work," he whimpered as I walked in the room. "I called in sick. I'll stay out of your way. I promise."

Oh please, dear God.

"I cannot . . ." I started. "I cannot work here with you around, crying like this. It's not a good idea. I have deadlines. I'm going to work somewhere else." I was too sick, too tired, and too disgusted to argue anymore.

But Joe was not about to give up that easily. I always preferred to go away for a little while, walk four miles, see a friend, anything to help me calm down before having one of our "discussions." Not Joe. He always had to have immediate resolution. I walked from the room. He followed me.

I spun around. That did it. "Look, Joe, let's just admit it. This is not working. It's not. We need separate apartments. I think you need to go."

Towering over me, he glared down into my eyes, an angry, bitter two-year-old trapped in a giant's body. "I am not leaving. I am not ending this marriage. No. You said you would move out!!"

Had I? Jesus, I couldn't even remember. Maybe I had. Maybe I'd said it in my sleep to get him to shut up. I couldn't remember saying it, and even if I had, I was changing my mind.

"You listen, Joe. I have lived in this apartment for nearly five years. It is the only home my son remembers having. He goes to school in this district. His friends are here, his life is here. Now would you please leave?"

He would not. One thought started flashing in my mind, as my motherly instinct to protect by any means necessary cranked up to full force: Am I safe here? I wasn't safe here. Even if Joe did not physically attack me—as I still feared he might—I was, emotionally, beaten to a pulp by this relationship.

I raced to my bedroom, pulled a suitcase from the closet

and began to cram clothes in it. Joe followed me. Stood above me. "No, don't. Don't go," he was crying, sounding less and less rational, if that was possible.

I ran back over to Henry's room to grab a few things for him, ran back to my room to shove them in the suitcase. Joe was sitting on our bed now, howling. "No, no, no, no, no, no, no," he cried.

"I have to go, Joe. This is all so wrong." With that, I started to pack my laptop computer. It was a prized possession of mine, one I had recently purchased with cash, a real achievement for me. It represented my independence, my success, what I could do if I set my mind to it, how far I'd come from being a waitress.

He reached out, swiped it from my hands, dangled it before me like a lion toying with a mouse. My tool of communication, the thing I used to pay the rent and feed my baby, the symbol of my self-esteem, now yanked from me. I had let men get me down before. I had sacrificed a lot to try to find one, keep one, find myself by looking to any number of them. And I had gone too far. The man I had chosen as my alleged lifelong partner stood ready to destroy me, to strip me of everything. This, I could tell, was just the start. Where would he stop? Or would he stop?

"Give it back."

"No." There was no sign of the cool, pulled-together businessman who left the house each morning to make big business deals, to convince the world he was a champ. I was afraid he was going to hurt me. No, wait, he had already hurt me, over and over. In less than a year, he had managed to outdo what my father had done to me in a lifetime.

Finally, I cried. I begged. Satisfied, I supposed, that this showed I was weaker than he, that I knew who was in charge, he gave it back. As I slung it on my shoulder, and turned to grab my suitcase, he leaped from the bed and lunged at me. As had my father a decade earlier, Joe, too, missed his mark. Fortunately, it was a cold day and I was wearing several layers of clothing. Grabbing for my shoulder, instead he got a handful of mostly sweater, and just a little me.

I ran then, raced for the door, not waiting to find out what he might do next. I wasn't fast enough. He beat me to the doorway, rose up to his entire daunting width and height, puffing up like an enraged blowfish, daring me to try and cross his path.

Now I really broke down. Suddenly I was five. I was the child whose only hope was to beg mercy. "Please, please," I cried. "Let me go. I'll call you. I swear. Just let me leave."

I weaseled past him, stumbled down the stairs, tripped out the front door. He followed me, stood on the front lawn still crying. I slammed the car door and hit reverse.

Marty listened to all of this in complete silence, measuring his words carefully when I finally finished and it was his turn. He chose, for the first part of his response, to speak to me as a lawyer.

"Are you afraid of him?"

"Oh, God, yes. I'm terrified. I am so worried."

Marty asked me a few more questions and determined that I should get a temporary protective order right away.

That decision made, he switched to friend and addressed the pregnancy. "I agree that you need an abortion. I think it's the best thing. But listen. I want you to wait a couple of weeks. I want you to talk to a therapist. I want you to be sure about this. You always said you would never have one. I don't want you to fall apart somewhere down the line over this."

We went to the courthouse and filed the protective order. We went to Henry's school and informed his teacher and the officials about the order. We went to Marty's apartment so I could rest for a few minutes. And as we walked in the door, he turned to me.

"When was the last time you ate?"

That he would think of such a detail made me weep. "I don't know. Yesterday maybe?" The nightmare of my life had killed my appetite, but whether I wanted to admit it or not, the pregnancy left me starving. Marty rummaged through his distinctly bachelor-stocked cupboards and resurfaced with a bag of pretzels, some stale Fig Newtons, and an energy bar.

"Look, I don't care if you're hungry. I don't want to hear it. Just eat, will you?"

He sent me off to put a stop on my mail. I did. That finished, my exhaustion hit me like a truck. I went to another friend and requested a place to sleep. And for two short hours, I escaped into the slumber of the dead.

25

"HEY, Hen, how would you like to stay with Grace and Alan and JohnHenry for a while? It will be like a vacation." I tried to sound cheerful as I picked my son up from school and drove him to our friends' place.

"That sounds fine, Mom. But how come?"

"Well, um, you see, Joe and I are having some problems, honey, and I think it would be smart for us to take a little break from each other."

Ever agreeable, Henry did not put up a fuss. And Alan and Grace went out of their way not only to make us feel completely at home, but to help me monitor him. Sometimes my child acted so calm in the face of a crisis, I worried that he hid his true feelings to spare me. He was amazingly overprotective for his age, ran to check on me anytime I so much as stubbed my toe and said "Ouch." I was in such a state of confusion I knew I could not be an adequate parent. They watched him closely, reported to me nightly any signs of stress.

He started calling Alan "Dad" frequently. This didn't

trouble me. He'd done this other times, just not as often. I took comfort, knowing he looked to Alan as a father figure. And for once I was happy that Henry and Joe had not bonded.

To be on the safe side, to alleviate any confusion Henry might have, I called James in St. Louis, told him the whole sordid tale. "James, I think it would help a lot if you called Henry regularly, let him know how much you love him." From that point on, James started calling every night.

I made an appointment for an abortion. Canceled it. I still felt no doubt that this would be the best move, but Elaine suggested I find a private doctor rather than a clinic, said it would be easier. And some of my friends wanted me to wait a little while, shared Marty's concern, worried that I might regret the decision later. So before rescheduling, I went to see a therapist.

First things first, we discussed the abortion. My main concern—aside from worrying about Joe's reaction—was how fine and guilt-free I felt about the whole thing. Did that mean I was in full and total denial? Granted, I had been politically pro-choice forever, had even marched at rallies. But personally, it was such a different story, my own uterus influenced too heavily by Daddy for me ever, until now, to exercise the right I had fought for for other women.

So, did I think that was a baby in there? Was that a possible problem? Oh no. Not at all. I had this feeling that this thing inside of me was less like a child and more like the Holy Spirit I had been waiting for forever, from the time I sat my skinny eleven-year-old ass down on that hard wooden bench for three hours one Good Friday and prayed for deliverance.

Finally, in the oddest, most ironic of ways, my prayers were answered by this thing inside of me. Finally I felt something like the lightning bolt I'd hoped for all those years ago. It was another sort of trinity, the trinity of me, myself and I. It was little frightened me at last spitting in the face of all the men who had ever tried to tell me how it was going to be.

It was stunning, this thing I felt. It was knowing I had made one dreadful error but knowing too, for once, that I did not have to spend my entire life serving penance for that error, being tied to this man who wanted to change me so much. It was as if this thing inside of me was what a friend suggested: a messenger who knew and accepted her fate before she chose me, an angel come to deliver me by fire from the hell of the man I'd married.

I hated telling a stranger so much so fast, but my therapist needed some history if she was going to help me. Condensing the events of my marriage, from how I met Joe to how I ran from him, I underscored what I could not deny was pure stupidity on my part again and again. Even this woman, trained to deal with people in crisis, seemed surprised at all I revealed.

I told her that I'd told Joe I would agree to one session with him to sort through some issues, offer him some closure on the abortion. She talked to Joe on the phone once and told me in no uncertain terms that the session I wanted for both of us would be pointless—given that he wanted reconciliation and I wanted him to fall off the earth.

But she and I did agree totally on the abortion. After hearing me out, helping me look at all sides of the situation and what the fallout might bring, she strongly suggested I follow my instincts and go ahead with the plan. I floated through the murk of the following week, sleepless and frazzled, waiting for my appointment to arrive.

Joe was beside himself over my decision to have an abortion. During this period, and for weeks afterward, he buried me under dozens of phone messages and e-mails, long, rambling tangles of words that were all over the board in sentiment.

One day he would say he was losing his mind. The next he threatened to try to legally block the abortion. Then, in the next message, he would feign calm, and offer to pay for the procedure. Once or twice, he offered me full custody if I would reconsider.

If he had been any other man, I might have considered this offer. But I didn't trust Joe. I could just see him, backed by the money of his wealthy extended Christian family, explaining to a judge that he hadn't really meant full custody, that he had been under severe duress at the time of the deal. I could see his lawyer arguing that because I had even contemplated abortion, I was unfit, that Joe should have full custody instead.

There was no way, *no way* that I would risk wrecking my life, Henry's life, and this potential child's life by setting myself up to be involved with Joe like that. I would not spend twenty years and money I didn't have and emotions I couldn't spare fighting him in court over and over.

The few times I spoke to him directly, before I realized the foolishness of such conversations—he took any words from me, even "Fuck you," as a sign of hope—he cried and cried, begged me to please come have dinner with him, let him play Frisbee with Henry (ha!), to come "home."

Home? It was my home. The son-of-a-bitch had bullied me out of my own place, and now he expected me to sashay back in the door, all hugs and apologies, and eat a bowl of soup with him? I was living out of a suitcase, sharing a single bed with my child, neither of us with more than two changes of clothes, let alone any of our other possessions.

He called my friends. He called Marty. He'd changed his mind. He was a good guy, he swore. I could have the apartment back. Too late. By then I wanted to move to a place where he could not easily find me.

The day before the abortion, I drove Henry to school. He had been so excited at the prospect of being a big brother. I had told him—and everyone else I knew—when I first discovered I was pregnant, never dreaming I would terminate. Now I had some serious explaining to do.

My son and I share an intense connection. I believe he knew, before I spoke to him about it, that something terrible had gone wrong. I say this because for the entire week prior to the abortion, he stopped his otherwise steady stream of eager questions about his future sibling. Now I truly believe that he sensed the end was near, and he delicately broached the topic once more.

"Mom, how long until Halloween?"

"Oh, not until summer passes, honey. And it's still winter."

"No, I mean, how long exactly?"

"Eight months. Why?"

"Because the baby's coming around Halloween. That's when I get to be a brother."

This is when, as the rain hit the windshield keeping time with my tears, I told him how babies are like flowers, that some seeds grow and some do not. I told him I had an appointment with the doctor, that there might be some problems. I vowed to tell him about the abortion one day. But at this point, he had more than enough to cope with.

The following morning, early, I reported for part one of a two-part procedure. The doctor, a stranger, inserted a small tube in my cervix to begin dilation. Then he sent me off to pick up some drugs and get some rest, to report back in a few hours.

At the pharmacy, I picked up some sketch pads and colored markers for Henry and JohnHenry. I knew the next time I saw my son I would be heavily medicated. I wanted to leave some gift on the table to show I had been thinking about him. And I wanted, also, to leave him tools to express himself, should he need an outlet to deal with the news I would deliver to him the next time we did speak.

I went back to Alan and Grace's to kill the next three hours alone. I tried to work, gave up, retreated to the front porch. It was wet and cold and dark, and I sat watching my breath mingle with the smoke I exhaled from the cigarettes I had given up briefly, and now had resumed with a vengeance. Though it was barely noon, I drank a beer, too. After nearly a year of complete sobriety, I was back to my wicked ways.

My efforts to take the edge off were greatly enhanced when, as per instructed, I popped a pill forty-five minutes before my next scheduled meeting with the doc. I have no idea what the drug was, but it did the trick. I sat there, getting stoned, momentarily snapped back to reality by the ringing phone. It must be Grace, my designated driver, calling to make sure I was ready.

"Hello? It's me, Bridget." My sister, Bridget? How had she

found me at Grace's? And what was up with her bizarre timing?

She explained. My darling husband, who had never even met my family, who had spoken to Bridget only once, on the phone, the day after our wedding, had taken it upon himself to contact my pro-life family—yes, those same people who would advocate delivering a headless child rather than having an abortion—and inform them of my choice. Actually, I wasn't totally stunned; Joe had left a phone message hours earlier, in which I thought he'd mentioned my sister's name. He had carried through on his threat to do the most damaging thing he could think of.

There but for the grace of sedatives would I have gone into a tirade. Too late. I was high enough to not even break a small sweat, let alone raise my voice. Bridget said, "I really wish you didn't have to do this." I cut her off at the pass.

"Listen to me, Bridg. I'm gonna say it once. If you think I'm going to have his baby and run the risk of ruining Henry's life and mine, you're crazy. I appreciate your call, but I have to go. My appointment is in twenty minutes."

I hung up as Grace walked in. I told her about Bridget's call, and her mouth literally fell open. The nightmare was growing blacker by the minute.

The procedure was short, and I closed my eyes under the blinding light and squeezed too hard the hand of a nurse who appeared not old enough to have graduated from high school. I drifted off in the recovery room until they woke me and walked me out. I sat down like a zombie to wait for Elaine, designated driver number two.

Elaine brought me, and the lasagna she made to feed us for a while, back to Grace and Alan's. She put me to bed, sat with me as I drifted in and out of sleep, cried tears of sorrow and relief, thought about how much that had happened over twelve short months. One year ago, I was giving a poetry reading in New York City, basking in the laughter of my friends, the applause of allegedly jaded strangers. Now I was crying in someone else's bed, all of my own furniture and other possessions appropriated by some strange man I had convinced myself I simply could not live without. A man, salt-to-the-wounds, I was still legally bound to. My husband.

Marty appeared beside me, and I woke up long enough to wriggle over and put my head in his lap. "Marty," I whispered, crying softly. He stroked my hair, dealt with the awkwardness of our touching—how much we preferred the happy times, when we could joke about our mutual non-hugginess. Next came Grace—God, I was like Dorothy coming to at the end of *The Wizard of* Oz—and with her, my son, my real baby. He stood for a moment at the door, backlit from the light of the other room as I lay in my darkness, looking like some angel of mercy come to heal me.

Then he ran to me, knowing the verdict before I read it to him. "The doctor, Mom? Mom, did you lose the baby?" I nodded, and he wept a river, cried for our loss and held me tight until I drifted off again. Why had I put myself through all of this? Why had I subjected my innocent child to such horrors? Was the quest for one man really so important that I would destroy everything I had fought so long to build, just to have a partner?

Determined to make it up to Henry, myself, and our closest friends—the ones who never gave up though others had, dismissing me as too high-maintenance for their tastes—I forced myself to focus. Borrowing money against my incoming paycheck, I came up with a deposit on a new place. The only decent apartment I could find was three hundred dollars more a month than the place we fled. I did not care. If I was going to uproot my son from everything he considered home, from the school and kindergarten teacher he loved, I would do what I had to to afford him a decent new home.

Another loan. This one to pay five strong men to help me haphazardly pack all of my belongings in the few hours allotted to me by my husband's lawyer. We bundled things in sheets, tore the furniture down carelessly, hustled hustled hustled to beat Joe's return-from-work deadline. I unpacked equally fast, determined to provide some sense of normalcy, some familiarity of things, if not location, for my child.

I enrolled Henry in his new school, trying hard not to wince as I explained to the teachers and administrators that I had obtained a restraining order against my husband, who by its terms could not come near my son. Henry was not to go to the rest room alone. He needed to be watched constantly. These things settled, I took him to the pound, let him pick a puppy to try hard to make up just a little for all I had put him through.

26

"WELL, I'll tell you one thing. Your jeans are going to fit a lot better once they get this out."

Excuse me? I looked at the doctor performing my postabortion checkup and tried to discern if this comment came from a place of hideous chauvinism, pathetic bedside manner, or just a really, really bad sense of humor.

On the monitor above my head, as he ran first an external and then an internal exam (the latter involving a device I swear was purchased in an adult toy store), he pointed to the black mass floating above my uterus. "I'm not an expert in this area," he said, "so I can't say for sure what this thing is. But it is something. I want you to go to a specialist immediately."

"This thing" turned out to be a grapefruit-sized growth, defined by some of the experts as a tumor, others as a cyst containing solid matter. I clung to the former definition for a few reasons. First, tumor sounded so much more exciting and dramatic. Second, I was in such a low place, much as I wanted to, I found it impossible to think of the less-threatening "cyst." Third, I had said, on my first day staying with Grace, that Joe was like a huge tumor, that I had to remove him. And now, the symbol had manifested physically, a semisolid mass potentially threatening my life.

Oh, the irony. Oh, the possibilities. I could just imagine my husband hearing the news and, reverting back to his missionary ways, claiming this was what I got for having an abortion, this was God punishing me for the evil sin of my killing his child. I, of course, chose an equal and opposite spiritual spin, realizing that the discovery of "this thing" would have occurred much, much later—perhaps too late—if not for the abortion.

On the other hand, while it would have been convenient to use this tumor as an excuse for all the people who asked why my pregnancy had ended—oh, we had told so many— I refused. I had done what I had done for peace of mind, reason enough. That the doctors had, as a result, discovered this growth wrapped around my left ovary was an added blessing.

Four weeks, two more ultrasounds, and three more pregnancy tests later (leading me, terrified but incorrectly, to think the abortion had been botched), my ob/gyn announced that it was time to yank. Sometimes such cysts disappear on their own. Not this one; it was growing. We'd waited long enough. Time to say bye-bye.

For the second time in three months, I geared up for surgery. I tried so hard to think positive thoughts, but in the days before the operation, I could not fight back the feeling that surely I had terminal cancer, or that I would die on the operating table. Why not? It seemed that nearly every other possible catastrophe had hit within the last three months. Time spent with my son now was especially bittersweet. I did not want to frighten him, but I did want to hold him to me, to love him so hard, just in case. Just in case.

Grace and Alan took Henry the night before the big day, and I tried, with little success, to get some sleep on Elaine's couch. At seven, she walked me to the hospital, just across the street, waited for me to check in, and left, at my insistence.

In pre-op, I sat on the table being prepped by two nurses who resembled Cinderella's giggly godmothers. I had been strong in the waiting area. I had been strong putting on hospital-regulation garb. Now, as these women buzzed around me, I started to cry, absolutely petrified, desperate for someone, a friend, to hold me.

I apologized for being a baby, but they soothed me. "You're allowed to be upset," said one as she put some magic potion into the IV now dripping into my wrist. In no time, I was totally loopy.

Later, alone in the operating room, high as a kite, I waited. My doctor entered with her team. "Ready for some fun?" she asked. I passed out, woke up hours later, no clue where I was, curious what this thing shoved up my nose was, wondering why some strange woman was leaning over me muttering the word "benign." And what the hell was that ache in my abdomen?

Slowly, it dawned on me. Oh yeah, I'd spent a month living in the shadow of cancer, and now I was off the hook. Missing an ovary, granted, but clear of death's threat.

Or so I thought. I spent four days at home unable to stop friends and neighbors from doing everything but take a shit for me. I felt loved. I felt better. I felt surely that was it, the final test for the year.

And then the phone rang. My doctor. "Actually," she said,

"we found some abnormal cells in there." Abnormal cells? What did that mean. "Well, a lot of times it means cancer. Only we aren't calling it cancer." Oh great. What are you calling it then, Bob?

Martha explained. The abnormal cells were minimal and limited to a very small area. She felt confident that she'd eradicated them all, and given my good health (well, most of the time) she hoped for the best and expected nothing less from me. Frankly, I was way too fucking tired from everything that had already happened to argue with her. Fine. I don't have cancer. Yes, I'll come in for checkups every two months.

Next crisis, please.

A week prior to, and then immediately following my surgery, I received a series of e-mails that at first were simply odd, but which grew increasingly hostile. Some came from anonymous sources, others from people whose names I did not recognize. Normally, this would not have alarmed me—as a columnist, I often received fan mail and the occasional hate letter.

What struck me about these e-mails, what caused growing concern, were their bitter accusations that I was a baby-killer and that I had abused my husband. Aspects of my personal life were brought into question. On the one hand, I did write publicly about many personal things, including my abortion. But sometimes, a detail would be thrown at me from a stranger, a detail I knew I hadn't mentioned in my writing. Who were these letter-writers and where had they gotten their information?

There were other problems, more freakiness. Part of my job included moderating a public, electronic bulletin board.

Suddenly, in what was essentially my workplace, still more people I had never heard of began showing up (typically posts to the board were made by regulars). As in the strange private missives arriving in my e-mail box, here again I was ridiculed, labeled a murderer, likened to a Nazi, and asked intimate questions out of the blue about my failing marriage.

Sometimes, pissed off at what felt like job interference, I responded to these threats and taunts by attempting to tell my accusers, also publicly and within what I hoped was acceptable terminology, to go fuck themselves. Management would then receive a complaint and I would be chewed out. I was stuck. I could shut my mouth and take it or I could look for another job.

Already worn out from my marriage, the mess of my pending divorce, my two surgeries, and my move, I felt a major toll being taken on my mental health. I attempted to resign from my position as bulletin board host, although it was part of the best position I'd ever held. My manager pleaded with me to stay, to hang in there for at least one more month. I agreed, though the joy this job had once brought me had disappeared. It was with great trepidation that I logged on daily to do my duty, which now included reading vitriolic attacks against me on a regular basis.

Still, unbelievably, this was not the worst of it. Simultaneously, I was receiving what felt like an onslaught of correspondence from Joe. Unlike the old days, that courtship during which I couldn't wait for his next letter, now I winced whenever I checked my e-mail and saw his name in my in-box. He would go on and on about how I killed his baby. He also let me know that he'd gotten a great new job and would now be out-earning me. In addition, friends began to contact me—they, too, were getting similar e-mails. One friend informed me that Joe had sent her several private e-mails I'd sent him over the course of our marriage.

I was outraged. Each of these notes clearly violated the restraining order I got to replace the temporary protective order when it expired. Joe was aware of this, but didn't seem to care. He wrote, "I know this is breaking the restraining order. So what? What are you going to do, divorce me?"

How I wished it were that simple. It wasn't. Marty had been working the case and had tried to be reasonable with Joe. The stoic face he kept, though, was nothing but a facade. We were too close for him to continue representing me. He finally told me how much sleep he'd been losing worrying about me. And, too, our personal relationship had grown strained. Every time I saw him, business or pleasure, I burst out crying. Though Marty would never abandon me, these outbursts were obviously extremely difficult for him to endure. I longed so much to get back to the days when Henry and Marty and I just hung out, ate dinner, joked all the time.

Dawn, a deceptively delicate looking associate of Marty's, agreed to take over. After reviewing my legal file, which had grown thick with copies of crazy e-mails and bulletin board posts, Dawn called me into her office. "We," she said, in her lovely Texas twang, "are gonna hogtie this sonuvabitch." She offered me a choice: a dramatic but sure-to-be-torture courtroom war or an out-of-court settlement that would let her nail him quietly.

Fortunately, Dawn did not need a major production to get her point across. Whip-smart, she examined our options and wrote up a divorce decree that came down hard on Joe. When he balked—he did not want his "pristine" record sullied by the permanent restraining order I asked for—she pulled out her ace.

She presented my husband's attorney with a small sampling of the things Joe had written to me and about me. She hinted that, if need be, she would be happy to supply more examples of violations of the restraining order. Plenty more.

Now, Joe quickly agreed to sign the divorce papers. He also agreed to admit guilt on the nine counts Dawn offered as an appetizer, agreed to nine concurrent suspended jail sentences, was put on six months probation, and signed a permanent restraining order. If he ever came near me or my son, if he ever wrote my sister, my uncle, my friends, or my colleagues ever again, off he would go to the big house. (In exchange, he had his lawyer write into the divorce decree a shorter restraining order against me, as if I would ever, ever even look at a picture of him again, let alone get within 500 feet of him.)

Dawn, who'd watched me scowl throughout this process, who'd seen me cry when the stress of it all overwhelmed me, promised me that actually filing the divorce in court would bring relief. I found that hard to believe. We stood there in July 1997, and after explaining to the judge the atypical additions—such as the suspended jail sentences—included in the document, he granted the divorce, looked me in the eye, shook his head as if with great concern, and said, "Good luck."

In the elevator, on our way to the lobby, I smiled. Dawn was right. "That's the first time I've seen you happy in months," she said, beaming back. I hadn't gotten off scot-free, nor did I believe my world suddenly would be calm. But for that moment, relief swept over me. I was no longer legally linked to the man who had made my life hell.

Reflecting later over my awful, hurried choice to marry—and to marry a stranger at that—I couldn't not come down hard on myself. My naiveté regarding men, which I had for so many years joked about, no longer held the remotest bit of humor. In my rush to resolve my deep-seated, lifelong unhappy relationship with one man, I had immersed myself in another, far more distressing one. Compared to Joe, my father now stood, at worst, as a minor irritation. Ironically, Joe *had* managed to take away much of the pain of Daddy. But instead of replacing that pain with the love I'd hoped for, he'd blanketed it with his own brand of misery.

In my waking and sleeping hours, thoughts of Joe consumed me . . . just what he hoped for when he bombarded me with all of his letters and phone calls. My friends encouraged me to go out, to try to get back to the person I had been before. I could not. I was changed forever. Perhaps I would find a way to laugh spontaneously again. Maybe I could venture out on occasion. But for now, I was too battered by my marriage, too afraid I might run into Joe in public. Mostly, I just stayed at home.

27

WE were both fucked up, there can be no doubt, both lost in our own myths of what would make us better, what we thought would take away the hurts we had accumulated over the years. He, I believe, thought that by controlling me he could control himself after being so out of control for so long. I, I know, thought that by attaching myself to some fictional wonder man, I could fill the daddy hole that swallowed my heart again and again.

There was one major difference, though. I wanted to get better, finally, to move on to some steady inner calm within. Joe continued to lash out, to blame me for everything. If only I hadn't murdered his baby, if only I had come home like a good girl, if only I had listened to him, we could be so happy now.

I'd quit therapy shortly after the abortion, stubbornly determined to figure things out on my own. But a clinical depression drove me back. And so at last I sat on the couch, of my own free will, the child of a man who thought he was God, the woman with a savior complex, who at thirty-three just happened to be the same age as Jesus when he was crucified. And I announced I was ready for a resurrection. First I needed to kick the depression. Second, I had to—absolutely had to—find a way to quit running after all the wrong men.

A flirtation with Prozac jump-started me out of the darkness, then sent me hurtling too far, too fast, into the land of speediness. Insomnia resulted, which I attempted to quell by drinking heavily, daily, turning my body into a beaker of chemicals that should not be mixed under any circumstances.

Frustrated, I quit the Prozac, and fought my fascination with the bottle for what seemed like the hundredth time in my life. Though I seldom got drunk—I drank slowly, maintaining an even buzz over many hours—I drank far too much. Even I couldn't deny that I was relying too heavily, once again, on this liquid sedative.

And so I fought. And I struggled. And through it all, my friends just kept coming back to help. Alan and Grace continued the ritual that had begun when I first moved into the new place, taking turns sitting up with me at night, watching old movies, holding my hand, helping me through the terror that struck without warning. Elaine met me for tennis every morning, helped me bang and sweat out my depression. On my own, I walked for hours every day, willing myself to get better.

Slowly, realizing things could never, ever really go back to what they were—rigid caution was now and forevermore a necessary part of the picture for me—I came to a new place. I looked at my son, laughing at school, sleeping at night, slipping into my bed in the wee hours to curl up around me, and I considered how much we had already overcome, long before my foolish marriage.

Still, the child was happy. He was resilient. And that was not some self-consoling false truth I'd told myself. The therapist I took him to twice had to struggle to come up with some bad news, some proof of depression in him that simply did not exist. He had cried, appropriately, over the loss of the chance to be a big brother. He had voiced a full range of emotions at the moving, my surgery, my clear concern about Joe. He was not hiding feelings from me. And to be certain I wasn't merely seeing what I wished to see, I continued to check with our friends and his teachers, to ask for their help in looking for any signs of distress. None were found.

While I had grown quite humorless as Joe had turned up the heat again and again, my little man never seemed to lose his happy spark for long. His infectious laughter motivated me to make him smile again, laugh some more. He, in turn, did his bit to entertain me. One morning, as I begged for five more minutes of shut-eye, he clapped his hands together. "Up, Mom. Now. Says right here in the script the divorce is over. Let's go."

Go we did, now on a different road, but the direction forward, as it had been for so long before I took the wrong path that ill-fated April Fool's Day the year before. I stopped looking for the grand actions, the dramatic events that had defined so much of my life for so long. That bottomless need for attention, the need I had tried so many times to conquer with one man or another, was now sated by smaller, safer things. Putting Henry's underwear on the dog's head was as exciting as things got anymore. And the puzzled look on the pup's face, coupled with my son's fits of giggles, were suddenly plenty enough fun for me.

Before things went so wrong, fell apart so fast, I had a reputation as feeder. Growing up in a large family, I was much better at cooking for a dozen people than for two. Two, sometimes three nights a week, no occasion necessary, my kitchen would fill, and I happily fed my friends.

But I'd given up cooking almost entirely after Joe, relying on take-out or frozen microwave stuff. I was just too depressed to do more, to take care of anyone but Henry and me, and even that I did nominally. Now, encouraged by my son's relentless good cheer, I decided to have one of our famous homemade pizza parties, knowing my son would delight in his favorite food, would be thrilled to have our comrades join us again. Like the good old days.

The house filled. Marty, Grace, Alan, JohnHenry, Elaine, a number of the many others who had stood by us through the storm. I looked around me at these people whom I had, so unintentionally, nearly tossed aside for one man. I wanted to throw myself at their feet, beg for mercy, weep with gratitude.

Unnecessary. They were my family. They knew me. They loved me. They agreed that I had messed up but required no penance from me. None of them held my sins against me. Not one desired my publishing rights.

Tentatively, then more confidently, I let the feeling of security those friends provided wrap around me. I knew that, not far away, there was a man who wished nothing but the worst for me. I shut his picture from my mind. For that moment, I was happy. For that evening, I laughed.

My guests shuffled out hours later, and finally I tucked the exhausted little man in his bed. As I had since he was a tiny baby, I sang to him his nightly lullaby, a little tune from *Jesus Christ Superstar,* sung by Mary Magdalene to her savior.

> Try not to get worried
> Try not to turn on to
> Problems that upset you.
> Don't you know
> Everything's alright
> Yes everything's fine.
> And I want you to sleep well tonight
> Let the world turn without you tonight
> Close your eyes
> Close your eyes
> And forget all about us
> Tonight.

Henry hummed along with me. Wiped off the kiss I planted on his forehead. And drifted off.

We were not better yet. But we were getting there.

October 1997

Dear Henry,
My mother took so many pictures of me and my sisters and brother when we were growing up. She took moving pictures. She took still pictures. Most of these have sat in boxes over the years. I knew they were there. She even sent me a bunch once. But I hardly ever look at them. Hardly ever go back through her files.

Mostly, I examine pictures in my mind. I was born with a memory that lets me record events and never forget them. Sometimes, this has been a problem for me. Sometimes, an image flashes through my head of my daddy and me or your daddy and you—and often these are not the happy pictures I want them to be. Often, I remember not because I want to, but simply because I cannot forget.

For example, there's this one mental film I have. You were five and I was thirty-two. You were about to graduate from pre-school and, to celebrate the beautiful garden you and your classmates had planted, your favorite teacher wanted to find a birdbath to add.

You told me this and I took it upon myself to find that monument, to give a permanent gift of gratitude to your teachers, who had helped us so much over the years. I headed off to the local lawn-art broker to select the perfect concrete adornment.

But I was distracted from the birdbaths by a statue of St. Francis, patron of animals and children, every Catholic's fa- vored garden centerpiece. Though I knew the school might re-

ject it on the grounds that it was religious, I simply could not resist. I was like my father in that sense, often unable to go along with a specific request, needing to put my own stamp on things.

As it happened, I had given my truck away not long before, tired of dealing with its heft and quirks. So I'd brought along the stroller you had long outgrown, and I loaded my purchase—all seventy pounds of him—into the carriage for the mile walk to school. It was at least ninety degrees that afternoon. Sweat poured off my body, down my neck, and deep into the scoop of my sleeveless man's undershirt.

As I glanced down at the rivulets of perspiration winding their way into my cleavage, a funny thought occurred to me: I was my father. I was dressed exactly as he dressed—same undershirt, same khaki pants. I sported a prominent tattoo on my bicep. I wore a look of grim determination identical to his. And I reeked of the self-righteousness of my task, knowing but pretending not to care that passersby probably wondered what the hell I was doing strolling a saint down the main street of town in a baby stroller. Only one other person I could think of would have the nerve to do such a thing. Daddy.

I want you to know this because I want you to know something it took me far too long to realize. No matter how old you grow, no matter how far you run, you will always be who you came from. Me? I have complained about my daddy forever, rarely said a good word about the man in years. But you know something? I am him. Well, perhaps just part him. Part my mother. Part me, myself, and I. But no matter how much I've tried to deny it—and believe me, I have—there is much of my father I will never shake. I can't ever imagine liking him. Then again, I will never forget gifts he gave me: a love of music, all sorts; a love of the ocean; a wicked sense of humor. These things, as well as the anger I inherited and the bitterness I have not escaped, have shaped me. As you, no doubt, will be shaped by my actions. Your daddy's, too, even though he isn't here so much.

Over the years, people have accused me of hanging on to my anger and my pain. Let it go, they say. Let it go and you will find peace. But I don't hang on because I want to. I do not hang on because I enjoy wallowing in the sorrow, the thing others call self-pity. I simply have this big shoebox in my head, and it is full of pictures as real as any tangible souvenirs. Some of these pictures, sadly, are dark ones. But there are plenty of wonderful ones, too.

Of all the pictures my mind has kept of you and me over the years, one stands out most of all. On my wall, above my desk, hangs a receipt from the Mogador Cafe, a tiny basement joint in the East Village of New York City. Total: $4.95. This check is dated 2/19/1996. To me, it's like a frame for the image I hold dearest of me and you, my perfect little boy, in a moment of quiet happiness.

We went there on the last day of your second trip to that big city. We'd spent a long week wandering the snowy streets. At home in Texas, you'd once asked me, "Mom, what are snow pants?" Now, you wanted to jump in every pile, every little mound, even if it was filthy from the exhaust of a million cars and trucks.

At first I was impatient, tried to hurry you. You paid no mind, though—this was such a treat for you. It was so wonderful to see you find so much fun in something so simple, snow I took for granted growing up in the North, snow I grew to curse when I was old enough to shovel it, to drive in it. Snow I ran from as I headed South and stayed there (with few exceptions) for most of my adult life.

We hadn't planned to go to the restaurant. We had a plane to catch when we left Jonathan's so early that morning. I had this silly idea that a little toy store would be open at that hour. Of course, it wasn't. We moved on. I pulled my little rolling suitcase behind me. You pulled your little rolling suitcase behind you.

There were only a few customers and a young, beautiful waitress in the Mogador. She looked so fresh, so happy to be out in the world, even waitressing at that hour, that I smiled. Remembering how I used to feel that way. We set our luggage in a corner, ordered breakfast, and I smiled again when she charged us so little.

I love that picture of us, sitting there, talking about our trip and all we'd done as we looked out and up through the basement window to the quiet street above. After a week of moving, moving, moving, now we sat. Still. Now we took our time.

This was a picture I recalled time and again throughout my marriage. Joe and I would fight over some little thing or some big thing. And I would think back to you and me in that restaurant. It was that very night, once we were home, that I first heard from Joe. That very night I answered him and started something that would change us so much.

I never thought we could get back to that place. To just you and me together. I thought I had wrecked things for good when I brought that man into our lives. Cursed myself for being so blind to the happiness we already had—you and me and all the friends who loved us so much already. Even when I realized—and acted on that realization—that I could leave, that I was strong enough, that we could start again, I could not stop thinking about how foolish I had been, how much I had endangered us.

I am sorry for some of the things I put you through, Henry. For the things I put myself through. But I try not to regret them, son. Because no matter how much harder I might have tried—to be "good," to follow the rules, to "settle down"—I promise you that we would have hit bumps anyway.

The other day, I wanted you to fix your math homework and you, tired of school and wanting to play Nintendo, shot me an exasperated look. "Mom, everyone makes mistakes," you said.

Yes, we do, honey. And how glad I am that you know this already. How much I hope you remember this, that it helps you as you stumble through life. Try not to waste time as I did. And I don't mean time wasted making mistakes. I mean time wasted beating yourself up for those mistakes. Believe me, there are plenty of other people out there willing to do that for you.

One night, not long after we moved into our new house, I talked to you about my mistakes. I was still really scared. Still not sure how we would pull through. But I wanted you to feel safe. So I told you the truth. I asked you if you knew what the next step was. You looked at me—we had been swimming all day and you were fading fast—and in your little sleepy voice, somber and straight, you whispered, "Yes, Mom. You need to get back on the horse."

Promise me, promise me. Get back on that horse every time, baby. And I promise not to ask anything more.

You inherited my memory, son. You've made that clear

since you were two. Not a day passes when you don't turn to me and ask me if I remember that day when . . . I can't always remember at first, but you offer the details, and you're always right.

I wonder what pictures you'll look at most in the shoebox of your own mind. I wonder if your memories will be so strong that you will have to organize them like I do, make little movies, write little stories, to help you wade through the things that, like me, you will not be able to forget.

One day, honey—maybe soon, maybe when you are fifty—we will go back to that little restaurant in New York. And we will order a feast. And we will take our time. And we will smile at the young, beautiful waitress just starting her journey in life. I wonder if you'll recall our other breakfast there. That one moment of calm in our gorgeous storm. I wonder what stories you'll tell.

I can't wait to sit and listen.